Sitting across from him, Andi held her water bottle out to propose a toast.

"To *Drifting Dreamer*," she said, tapping her bottle against Zeke's. "I can't stop thinking about what I may uncover about her next."

Zeke threw his head back. "Oh, no. Now every day I'll wonder if something new has turned up."

"I'll keep you guessing, section by section," she said, cocking her head. "It's tempting to start taking apart every inch of the boat. No telling what we'd find under the bunks."

"But maybe it's better to keep the suspense going," he said, surprising himself.

Her expression changed. "Funny, isn't it? A boat named *Drifting Dreamer* simply showed up here one day without fanfare or even much preparation."

"So did you," Zeke teased, his voice low and right on the edge of flirtatious.

Dear Reader,

Welcome back to Two Moon Bay, a small town on Wisconsin's Lake Michigan shore. In the third book in the series, several characters from *Girl in the Spotlight* and *Something to Treasure* are back and two have a story of their own. *Love, Unexpected* proves romance can tap us on the shoulder, even if we've closed our hearts to love.

Andi and Zeke find they share a passion for restoration and strike a deal to make the boat *Drifting Dreamer* beautiful again. Curious about the dreams behind the ship's name, the two search for answers while they bring the vessel back to life. As they discover what can—and can't—be restored, they confide their secrets and maybe even spin new dreams.

I hope you enjoy Andi and Zeke's special summer in *Love, Unexpected*. You can visit me and add your name to my mailing list at virginiamccullough.com. Find me on Twitter, @vemccullough, and Facebook, Facebook.com/virginia.mccullough.7.

To one more happy ending,

Virginia McCullough

HEARTWARMING

Love, Unexpected

Virginia McCullough

If you purchased this book without a cover you should be aware that this book is stolen property. It was reported as "unsold and destroyed" to the publisher, and neither the author nor the publisher has received any payment for this "stripped book."

Recycling programs
for this product may
not exist in your area.

ISBN-13: 978-1-335-63362-0

Love, Unexpected

Copyright © 2018 by Virginia McCullough

All rights reserved. Except for use in any review, the reproduction or utilization of this work in whole or in part in any form by any electronic, mechanical or other means, now known or hereafter invented, including xerography, photocopying and recording, or in any information storage or retrieval system, is forbidden without the written permission of the publisher, Harlequin Enterprises Limited, 22 Adelaide St. West, 40th Floor, Toronto, Ontario M5H 4E3, Canada.

This is a work of fiction. Names, characters, places and incidents are either the product of the author's imagination or are used fictitiously, and any resemblance to actual persons, living or dead, business establishments, events or locales is entirely coincidental.

This edition published by arrangement with Harlequin Books S.A.

For questions and comments about the quality of this book, please contact us at CustomerService@Harlequin.com.

® and TM are trademarks of Harlequin Enterprises Limited or its corporate affiliates. Trademarks indicated with ® are registered in the United States Patent and Trademark Office, the Canadian Intellectual Property Office and in other countries.

Printed in U.S.A.

After a childhood spent on Chicago's sandy beaches, **Virginia McCullough** moved to a rocky island in Maine, where she began writing magazine articles. She soon turned to coauthoring and ghostwriting nonfiction books, and eventually began listening to the fictional characters whispering in her ear. Today, when not writing stories, Virginia likes to wander the world.

To contact the author, please visit virginiamccullough.com, or find her on Twitter, @vemccullough, and Facebook, Facebook.com/virginia.mccullough.7.

Books by Virginia McCullough

Harlequin Heartwarming

Girl in the Spotlight
Something to Treasure

Visit the Author Profile page at Harlequin.com for more titles.

For my two grown children, Laura & Adam—
to paraphrase Rat in *The Wind in the Willows*,
they've had some experience
"messing about in boats."

CHAPTER ONE

ZEKE DONOVAN DIDN'T like his choices. He could simmer inside, or maybe stomp around the dock. Or he could let loose and holler at somebody. But as frustrated as he was, he knew perfectly well he wouldn't do any of those things. He wasn't the simmering, stomping, hollering type. Especially not when it came to his dad.

Planting a hand on his hip, Zeke filled his lungs and let the air out in a long sigh. On the few occasions in the last few years he'd been angry at his dad over mistakes or mix-ups, Zeke always ended up feeling guilty. Besides, anger didn't solve anything. Today, like other days, he'd just have to figure out a way to clean up the mess Dad left behind.

Mess was a good word for the ancient motor yacht gently rocking at their Donovan Marine Supply dock in Two Moon Bay. By ny standards, the boat was fifty feet of peeling varnish, not to mention the cracks in the wooden cabin house and rails. The sooner Zeke could find a way to get the eyesore off his hands—and off his dock—the better.

Early that morning, before they'd even flipped their sign from Closed to Open, Zeke learned *Drifting Dreamer* would be delivered to their dock in Two Moon Bay that day. Like a switch had flipped on inside his head, Dad suddenly remembered he'd inherited a yacht. The memory surfaced after a call from a lawyer's office downstate in Kenosha confirmed the boat would arrive by noon. How this derelict motor yacht ended up settling a twenty-year-old debt was a question still waiting for an answer.

Zeke glanced at his dad and then studied the papers he held. "The original letter is dated in March, Dad." He pointed to a date in the body of the letter. "There it is, right there at the end, the estimated delivery date in June. *Today*."

Frowning, Art Donovan said, "I meant to tell you about that letter from the law firm. But I must have stuck it in the drawer in my nightstand."

Out of sight, out of mind, Zeke thought.

This shouldn't have surprised him, but it did. His dad often forgot day-to-day events, but typically remembered details of his dealings with a customer from years ago. Unfortunately, stashing the March letter in a drawer in his room was like him, too. Zeke worked with his dad every day, but at no time in these last few months had the letter from the law firm surfaced.

The letter was addressed to his dad, Arthur Donovan. The facts confirmed that a man named Terrance Smyth had died and bequeathed this very old, but classic yacht to his dad to settle that debt. Zeke slapped the sheaf of legal documents against his thigh. "Do you remember the guy who stiffed you, Dad?"

"You bet I remember him." Art flapped his hand toward the boat. "I spent a couple of months trying to track him down to pay for the hardware I sold him to outfit his boat—about two grand worth of top-of-the-line stainless steel. I almost found him, but he disappeared again. I finally gave up. Wrote it off as a bad debt and moved on."

Art shook his head and jabbed his finger in the air toward the run-down boat. "But it wasn't this boat he was outfitting, not *Drifting Dreamer*. What I sold him was hardware for his fiberglass sailboat."

None of that really mattered. "We might as well have a closer look." Zeke stepped from the dock to the deck of *Drifting Dreamer*. He bounced a few times to test its strength before glancing over his shoulder and nodding to his dad. "Come on aboard. Seems sturdy enough to support us. At least it's teak and probably cleans up pretty easily. The deck might be newer than everything else topside."

From the aft deck, Zeke quickly scanned the boat from bow to stern. "Since you own this baby, such as she is, free and clear, we might as well see what we can salvage. Or…"

"Or what?" Art asked.

"Beats me." Zeke grinned at his dad, his mood softening enough to bring back his sense of humor.

For the next few minutes, Zeke pushed away worrying thoughts of his dad's odd memory lapses. Were they really happening more frequently, or did it only seem that way sometimes? Like now, when a fifty-foot boat showed up unannounced. The one bright spot was that unlike some of his dad's other mistakes, this one wouldn't hurt their marine supply business, except in lost time spent ridding themselves of the run-down yacht. But still, how could anyone, even a forgetful person like his dad, let an unexpected inheritance this substantial slip his mind?

Thinking back twenty years, Zeke had been away at college and had no memory of this bad debt. Dad obviously had handled it by himself, as he had everything connected with the family business.

"Hey, Zeke," Art called from the wheelhouse, "*Drifting Dreamer* must have been a beauty in her day. Not everything's old, either. She's got electronics they didn't make back in 1939."

"I can see that," Zeke said honestly, looking at the spec sheet. Even the diesel engine was only six years old and showed its good condition with a healthy hum when the two guys hired to deliver *Drifting Dreamer* had maneuvered between the pilings on the dock. Newer equipment aside, on closer inspection, the overall condition of the boat was every bit as sad as it appeared at first glance. The remaining traces of varnish on the mahogany trim and wheelhouse were only reminders of the yacht's better days. Zeke grimaced at the sight of blackening wood and cracked joints and seams.

"All the hardware is bronze," Zeke called, trying to insert a positive note. "That's worth something." If they scrapped the boat parts, they'd recoup the original two thousand dollars—with interest. Zeke gently kicked the toe of his shoe against the row of wooden bins under the rail of the aft deck. They rarely saw that high-quality mahogany anymore, except on the luxury custom boats very few people could afford.

When Zeke went into the main cabin, his dad was peering inside the oven of the newish stove, another item on the spec sheet that puzzled Zeke. Someone had a plan to bring back *Drifting Dreamer*. But who? Zeke shook off the question. It intrigued him, like a mystery, but it didn't matter. He and his dad needed a new plan. Now.

To start, Zeke supposed they could ask Nelson White, their old friend who owned the marina and boatyard next door, to haul the boat out of the water, so they could begin salvaging whatever was valuable and get rid of the rest. But then he muttered, "A little sweat and sandpaper could help. To get her ready to sell, I mean. Maybe there's life in the boat yet. We don't *need* to junk her."

His dad grinned and cupped his ear, acknowledging the groan of the pump that ran for a few seconds before coming to a halt with a clunk. "The bilge pump works."

"See? Another selling point. Besides, we know for sure she's seaworthy enough to make the trip from Kenosha."

According to the paperwork, the nearly eighty-year-old yacht had been built in Duluth, Minnesota, and launched in 1939. It was a Bergstrom 50, a legendary design. That alone made her a classic, Zeke thought. From the attorney's letter, Zeke learned Smyth bought the boat four years before he died. It had been sitting under a tarp in a boatyard, the victim of years of neglect.

He'd added a note in his will about it being better late than never to make restitution.

"Man, oh, man, you don't have this much storage in your house," Art called from the forward cabin.

"That big, huh?" Zeke was amused by his dad's remark, even knowing it was his responsibility to resolve this result of a twenty-year-old problem. As a kid, he and his dad had been referred to as Art and his boy, Zeke. Even when he'd been almost thirty years old he was still Art's boy. But over these last years, the situation reversed. Now people around town called them Zeke and his dad, Art. The shift was subtle at first, and really shouldn't have mattered. But it did, mainly because Art had changed over the years, and Zeke had all but forced his dad to leave the apartment over their store and move into his house down the street.

"Must have cost a small fortune," Art said as he came out of the cabin. "But there's a lot of pride in this old yacht."

Standing in the galley, Zeke agreed with his dad. It was built to be a showpiece and was made with the best materials available in the 1930s. In his mind's eye, Zeke could take himself back to the day *Drifting Dreamer* was launched. The original owner, whoever it was, had chosen that name for a reason. Maybe a couple had her built, or it could have been a family. What kinds of dreams did they have mind?

"Kinda musty in here," Art said, wrinkling his nose. "I can hardly smell anything anymore, but I got a whiff of old-boat odor. Maybe a little mildew mixed in. But it's probably just the smell of a boat that's been closed up too long."

His train of thought interrupted, Zeke reached up and opened the porthole above the sink to let in a little fresh air on the sunny day.

"I suppose we better get back to the store," Zeke said. "We won't solve this problem today. But who knows? Someone might come along with money to burn and make you an offer, Dad."

"Yep, and we left Teddy alone," Art said, "not that the little mutt gets himself into too much trouble. I'll take him for a walk."

Zeke smiled at that characterization of the dog that had maneuvered his way through the back door of their store one day, plunked himself down and never left. In his pocket, Zeke's phone signaled a text. As he read the screen, he got an immediate hit in his gut. He glanced at his dad, who was opening and closing storage lockers. But now they had another problem to solve. And right away.

"Uh, Dad, we really do need to get back."

He left out any mention of the customer's problem. Well, a Donovan Marine Supply problem now. If he said anything about his dad mixing up an order for one of their best customers, he'd just upset him.

Zeke quickly scanned the shabby cabin one more time. *Drifting Dreamer* would have to wait.

WHENEVER ANDI STERLING'S mood needed a boost, a little aimless wandering usually did the trick. But that Friday night, even meandering along Two Moon Bay's streets, Andi found her state of mind darkening as daylight faded into dusk.

She'd been in Two Moon Bay only a few days, but already she'd learned her way around the picture-book town. Ironically, despite not having a permanent place to live for herself and her daughter, Brooke, the town was beginning to feel like home. That evening, though, she deliberately avoided the shops and restaurants downtown and instead kept close to the waterfront parks and businesses.

Andi drew her hand across her brow, damp from the humid evening air. Since it was much too warm to let her long hair hang loose down her back, she tucked the stray wisps into the twist she'd fixed at the nape of her neck. "Stay put," she murmured, mocking a tone of authority.

Since she knew almost no one in town, she could ramble around unnoticed, almost as if she was hiding. And in a way she was. For now, she craved privacy, even anonymity. She couldn't say why that was true, but maybe it was because she had so many loose ends in her life and didn't want to try to explain them.

Crossing the block-long park, the aroma of brats and burgers cooking on grills caught her attention. Couples and families were having old-fashioned cookouts around the clusters of wooden picnic tables and benches. The pleasant scents carried over to the party-like atmosphere of the Two Moon Bay Marina, a hot spot in late June. The breeze carried the hum of conversation and bursts of laughter, and a few boats were motoring out of the protected yacht basin and into the bay for a late-evening sail.

As Andi approached the well-lit docks, she spotted the tour boat with the almost whimsical name, *Lucy Bee*. Brooke had been on a trip on that boat with her stepmom, Lark, last summer. It amused Andi that Brooke was way more familiar with Two Moon Bay than she was thanks to her dad—Andi's ex—living there.

A loud cheer drew Andi's attention to a deck party on a large yacht, where a big-screen TV showed a baseball game. But then her eye was also drawn to a small run-about tied at the dock, where two teenage boys sat across from each other, phones in hand, so engrossed in video games or texting they were oblivious to what was going on around them.

Couples, parents, kids. Everywhere Andi looked she saw people busy having fun. But a few men and women weren't too preoccupied to raise their hands in a sociable wave as she passed by. She was all smiles as she returned the greeting and kept walking as if she had somewhere to be.

Soon, Andi left the well-lit marina behind and reached an empty stretch of grass she knew led to a pair of docks belonging to the marine supply store. She and Brooke had ventured this way a couple times over the last few days, either on foot or on their bikes. They were usually taking the long route to the park or the Bean Grinder, where she and Brooke—and apparently all of Two Moon Bay—found their favorite coffee drinks and other treats.

A wave of nostalgia gently washed over her. Only recently had she fully accepted that the days when Brooke could be distracted with trips to the park or luscious cookies were fast disappearing. At ten years old, Brooke was growing up and asking hard questions. Like when was her mother going to get another job, and where were they going to live in their new town? At the moment, Andi didn't have answers. No matter how hard she tried to keep up a cheerful and optimistic attitude about their move to Two Moon Bay, Andi still had regrets—and doubts—and they couldn't help but spill over onto Brooke.

At least once a day, Brooke pointed out that she had no friends in Two Moon Bay. Andi gave her pat reassurances that she'd make new friends at riding camp and, later, in her new school. Brooke had already spent many weekends with her dad, who'd moved from Green Bay to Two Moon Bay late last summer. Miles and his new wife, Lark, had moved into a lakefront home. Her ex's remarriage and move became the chief catalyst for Andi's decision to relocate. For one thing, it would be so much easier to keep their shared custody agreement working smoothly—as it had for years. Those long drives involved in taking Brooke back and forth to each other's houses in towns an hour away had grown old fast. Moving closer made a lot of sense, especially because Andi no longer had a job to anchor her in one place.

Andi pushed aside her job worries. Finding a place to live was a much bigger challenge. And she needed a house or an apartment right now. She and Brooke were staying in a cottage Lark owned and had lived in with her son, Evan. It was cozy and homey, but it was available for only another week, because Lark and Miles were expecting guests and were putting them up in the cottage.

Away from the lights and the party atmosphere of the marina now, Andi kept walking across the grass, alone with her bundles of mixed feelings. She ought to be grateful she could stay in Lark's cottage. Well, she was grateful. But as much as she liked her ex's new wife, Andi was embarrassed she needed to accept Lark's offer.

At the moment, her daughter was spending an exciting weekend in Chicago with her dad and Lark, and Evan, Brooke's stepbrother. For Brooke, the high point was the plan to ride the Ferris wheel at Navy Pier. She'd been talking about it for weeks.

Suddenly, the humidity on the hot evening seemed to trap her, and she brushed her hand across the back of her neck. The ground was soft under her feet as she slipped deeper into the darkness and approached the quiet docks. An isolated spot, it was peaceful and set apart from the marina, where people were always coming and going.

The docks belonging to Donovan Marine Supply were usually empty. She'd seen only one boat tied up there and it was gone by the time she and Brooke had passed by again on the way back to the cottage.

Tonight was different, though. Something had changed. Even in the dim light, she saw what looked like a large boat tied up with a row of fenders hanging from the rail to protect the hull from bumping against the wooden dock. The boat was closed up, with no light coming from inside. But even in the yellowish glow coming from the low light mounted at the end of the dock, Andi saw that the boat was amazing.

An amazing wreck.

The boat in front of her was unlike any yacht or runabout she'd seen at the Two Moon Bay docks—or anywhere else. This boat was a pile of ruined varnish and cracked or missing wood. From what she could see the boat was dying from neglect. Andi almost laughed out loud. Those were the exact words she'd used when she'd first seen the house she and Miles bought right after they were married. That house was such a wreck the cracks in the plaster had looked like roads and highways on a map. Someone had painted over the original oak woodwork, and the kitchen would have made a great exhibit in a Depression-era museum. But the previous owner's estate had installed a new roof and repaired the foundation. Andi had instinctively known the house had strong bones, but badly needed a face-lift to restore its glory.

Staring at the boat, Andi had a feeling the

yacht was a lot like her old house. For sure, the fixer-upper boat's to-do list would be as long as the dock itself. What a huge undertaking. Then why was her heart beating a little faster? She immediately dismissed her own surprising reaction. Did she really want to clutch a scraper in her hand and get to work? As a matter of fact, yes, it was an appealing idea. She didn't know a lot about large motor yachts, but something in her longed to brighten up this floating mass of wood.

Andi started when her phone vibrated in her pocket, but she guessed it would be Brooke and hurried to answer.

"Hi, Mom."

Better than cheery, Brooke sounded excited.

"Well, hello. Are you enjoying yourself in the big city?" Her mood lifted at the sound of her daughter's voice.

"We're at Navy Pier eating fudge ice cream," Brooke said. "We rode the Ferris wheel, and it was great. And we went to the aquarium today. You should see the sharks—and the dolphins."

"Sounds like fun." She walked away from

the dock, but before she got too far, she pivoted and took another look at the boat. Nothing in the marina was as isolated as that lone yacht.

"Wait, Mom. Dad wants to talk to you a minute."

"Okay, put him on," Andi said, taking a few more steps away from the boat.

"Hey, Andi," Miles said, "any news?"

"About a roof over my head, you mean? And Brooke's." Andi winced at the sarcastic tone coming out of her mouth. Where had it come from? Frustration? Misplaced resentment? Miles didn't mean anything negative by the question.

"Oops, sorry, Miles," she said quickly. "Don't mind me. I'm mad at myself. Somehow, this move didn't go at all the way I planned it."

"It *will* work out. And like I told you, you can stay in the cottage another week or so, and then move back in when our guests leave."

Andi knew exactly what was coming next. If she still hadn't found a place to live, she and Brooke were welcome to stay with Miles and Lark. They had plenty of space, and

Brooke had her own room fixed up exactly as she wanted it. She spent almost half her time in Miles's house, anyway. Andi would be welcome to the guest room. It was a generous offer. Andi knew that. Just like she knew she *couldn't* bring herself to stay there.

"We talked about that, and you know how I feel, Miles. It would be too odd for Brooke. She's used to going between my house and your house. It's been her life since she was a toddler. She adjusted well to being with you and Lark and Evan. But stay in your house? I don't think so."

"You wouldn't be here for long. Only until things settle in for you in Two Moon Bay, Andi. It would only be for a week or two."

"Look, I'll get vacation rentals a week or two at a time, or we'll stay in one of the residential hotels," she said, annoyed by the turn of the conversation. "It's not the best solution, but it's better than being with Brooke in the same house with you and Lark and her son." Such a nightmarish solution. Andi would do almost anything to avoid it.

"You make it sound like a punishment for something," Miles said, uncharacteristic resentment seeping into his voice. "You're telling me you'd rather be alone with Brooke in a hotel than with her in my house."

"Yes, Miles, that's precisely what I'm saying." She paused. "Give me a minute to spell this out for you." It was hard to gather her thoughts with the background noise coming from Miles's phone. Between a loud blues band, a mix of voices and the wind producing a static sound, it was nearly impossible to hear him. She kicked her voice up a notch. "I'm on my way back to the cottage now. Can we talk later? I'd like you to understand."

"Okay, I'll call you in an hour or so."

With the call ended, Andi retraced her steps back across the grass and through the marina and down a few blocks of the waterfront street. She was soon unlocking the front door to Lark's cottage on Night Beach Road. She fixed herself a plate of cheese and crackers and made short work of what she decided was dinner. Then she poured herself a glass of merlot and sat in the window seat to wait for Miles's call.

Andi barely knew Lark, but it was easy to picture Brooke's stepmom raising Evan in this cottage, working at her desk in front of this large picture window with its view of the lake. It was still Lark's office, except when she and Miles had company staying here, like now. Then she worked in her office in their new house just down the street.

Andi thought about all the reasons she believed moving to Two Moon Bay was good for Brooke. But the logical, sound reasons for making such a major change only explained about 90 percent of her rationale. Andi hadn't confided to anyone about the other reasons that pushed her toward her decision. It was hunger, she thought. She was hungry for something different in her life. After years of successfully managing a large medical practice, she'd been a casualty of a merger with a larger medical group. Luckily, she was a saver so she wasn't living hand-to-mouth. She'd also accepted a few temp assignments over the last eighteen months and that helped cover her expenses. She had the luxury of holding out for a good professional opportunity.

When she'd first started her job search, a couple of medical practices had come looking for her, even coaxing her to agree to interviews, but they made such lowball offers she'd turned them down flat. She was determined to think bigger, not smaller. Or, what was stopping her from changing fields altogether, maybe taking off in a new direction?

Deciding to move to Two Moon Bay had been bound up in that exciting notion of a fresh start. All that work to renovate her house increased its value and the profit from its sale bought her more time to figure out what she wanted. The sale happened much faster than she or the Realtor had anticipated. The offer was well above the asking price, but in order to take advantage of it, she'd agreed to a closing date that allowed her almost no time to find a permanent rental.

Andi sipped her wine and stared at the narrow reflection of the new moon breaking through the haze over the lake. Where had her logical mind gone? None of these short-term problems would matter if she was judging her situation rationally. These were setbacks, minor at that, but they brought back long buried memories of other times she'd just as soon forget.

Like the air, the lake was still tonight. That sad old boat she'd seen was probably barely moving at the dock.

Odd that she would think of that boat. But there was something about it. But what?

Miles's call broke into her thoughts.

"So?" he asked.

"So," she said back, "here it is. You know I agreed to get out of the house in Green Bay without enough time to organize the move or find a rental, let alone buy a new place. I feel bad about that. Here I am, with my reputation as a hotshot manager, but I *mis*managed this entire situation."

"But I keep trying to tell you it's okay," he said with an impatient sigh. "We all know it's temporary. We have room for you. This is about you, Andi, not me…or anyone else."

Lark. He means it's not about her. But Andi knew that. Using her thumb and index finger, she rubbed her forehead as if that action could produce the words that would help him understand. "I know this sounds overblown, but it feels chaotic, Miles," she finally said. "On some level, not having a job or a house reminds me of the days after our divorce when I made so many mistakes."

She was talking in code, as if not spelling it out would soften the blow. Who was she kidding? The blow was landing on her, not

Miles. "I married Roger so fast, and it was such a disaster. The next year was a mess. You were the one who kept life stable for Brooke."

"Oh, Andi, that was years ago," Miles said softly. "I can't believe you're linking that old mistake with this situation. They're entirely different. Anyone would have jumped at the offer you got for the house and figured out how to meet the terms later."

Andi laughed. "You're right, logically, that is. I guess this is stress talking. And Brooke was crabby about packing up so fast. That's what brings up the same old feelings that I failed her—again. But I'd rather we move into a residential hotel until I find something. Better than having her mom staying with her dad and his new wife. A woman her dad knew long before he met her mom. It's complicated, Miles." Unintentionally, the volume of her voice had increased so she was almost hollering at him. "Sorry, Miles, I'm not mad at you."

"I get it, but you're being too hard on yourself. I've never criticized you as a mom. *Never.*"

Now he was getting mad. Another unintended consequence of the quandary she'd created.

"And one more thing. You're taking Brooke's bad moods way too seriously," Miles said, his voice normal again. "Change is hard."

Andi let out a long, weary sigh. "That's true. But her riding camp starts soon. I'm hoping being around horses will improve her attitude."

With a laugh in his voice, Miles said, "She's told Evan all about her camp in great detail. That kid is so patient, and he's only fourteen."

"It's worked out well for you. The move, I mean, and you and Lark."

"Yes." He paused. "I'm not trying to hurt you with this offer of a room in our house. Neither is Lark."

His gentle tone triggered the growing fullness behind her eyes, but she wasn't ready to let down her emotional barrier, not even with Miles. "True enough. But try to understand what's behind my thinking. You and I get along well, and all that, and as much as I rooted for you and Lark, I simply can't be under the same roof with you two." She snickered. "That was blunt enough, I hope."

"Handle it your way," Miles said matter-of-factly. "I won't bring it up again."

She felt lighter. A burden was lifted, and suddenly a hotel suite didn't seem so bad. She was tempted to tell Miles about other things going on with her, but she held back. They were friendly, but he wasn't an intimate friend. Besides, she didn't even know what was going on inside her, or why she was stirred up about change.

They ended the call and Andi immediately searched for local hotels that offered the kind of room she and Brooke would need. Of course, she thought, when the Sleepy Moon Inn came up. She'd seen it on the edge of downtown, only a few blocks away. She searched the site for vacancies, and when the information came up, she made a reservation and breathed a little easier.

Thinking about her exchange with Miles, she realized it was a good thing she hadn't spontaneously confided her nagging wish for *something different, a new direction*. Wow. Those were the words she'd used years ago when she'd foolishly told him she wanted a divorce, claiming marriage—to anyone—wasn't right for her and she needed another path.

Andi shivered inside, thinking of how ridiculous that sounded to her now.

Enough. Look ahead, not back. Her personal motto, particularly after her job ended.

Andi slipped out of her jeans and tank top and pulled her sleep shirt over her head. Going through her nightly routine helped put a stop to the useless journey into the worst part of her past. As she smoothed moisturizer across her cheeks, she struggled to recapture her excitement over the decision to move to Two Moon Bay. But the move itself was only one part of it.

She felt her old patterns shifting. Maybe it was because Brooke was growing up and needed her less. In any case, the changes weren't limited to the mundane stuff, like finding an apartment or a predictable, if dull job in the same field. Except for a couple of huge mistakes, each involving a man, she'd lived cautiously, maybe too much so. She was always guarding against throwing her life—and Brooke's—into disarray. Now she wanted more.

Andi fluffed the pillow and turned on her side. Closing her eyes, she decided that if she ended up in the hotel suite, she'd turn it into an adventure for herself and Brooke. She'd convince Brooke it was like camping out but without the bugs. Whoever built that run-down old boat she'd seen earlier must have wanted something out of the ordinary. So why shouldn't she?

CHAPTER TWO

ZEKE STOOD BEHIND the counter and packed small orders, but kept one eye on his dad going through the routine of leashing Teddy and taking him out for a walk around the block. As always, Art opened the front door, then turned around and said, “Exercise for man and beast.”

“That’s right, Dad,” Zeke responded, as if on autopilot. Talk about a rut. Same walk, same quip every morning.

When the door closed behind the man and the beast, Zeke counted on fifteen minutes to catch up after yesterday’s glitch. He’d put over one hundred miles on his truck driving to exchange orders addressed to the wrong customers so that each package got to the right person. Fortunately, the people involved had done business with Donovan Marine Supply for years. Don’t worry, they’d said. They understood. But how could they? Zeke sometimes had trouble understanding what was happening to his dad.

Correcting these mistakes not only took time, but it also meant leaving Dad alone in the shop. Now, before he got too deep into handling the orders that had come in online overnight, Zeke hurried to the section his dad has stocked the day before. Familiar dread settled in his chest as he prepared himself to double-check the pricing and placement, and, if necessary, fix mistakes.

Crouching to look at the cost of the existing stock of various sizes of nylon line, Zeke matched them against the pricing on the new order. He let all the air out of his lungs and his breathing returned to normal. But that didn't clear his conscience. No matter how well he prepared himself, he couldn't fight off little stabs of guilt every time he did precisely what his dad had accused him of—going behind him to check his work.

Maybe he wouldn't feel like such a sneak if his dad's memory lapses, or more typically, loss of focus, occurred every day or even every week. But they didn't. Most of the time, his dad's work lived up to the standards their customers expected from Art Donovan, and that Art expected of Zeke. But even occasional glitches cost them money—and goodwill—all the same.

Zeke checked the last of the new stock of stainless deck hardware. Satisfied it was in good shape and priced correctly, he went back to orders on the computer.

Zeke's mood lifted when he saw the orders for two anchor packages—anchor, chain and line. Not bad. They hadn't even opened the door yet and they already had a substantial sale scheduled for customer pickup later that day. He moved on to the next order, this one for paint and varnish. That made him think of *Drifting Dreamer.* As he'd gone to sleep last night, the old yacht hung out in his thoughts. What had happened that turned such a classic boat into a wreck? One thing was sure—if they decided to sell fast and get it off their hands, the new owner was going to need a whole lot of both paint and varnish.

Or maybe he'd take on the job of giving that yacht a new life and recover the costs in the sale price. It was an appealing idea Zeke made himself shake off. He barely had time for the occasional building restoration job that came his way. Where would he find time to restore an old boat? He shouldn't go down this road, anyway—the one where he saw the boat like she was a person with a brain and a heart and whose glory days were behind her.

Zeke heard the back screen-door hinges squeak, the signal his dad and Teddy were back.

"Hey, Zeke, there's a lady down by the boat," Art said, coming around the corner to the counter. "You know, that old yacht from yesterday."

"*Drifting Dreamer*, Dad," he said drily. "She's the only boat we own." Was there more to the story? "Uh, did she have a question or want something?"

"I don't know. I didn't talk to her. We have too much to do around here to stop and chat to a stranger. Even a good-looking one. The gal has some long hair." Art let go of the leash and in a flash, Teddy turned and made a beeline for the back door.

"There goes the dog." Zeke bit his tongue before he could snap at his dad, who hadn't hooked the latch on the door to keep Teddy inside. "I'll go get him."

Teddy was out the door and headed for the dock, but Zeke managed to grab the leash off the grass and slow him down. "Hey, buddy, you can't go out by yourself." The dog pulled on the leash and led Zeke straight for the woman standing on the dock looking at the boat. He saw what his dad meant. Her dark hair fell more than halfway down her back.

"Okay, Teddy, we'll stay out a little longer." He let Teddy take him to the woman, who was tall and slender, and wore jeans and a red T-shirt. When she saw him coming, she lifted her sunglasses and perched them on her head. In her other hand, she held a giant-size Bean Grinder to-go cup.

"Good morning," she called out, smiling. "I suppose I'm trespassing."

He was tongue-tied. By a pretty smile and long legs. He raised his hand in protest. "Probably so, but we won't call the sheriff, at least not yet."

"I see. I have to prove myself first." She held up the cup. "I'm armed only with the Bean Grinder's morning mix."

"In that case, we'll..." Zeke watched Teddy sniffing the woman's sneakers. "I was going to say we'll call off the dogs, but, too late."

She reached down and scratched Teddy

behind his ears. “No problem. I’m not afraid of a curious dog. I was out walking last night and saw this boat, but it was dark so I couldn’t see much. Something made me walk over this morning to get a better look.”

“Well, you’re only our second visitor since the boat arrived yesterday morning.” He explained that Nelson White, the owner of the marina and boatyard next door, had also wandered down to see the new arrival. Zeke nodded to the boat. “Nelson probably thinks the *Dreamer* is an eyesore bringing down the neighborhood.”

Zeke pulled on Teddy’s leash to stop him from circling the visitor and wrapping the leash around her legs. “What do you think?” Why had he asked that? Just to keep her from walking away?

“Right now, I’m thinking your dog is using his nose to learn all about me and where I’ve been this morning.” Her smile grew bigger as she stared at Teddy.

“That’s no doubt true.” Zeke eagerly grabbed the chance to play along. He hadn’t had this much conversation with a stranger—a female stranger—in a long time. Well, except for customers. What else had he been missing? "His name is Teddy, by the way."

"Theodore Donovan, I presume," she said, deadpan, as she pointed to their giant sign mounted high enough on the building to be visible from the water. "Hmm, sounds like he should run for office."

Zeke laughed from deep in his chest. "We never got as far as Theodore. He's plain ol' black-and-brown Teddy. And now he has a last name. We won't tell him, or he'll get a big head."

She narrowed her eyes in amusement. "If Teddy is like most dogs I know, he's probably spoiled rotten and already has a big head."

Her dark blue eyes glanced down at Teddy and then to the side to take in *Drifting Dreamer*. But, he noted, she now seemed to be studying him. "I'm Zeke, and as it happens, my real last name is Donovan."

He offered his free hand and she switched her coffee cup so she could grasp it. "I'm Andi Sterling. And I'm new in town."

"I figured that out," Zeke said. Her soft hand, extra warm from the coffee cup, gripped his.

"How so?"

No good reason, he thought, but that was no answer at all. "Because you don't look familiar. Sometimes I think I've met most everyone around here at least once."

"Well, now you know me, too. I've only been in Two Moon Bay for a few days." Suddenly, her expression changed from lighthearted to serious.

"Were you curious about the boat?" He gestured to the stern. "*Drifting Dreamer*. The name mostly wore off with the other paint." The hull once had been glossy black with the name painted on in bronze gold.

"You own the boat?" she asked, not looking at him but at the yacht.

"We do." Seeing it through her eyes, he quickly added, "To make a long story short, we inherited it. Uh, as is." That should explain its sorry state.

She turned her head to look directly at him. "Are you and your wife planning to keep it…her?"

Zeke waved her off. "Oh, no, I'm not married. I should have explained. My dad and I own the boat. Well, not exactly. It really belongs to him." Zeke shook his head, frustrated by the way he tripped over his words, sounding like a goofy teenager. "If you can believe it, a guy who owed Dad money left it to him in his will. We haven't decided what to do with it, but the guy settled, sort of, a twenty-year-old debt."

"Twenty years? Wow. That's an incredible story."

She shifted her weight from one foot to the other and took a sip of her coffee, showing no sign she was ready to leave.

Maybe the boat really did intrigue her. "Uh, would you like to go aboard and take a look inside?"

The bright smile was back. "I thought you'd never ask."

"Really?"

"Of course." Her blue eyes flashed flirtatiously. "Curiosity is killing me."

"Sorry, I'm just sort of shocked."

She exaggerated a look of wide-eyed innocence. "You mean because the boat doesn't look so good?"

Another laugh rose from deep inside. "No kidding."

"Okay, confession time." She gestured to the boat. "I don't know the first thing about boats. But I've restored a house over a century old and badly maintained for at least thirty of those one-hundred-plus years. I know very well how old, neglected things can be brought back."

She'd restored an old house? Hmm…intriguing. "Old and neglected. That about sums it up." He stared at *Drifting Dreamer* for a few seconds. "You go on aboard. I'll go get the key to open her up."

She nodded and, after only a couple of seconds of hesitation, climbed from the dock to the deck.

Taking the dog with him, Zeke hurried back inside the store, and found his dad sealing up a carton. As he unhooked Teddy's leash, he eyed the box with suspicion, memories of fixing yesterday's order mix-up intruding into his otherwise pleasant thoughts. He'd have a look at the cartons later before they had a chance to go out. He opened the top desk drawer in the office and grabbed the keys. "Hey, Dad, the woman with the long hair? Her name is Andi and she's curious about *Drifting Dreamer*. I thought I'd show her around."

"That so? Maybe she wants to buy it?"

Zeke frowned. "I hadn't thought of that,

but she said she restored an old house. So, who knows? Maybe she won't be able to resist the challenge."

Art looked over his bifocals and frowned. "Don't be long, son. We've got orders to fill."

"Got it, Dad." Zeke told Teddy to stay and let the screen door close. Teddy immediately started whining and Zeke stopped. "Andi's right, buddy, you *are* spoiled." Relenting, as Teddy surely knew he would, he said, "You stay close by. No running off."

Teddy trotted to the boat, beating Zeke there. He wasted no time jumping from the dock to the deck.

"I bet Mr. Theodore follows you everywhere," Andi joked.

"More or less," Zeke said. "I think of him more as my dad's dog, but we're both responsible for keeping the little stray."

"The dog apparently has good instincts." She flashed a beaming smile that once again showed her pretty white teeth.

He opened the padlock to the cabin doors and went down the wooden companionway into the saloon, or what he thought of as the main cabin. Andi followed close behind.

"What do you think? First…no, second impressions." He was aware that being aboard *Drifting Dreamer* wouldn't do much to alter an initial impression. It would probably only make reality hit home harder.

"I think this boat has a past," she said, following him into the center main saloon, "and I'd sure like to know what it is. Simple curiosity, I guess."

A past? Had she read his mind? That question had turned over and over in his mind last night. It had kept him wide-awake and thinking hard. From the moment he'd secured the dock lines, he'd wondered what this boat had been up to during her better days. It was a mystery he wanted to solve.

"I get it. I've been asking myself that, too. Unfortunately, we know very little, except what the spec sheet told us. She was built in 1939 in Duluth at the Metzger Boat Works. Pretty famous builders, those Metzgers. The listed owner is C. Peterson. We think the boat has been in the Great Lakes since her launch, but we can't say for sure. Somehow, she ended up in the hands of Terrance Smyth—he's the guy who owed my dad money."

Andi gestured around the all-mahogany

interior. "Someone named her *Drifting Dreamer* for a reason."

He'd thought of that, too. "Not that long ago, someone bought the diesel engine and new pumps and other gear, including a propane stove, so that person must have intended to do something with her. The galley is ready to go. And the boat is seaworthy. Made it up here from Kenosha, anyway."

"Maybe the plan was to get her running and then fix her up," Andi said. "Kind of like the way we lived in the house while I worked on it."

We? Who did that include?

"I'm guessing the deterioration and damage started decades ago."

Andi wrinkled her nose as she continued looking around.

"The stale smell of a closed-up boat." He led the way to the large wheelhouse, where the engine controls, the compass set in its bronze housing, the old-fashioned depth sounder and the newer radar were in place and ready to go.

"His new frontier," Zeke said, pointing to Teddy, who'd wasted no time in sniffing the corners and wagging his tail in excitement.

"Now that the dog has discovered the boat has an inside, he'll want to make it part of his regular rounds."

They went back into the main cabin and she continued studying the boat with a dreamy look in her big, dark blue eyes.

"Some people still call these areas of a boat the saloon," he said, standing in the middle of what was the boat's equivalent of a combination kitchen-dining area and living room. "Although that term only applies to high-end yachts. So maybe main cabin is more like it." He noted that she was deep in thought, her full lips pursed in concentration.

"This certainly was a high-end yacht," Andi said. "You could seat eight or ten people around the table." She moved inside the largest stateroom. "And this is almost like a regular bedroom."

"So is the other cabin in the bow. It has two single bunks," Zeke said. "I was surprised to find bunk cushions still packed in the canvas covers they were delivered in."

"Whoever had this boat built must have had quite a vision," she said, running her hand down the once smooth wood of the hanging locker. She tugged on the handle of one of the double doors and it broke free. "This is more like an antique armoire than an ordinary closet. It's as big as some of the closets I've seen in older houses. All this mahogany in a house would boost the price a notch or two."

Only yesterday, he'd seen mostly the boat's decay, but now, watching her study the fixtures, assessing everything, possibilities started clicking through his brain. He knew a thing or two about restoring buildings, and that's what fixing up this boat would be about. Restoration. *Drifting Dreamer* could be more than presentable. She could be a classic gem again.

"You're right about the quality of workmanship, and about vision, too. I wish we had better records. I know one thing for certain. No one builds this kind of yacht on a whim—or on a shoestring. And back in the hard times of the 1930s, any boat builder would have been happy for the business."

Andi nodded in agreement. "My grandpa talked endlessly about the Depression. Not much call for luxury yachts, I imagine, except for the very rich and very lucky. But *Drifting Dreamer* is a *fantastic* name."

Again, Andi ran her hand across the wood, this time one of the bulkheads. "Lots of black blotches in the wood under the peeling finish."

Suddenly self-conscious about staring at her long, graceful fingers in constant motion, he cleared his throat. "We haven't chewed over all the options yet, but my dad and I have to figure out what to do with her. We could sell off fixtures and bronze fittings. I know a woman who buys salvaged wood to make one-of-a-kind mirrors and picture frames. That would bring some money."

Andi's mouth dropped open. Pointing to the floor, she said, "You mean you'd *dismantle* this boat?"

Whoa, what a reaction. But it was one solution and he'd defend it. "Well, yes, scrapping her is one option. We have to be realistic. The pieces could be way more valuable than the whole boat intact."

"Unbelievable." Andi shook her head and pursed her lips in disgust.

She disapproved? This woman who didn't know the first thing about him? He shouldn't care, but he did. "Uh, that was our *first* thought. But then we figured since the hull seems sound there may be some life in her yet."

Andi nodded. "I'll bet there is."

Zeke decided to throw out another option. "We could also sell her as is." What if she was an interested buyer? He shouldn't immediately assume she couldn't or wouldn't buy a yacht. Even a derelict boat. What did he know about her? He glanced at the teak cabin floor, dried out and gray, but still sturdy. "My dad would probably like that plan better."

Silence. At the mention of his dad, his words took on an unexpected sadness and hung in the air. Meanwhile Teddy's nails clicked on the floor as he scurried across the cabin and broke the silence. Zeke heard himself breathe.

"I have a question." She abruptly faced him full-on. "What would you charge to rent this yacht to someone? For the summer, I mean."

"Rent? You mean to someone who wanted to *live* on *Drifting Dreamer*?"

She extended her hand and flashed an isn't-that-obvious? look. "That's exactly what I mean."

What was with the sharp tone? He supposed he'd annoyed her by not taking her question seriously, but he wouldn't make that mistake again. "Why do you ask?"

Leaning to the side, her gaze traveled up and down the largest cabin, taking it all in. "The essentials are here, Zeke. The stove has barely been used. The staterooms—cabins—could use a good cleanup." Casting a pointed look his way, she rolled her eyes. "They clearly need more than that, but you know what I mean. People don't build a fifty-foot boat they can't live on for extended periods of time. As long as the plumbing and electrical systems work, she could be made livable in short order."

Zeke leaned his weight against a bulkhead and crossed one foot over the other. Why would she ever consider moving aboard a boat that needed so much work? Or on a boat at all? Even one in tiptop shape. On the other hand, she'd said she restored an old house. At one time, restoration work was the focus of his life. That thought allowed him a little insight, maybe a hint into what made her tick. Behind those mysterious eyes. And the pretty smile. She'd sparked his curiosity before she'd spoken even one word.

He folded his arms across his chest. "Call me crazy, but what would prompt you to want to live on *Drifting Dreamer*?"

She stared at the floor. "It's not so complicated, Zeke. I need a place to live." She raised her head to look him in the eye. "Correction. My ten-year-old daughter and I need a place to live for the summer, and then when the tourist season is over, I'm sure I'll be able to find a permanent place here in town. Right now, summer rentals are scarce in Two Moon Bay, and we'd end up moving every couple of weeks."

A ten-year-old. A single mom and her daughter living on the boat? He was caught completely off guard. "Where are you staying now?"

She lifted her palms and let her head drop back. "I might have known you'd ask..."

"I'm sorry. I didn't mean to pry." Wait... why was he apologizing for asking a question anyone would?

"No, no, it's okay. I'm just teasing. Of course you'd want to know." She took her sunglasses off the top of her head and rearranged the white headband that held her hair off her face. "It's complicated. At the moment, and for the next few days, I'm staying—are you ready for this?—at my ex-husband's new wife's cottage on Night Beach Road."

"Ex-husband's new wife's cottage." He pointed his finger downward with each word as if connecting the dots.

"We share custody of our daughter, Brooke, and at the moment, she's in Chicago with her dad and Lark—that's his new wife." She grinned. "Newish wife."

"Brooke? Lark?" he blurted. "Then Miles is your ex-husband?"

The muscles in her face relaxed, showing visible relief. "Why, yes. Do you know him—them?"

Zeke laughed. "Lark and Miles are friends of Dawn Larsen and Jerrod Waters, the guy who runs the diving trips out of the marina—they're friends of mine. He has the tour boat, too. And I've met your little girl a couple of times."

"Do you mean *Lucy Bee*? It's docked at the marina?"

He nodded. "Matter of fact, Dawn and Jerrod have been married less than a year."

"And Miles was at their wedding," Andi said, chuckling. "Now I'm putting all the pieces together. Jerrod has a little girl, Carrie. Brooke has mentioned her."

"Right." Zeke led the way back to the deck. Teddy followed Andi and immediately flopped in a sunny corner and curled up, as if tuckered out from his tough morning of sniffing and endearing himself to his new friend.

"The dog has apparently heard all this before," Andi quipped.

"Right. He knows most of the players in our conversation, so it's very ho-hum to the family mutt." He hadn't joked around this much in a long time.

Way too long.

"For a minute there, I forgot that, of course, being on the waterfront you'd know Jerrod and Dawn and the rest of the crowd."

Zeke pointed down the waterfront to Nelson's marina, where Jerrod's boats were tied up at the main dock. "Jerrod keeps his boats at the marina all summer. I got to know Miles at a couple of events at the yacht club."

He turned the other way and pointed toward the glass-and-wood building down the shore. "That's the yacht club, but it's more than that now. They plan to have music on some weekends and they rent it out for weddings and parties."

Andi absently looked beyond him to the water, as if suddenly distracted. "I've walked down that way a couple of times since I've been in town. Brooke has told me lots of stories about the people you mentioned."

Zeke told Andi about what was supposed to have been a send-off party for Jerrod and his crew at the end of the season. "They were heading back south for the winter. But Jerrod and Carrie didn't leave. Asking Dawn to marry him led to a big change of plans for Jerrod and his crew."

Her laugh sounded a little forced when she said, "Such a chummy place. Brooke loves being here with her dad."

Zeke couldn't tell if her tone was wistful or resentful. Not an area he'd probe, in any case.

"We had to limit the time Brooke spent with him last year because of the distance. She was here for weekends, except when he was away doing one of his talks. But Miles and I both ate up way too much time on the road shuttling her back and forth."

"And now you've moved here." Given her connection to people he knew, Zeke was even more curious about her.

She ran her hand down the back of her head, subtly fidgeting with her hair. "Yes, I moved, but for various reasons, I ended up leaving in kind of a rush. Brooke and I have been here a week."

Zeke listened as she added a few details about hunting for a new job, too.

"So, I got my big idea about living on your boat because I can't stay at the cottage. Miles and Lark will have visitors from out of town staying there soon."

In a shot, her expression had gone from lively to troubled. She idly patted the back of a deck chair. "I'm sorry to have bothered you. I know this was kind of a wild idea." She walked past him and stepped off the boat.

Now she was running off? "Wait a second, Andi. Where are you going?"

She put her sunglasses back on, but before her eyes disappeared behind them, he saw them change again. Now she looked upset, even sad. "I've taken up too much of your time."

"Aren't you going to wait for my answer?"

Zeke had numbers running through his head, but they seemed meaningless. He'd never been a landlord before. If she wanted to live on the boat, what was to stop him from letting her? Well, given some time to think about it, he could probably come up with all kinds of good reasons why it was a bad idea. But he didn't care. He and his dad could use a little life around the store.

"Answer?" Her sunglasses went back to the top of her head. She squinted in the bright sunlight.

"You asked what I'd charge."

"Are you serious?"

"I was about to ask you that." Some banter saved him from admitting he had no idea what kind of deal to make.

She folded her arms over her chest and tilted her head. "I was…*am*. But how do I know you won't start salvaging all the valuable parts out from under me?"

He choked back a laugh at the teasing question. He didn't *want* to scrap the boat, especially a finely built yacht like this one. "Seems the longer I'm on the boat, the more I like her. I bet she cleans up nice."

"I've refinished my share of woodwork," she said with a shrug. "It's been a while, but I liked it. *Loved it*, actually. It was so satisfying to see the ugly transformed to beautiful again."

She might be a stranger, but he understood a little about her already. Zeke pointed to the store. "As it happens, I have the tools and supplies you'd need to take on that job."

"I just bet you do." She patted a bronze fitting at the base of the canopy. "I'll bet you have what I'd need to make this tarnished old bronze gleam in the sunshine."

"Donovan Marine Supply at your service."

She gave him a long look and stepped back aboard the boat. The air vibrated around him, like a low buzz. What? Zeke didn't even believe in that sort of thing. Electricity in the air and all that. Except in a real thunderstorm. Or did he? As of this minute, maybe it wasn't so impossible for the air to feel charged.

He cleared his throat to help him refocus. "We have power on the dock," he said to bring himself back to practicalities, "so you wouldn't have to run the engine to keep the refrigerator and lights on. And as you saw, the boat has a separate shower."

She flashed an excited smile. "It's got everything."

"You can use the washing machines in the mudroom in the back of the store. The second floor is like an oversize storage shed now, but it used be an apartment. I grew up in that place above the store. My dad and I live in a house down the street."

"Oh, so you live with your dad?"

"No, my dad lives with me." He played that statement back in his mind, knowing how annoyed he'd sounded.

Her face registered frank surprise "Sorry… I guess."

Zeke needed to explain, but that was complicated. Instead he waved her off. "Don't mind me. Let's get on with the arrangements." Ideas were coming fast now. "How about a barter deal? You and Brooke live aboard *Drifting Dreamer* for the summer. You'll make a start at getting the boat back in shape—cosmetically, anyway. I'll keep you in supplies." Grinning, he added, "And plenty of running water from Nelson's dock."

"You mean we could live here for free?"

"Of course, for free." He paused. "Really? You thought I'd charge you?" He brushed his hand across peeling varnish on the cabin. "And I'll certainly pay you for the hours you put in."

"Pay me?"

"Well, yes. This is a big undertaking." A new question came up. "I didn't think to ask. Do you have a job now?"

"Nope. I thought I might look for something part-time. Maybe see if one of the shops needed extra help for the tourist season. Mostly, I'm concentrating on getting set up here in Two Moon Bay and making sure Brooke is adjusting and all that. But I'll keep sending my résumé out as well, I suppose. The thing is..."

She stopped talking and with her forehead knitted in a deep frown, she stared off into space. He didn't know how to finish her sentence, but apparently, neither did she. But this woman he barely knew was fired up to make a change. He wasn't sure what she had in mind specifically, but somehow, he understood.

The sound of his cell phone interrupted his train of thought. He looked at the screen. His dad. Not a crisis, just a customer with questions. "I'll be right back. Don't go away."

She glanced at him with a faraway look in her eyes, as if the phone had startled her out of her private thoughts. "I won't."

He hurried off the boat, but Teddy stayed curled up out in the sun on the deck. Zeke smiled. That dog had found his second home. As he opened the door to the shop, he was still in a daze. From the looks of things, it wasn't going to be the same old kind of summer.

THE LIST-MAKER side of Andi was fully engaged. Almost too much so. Jobs swirled through her head looking for a place to land on her priority list, starting with happily canceling the reservation at the Sleepy Moon Inn. Minor decisions about what to pack and move aboard, and what to stash away in storage, were mixed up with the details of the gigantic job of making *Drifting Dreamer* livable in the next couple of days.

Ready to jump out of her skin, both excited and nervous, she warded off the questions coming from inside her about the wisdom of her decision. How could she explain the impulse to dive into a job like this? Until this surprise had come along this morning, she'd all but forgotten the buzz and tingle in her body that an unexpected stroke of luck could bring. It filled her with so much energy she had to do something to burn it off.

After downing half a peanut-butter-and-jelly sandwich, Andi put her bike in the rack on the back of her car and drove south down Night Beach Road until it curved and merged with the county road that led to the beach at Sibley State Park, only a quarter mile away. The line of cars on the side road provided plenty of company on the perfect seventy-degree day. She walked her bike out of the parking lot and started pedaling at the start of the dirt bike path that wound through several miles of dense forest.

She inhaled deeply, nearly euphoric from the damp earthy scents filling her nostrils that were the opposite of the stale odor that had permeated the boat. *Drifting Dreamer* may have been closed up for decades. As Andi slowed her pace, her body buzzed from exertion, but she was also filled with the energy of hope. In her small way, she'd bring *Drifting Dreamer* to life, starting with airing the boat to banish the stale smell. She'd fling open the portholes. Right. She smiled at the image of herself flinging bronze portholes wherever. But she'd certainly open them as wide as she could. Her mind jumped ahead to the process of restoring the wood, the fixtures—everything. Like Zeke had said, he had the tools she'd need for each job.

Zeke. Now he was a puzzle. An appealing, attractive puzzle. And none of her business. But she couldn't deny the unfamiliar feelings he'd brought up. The sense of fun, teasing, joking about Teddy. She'd had trouble keeping her eyes off of him. Even at five-ten, she'd had to tilt her head back to look him in the eye—light brown and very warm eyes. His full head of unruly dark blond hair suited him, somehow matched his casual jeans and the T-shirt with the store's logo on it.

Their time together that morning had been interrupted by a call on his cell from his dad and Zeke has asked her to wait while he hurried off to help deal with a customer. When he'd come back, he'd brought an outdoor electrical cord and tested the interior lights and the fridge. They'd started a list of mundane items, like light bulbs and ice trays. Together, they'd motored to Nelson's fuel dock and flushed the water tanks,and Zeke showed her how to fill them. He'd checked all of the equipment on the boat against the spec sheet. A couple of exhilarating hours flew by, not only because she saw proof that *Drifting Dreamer* would be a fun temporary home, but, with her imagination clicking along, she also saw the yacht's potential to make a comeback. Kind of like an old band getting back together to relive the glory days. Grinning at her comparison, she realized she was eager to dive into the work.

Watching Zeke, listening to him explain the controls on the hot water heater, she'd wondered about his other work. Restoration, he'd said. That piqued her interest. And why had he *drifted* away from it? Her word, not his.

After about five miles on the deserted dirt path, the woods ended and the paved path set back from the beach started. The cooler air now carried the slightly fishy scent of the lake and the beach. She shared the trail with walkers and adults and kids zipping along on Rollerblades. A few brave souls, mostly kids, had waded into the cold water and squealed as they bounced up and down to keep warm. She watched a couple of adults scurry back to the warm sand.

Andi could have shouted with joy herself. She'd taken on a big job, but for a couple of months, she'd wake up every day and do something that didn't involve a medical file, test result, patient inquiry, or insurance paper. Never had she imagined living on a motor yacht—in any condition.

By the time she stopped at a turnout to rest her legs before finishing the loop back to the parking lot, she'd burned off not only the nervous energy, but also any lingering self-doubt, too. Instead, she was filled with overwhelming confidence that she'd done the right thing. Rather than struggling to create a normal life for Brooke from a hotel suite, the summer with her little girl stretched long and sweet on the water.

From the minute she'd met Zeke, she was as curious about his dad as she was about him. For one thing, why had Zeke snapped at her over her question about living with his father? His only prickly moment. None of her business, of course, but Zeke had learned about Brooke and Miles. She might have known he'd already met them both, especially since Miles and Lark were part of the waterfront community in Two Moon Bay.

Did Zeke need to know about her second

ex-husband? Of course not. Why had she even thought of it? No matter how much time had passed, whenever Roger came to mind, a heavy sensation settled into every muscle in her body. Those memories still had the power to make her feel bad about herself.

Andi walked her bike to an empty picnic table in the turnout and pulled her tablet out of her backpack. A few minutes later, she had a new document with to-do lists side by side on her screen, each with items under the headings Before and After, in reference to the move. It took no time at all to create a couple of long lists.

Done with her lists for the time being, Andi texted Miles, telling him she'd found a place. She added, Details later, want to surprise Brooke.

And what a fun surprise it was.

And mysterious, she thought, as she got on her bike and began pedaling back to the parking lot. But if *Drifting Dreamer* was a classic design and had been built in a well-known boatyard, there would have to be some record of her somewhere. A boat registry? Or boatyard records? It couldn't hurt to do a little online research.

IT WAS LATE that night before Zeke had a chance to do even a quick search. And it was a fluke that a notice in a Duluth newspaper led to the first mention of the boat that was bobbing in the breeze at his dock. It seemed that someone named Charles Peterson had thrown a launch party in September of 1939 for *Drifting Dreamer*. He must not have had much time to use it that late in the year, not up in Lake Superior.

Zeke's first thought was how many Charles Petersons probably lived in Minnesota in the 1930s.

"Well, we have one clue, Teddy," Zeke said to the dog snoozing at his feet. "Are you impressed?" The dog opened one eye. Zeke laughed. He bet Andi would find this news quite intriguing. It wasn't much, but it was a start.

He sat back in the chair, staring at the man in the photo standing on the dock next to his boat. Now, almost eighty years later, a woman he didn't know was moving onto a boat he'd never heard of forty-eight hours ago. It made him wonder what would happen next.

CHAPTER THREE

"JUST TELL ME where we're going. Why can't you let me in on your big secret?" Brooke asked in a crabby tone.

Andi was more than a little crabby herself. She frowned at her pouty little girl. "You'd think I was punishing you. I told you, this is a *surprise*."

Andi shook her head. A surprise that showed every sign of landing with a thud. The rain had started in the middle of the night. It had let up a little in the last hour or so, but not much. It wasn't the rain that bothered her. She'd put a couple of umbrellas in the car and they had rain jackets, although Brooke's barely fit anymore. Andi had already added buying her a new one to her expanding list of things to do.

Brooke squirmed under her seat belt. "I wish my riding camp was starting today."

"I know you do, sweetie, but it's not much

longer. Right after the Fourth of July. Then you'll get to ride horses every day."

When had Brooke started talking about horses and longing for one of her own? Maybe five years ago. She'd already named her horse-to-be. Magic was the first name she picked, and Magic it had stayed. Andi and Miles had agreed to wait until she was twelve before letting her have a horse of her own. By then she'd be old enough to take on the responsibilities of owning a horse, and could earn money doing chores to help pay the boarding fees at one of the nearby stables. Two more years.

"Just think, by the first day of your camp, we'll be settled in our new place."

"Did you find us a house like Dad's?"

Andi shook her head. "Nope." Naturally, Brooke would compare everything to Miles's huge new house.

"Then it must be a cottage like Lark's," Brooke said confidently.

Keeping the spirit of surprise and intrigue going, Andi shook her head again.

"I know, I know," Brooke said. "You rented a cool apartment above one of those stores downtown. Maybe on top of the bakery or the ice-cream shop."

Great, that sounded appealing, even to Andi. "I'm thinking you'll never guess. But it's lots of fun."

Brooke had come home last night full of stories about Sue, the dinosaur at the Field Museum of Natural History. And the bus ride to the zoo? The most exciting ride ever. Who knew public transportation could be so exotic? One day, Brooke announced, she would move to Chicago and live in a building and ride an elevator up to her apartment, where she could see the whole city from her huge windows. Andi hoped her daughter would have everything she dreamed of. It was a nice idea. Maybe that idea would stick, just like Brooke's desire for a horse had lasted.

Lark's cottage was only a few blocks from Donovan's, Andi's shorthand for Zeke's store and docks. With Brooke sitting next to her with her forehead wrinkled in thought, only the slap of the windshield wipers broke the silence. *Please, please don't rain all day*, she begged the gods of weather. Yesterday, she'd opened hatches and portholes to air out the boat and cut through the stale odor clinging to everything. She'd used her hand vacuum to clear away the first layer of dust and then wiped away the grime stuck on the woodwork in the staterooms. Then she'd finished up her workday by making up both bunks in the second stateroom, Brooke's room. Satisfied she'd put the boat in suitable living conditions, she'd gone back to the cottage to wait for Miles to drop off Brooke.

Before leaving the cottage this morning, she encouraged Brooke to pack up a few of the wooden and ceramic horses in her collection, hoping the smile she sent Brooke's way conveyed the air of fun mystery she intended. "There's a perfect place for them in your new bedroom," she'd said.

Andi was eager to share her excitement about restoring *Drifting Dreamer*. She'd explain to Brooke that the two of them would always remember the year they lived on a yacht all summer. It would be their special adventure. She'd tell her that even this rundown boat could be made beautiful again, just like she'd made their house in Green Bay beautiful. Not that Brooke could remember the months stretching to years of hard work that had made that happen.

Andi pulled into a parking place at the Bean Grinder and took Brooke inside with her to pick up coffee, a carton of milk and two blueberry muffins. "We'll have our treat at our new table." Or if the rain and wind let up, they could sit under the canopy at the deck table.

Brooke, distracted by all the pastries in the glass case, nodded but said nothing.

It was still drizzling when they parked at Donovan's. "I'll take the bag and coffee, you take the milk carton. Put up your hood and follow me." She tried to keep her voice upbeat and light, but seeing the boat in the rain threatened her good mood, never mind Brooke's impatience cutting into her positive attitude. Andi winced at the sorry sight of *Drifting Dreamer*. She didn't look pretty under a clear sky, but in the rain, she was a real shipwreck.

When they reached the dock, Andi jolted, surprised to see Zeke appear on deck and lift his hand in a greeting. He was dry under the deck canopy.

"What's going on?" Brooke asked.

"Well, this is *Drifting Dreamer*, our new home. Only for the summer." Andi stepped aboard, looked behind her and pointed to the deck. "Just take one step and you'll be aboard." She nodded to Zeke. "I hear you've already met Zeke. He and his dad own the marine supply store and this dock, and now he owns this boat, too. I'm going to help him fix her up."

Greeting her with a big smile, Zeke said, "Nice to see you again, Brooke. I met you at a party at the yacht club."

Brooke stared at him, frowning.

Andi turned to Zeke and, keeping her voice low, asked, "Did something happen?"

"When the rain started in the night I got to thinking that I'd seen a couple of signs of leaking, so I came to check it out."

Andi looked inside. Rolled-up towels were catching water landing on the counter. The source of the steady drip was a row of portholes on the port side. Buckets were catching water coming through cracks in the cabin roof and housing.

"Oh, no," Andi muttered under her breath.

"I don't want to live on a leaky old boat," Brooke said with a quick shrug.

Andi laughed nervously. "I know it doesn't look so good now, but it will. You'll see."

"We can get these leaks taken care of in no time. Before the boat was brought up here, she was covered up with a canvas tarp," Zeke said with his focus on Brooke. "She's been out of the water a long time. When that happens, the wood dries out and even the hull takes in water through the seams. But we'll seal up everything. The place where you're going to sleep is dry."

"This isn't the surprise I had in mind, Brooke." Andi put her coffee and the bag on the deck table. "But, like Zeke says, the leaks can be fixed right away." Desperate to sound bright and optimistic, she added, "I didn't get to tell you the rest of the plan. This summer, I'm going to strip off all this old yellow varnish and sand the wood and make it gleam again. I can do this while we live here. We'll even eat outside on the deck all the time. Like a picnic every day."

Zeke nodded, his expression encouraging.

Brooke looked at the milk carton still in her hand. "I don't care. I don't want to eat outside. This isn't a house."

The rollout of her big surprise had gone so wrong, but Andi struggled to keep her voice steady, even firm, when she spoke. "That's true, Brooke, but lots of people live on boats just like this. It's a special kind of adventure. Some people live on motor yachts and sailboats and move from port to port, always exploring something new."

"You have everything you need here," Zeke said. "Even a shower and plenty of hot water. And your room has two bunks and a closet."

"You can have a friend here to spend the night," Andi said, flashing a grateful look to Zeke. She needed all the help she could get and was quickly running out of ideas. "Let's go see the inside."

"My friends are in Green Bay. Remember? We *moved*." Her mouth tight, Brooke pivoted halfway around and stared off the stern into the distance. "There's no one to invite."

"There's that little girl, Carrie." Andi cast a hopeless look at Zeke, immediately regretting her suggestion. It had come to mind only because Carrie's dad, Jerrod, ran diving trips, and Brooke knew the girl through Lark and her friends.

"Carrie's *six*, Mom."

"I know, I know. But you've mentioned her a few times. How nice she is. That's all." She turned to watch Zeke, who had gone inside the cabin and was making a show of checking the towels and buckets.

They'd reached an impasse. "We can talk this out later, Brooke. Come over to the table and have your snack."

"Okay." Brooke sat in the chair at the table. She yanked at her rain jacket and the snaps let go.

Good idea, Andi thought, as she slipped out of her jacket. They were dry under the canopy and the rain had tapered off to a drizzle, but humidity hung heavy in the air.

"You can take me to Dad's," Brooke said, lifting her chin a notch. "I'll stay with him this summer."

Her stomach dropped as she nearly shouted words of protest. But she held back her first negative response and closed her eyes. She would not overreact. She wouldn't yell. But no way would Brooke spend her entire summer with her dad. Given Miles's schedule, it was impossible, anyway.

She slid into a chair across from Brooke. "You know your dad has to go out of town to give his speeches and work with his clients, honey. He said he was flying out later today, in fact. His schedule isn't going to change. Besides, your dad and I have always had our own time with you. Now that we're living close by, it's going to be even easier to make sure you see him when he's in town."

With her jaw set, Brooke said, "Lark won't mind if I stay there all the time."

"But *I'll* mind, Brooke," she blurted. She paused to let that sink in. She'd hold her ground. For herself, but also to head off problems with Brooke's stepmom. Brooke had it wrong. Lark *would* mind. She had a son and a writing business to run. "This is a new experience for us, sweetie, just like your riding camp will be different and exciting. You need to give the boat a chance. I have a feeling you'll like it."

Brooke shook her head. "No, I won't." She took a big bite of her muffin and refused to meet Andi's gaze.

Andi saw no choice but to ignore Brooke's response. "Well, then, you finish up your muffin. I'll show you the rest of the boat." Andi picked up her coffee and muffin.

Going below, Zeke flashed a sympathetic look, prompting Andi to mouth the words, *It will be okay.*

"I hung around because I wanted to explain a few things about the leaks," Zeke said, his voice conversational. "Fortunately, the staterooms are okay. It's here in the galley and main *saloon* where the water's coming in."

Andi noted Zeke's raised voice and his emphasis on *saloon* wasn't lost on Brooke, whose face had taken on a look of curiosity.

Andi suppressed a smile. It would take a little more work to coax a question out of Brooke.

Keeping her voice casual, Andi led Zeke into Brooke's stateroom and patted the shelf. "I was thinking the horse collection could go here."

"Good place for it," Zeke said agreeably.

"I plan to start the exterior work on good weather days, the cooler the better," Andi said. "The rails can wait, but I can fill the cracks in the cabin house and start bringing that wood back. Both inside and out, I'll take the doors off the lockers and work on them away from the boat. Easier that way."

"Sounds good. There's plenty of room in our workshop, which doubles as a storage shed, but I'll get that cleaned out. We can store your supplies and tools there, too," Zeke said. "You can start whenever you want."

Out of the corner of her eye, she saw Brooke staring into the cabin, the unopened carton of milk still in her hand. Andi opened a heavy wooden door, exposing the empty shelves of the counter-size refrigerator. "If you don't want your milk now, you can put it in the refrigerator to keep it cold."

"That's a refrigerator?" Brooke asked.

Andi nodded.

"It's kinda small."

"The grocery store is right down the street. We'll shop a little more often. That's what people who live on boats do."

"Back in the old days, boats like this didn't have refrigerators," Zeke said. "They used to put blocks of ice inside of lockers like this. They called them ice chests."

Andi smiled at Zeke, noticing how his warm eyes communicated understanding. "Want to split my blueberry muffin?" she asked him. No harm in providing another subject to chat about.

"Uh, sure," he said.

Andi picked up the muffin off the table and put it on top of the refrigerator before using her fingers to split it more or less in half. "Help yourself."

"Nothing quite like a Bean Grinder muffin," Zeke said, breaking off a chunk and popping it in his mouth. "My dad and I go there for something almost every day."

"That place is one of the best things about living in Two Moon Bay." She kept her hands busy and periodically glanced at Zeke, who continued playing along with her game of slowly introducing the different features of the boat, taking a side trip only to extol the Bean Grinder.

The sound of a dog barking in the background got Zeke's attention. "Teddy," he said, frowning. "My dad must have brought him down." He went out to the deck.

Andi followed and laughed when she saw Teddy dash to the boat, dragging his leash. An older man, presumably Art, followed behind and tried to catch up to the fast dog. Zeke hurried off the boat and onto the dock and caught the dog by the collar in the grass. "Hey, Teddy, slow down."

"Is that your dog?" Brooke called out.

"He is, and he gets excited when he sees kids."

"Why?" Brooke went to the rail on the stern to watch the dog, the whole back half of him in motion, not just his wildly wagging tail.

Andi joined her, smiling to herself. Teddy the goodwill ambassador. Maybe he'd save the day. Her spirits soared when she noted the rain had completely stopped. The dripping below would stop, too.

"We don't know why he's drawn to kids, Brooke," Zeke said, "but he's always been that way."

Was that true? Andi wondered. Or was Zeke saying that to get Brooke's attention? Watching the dog jump around, obviously more excited than usual, she thought maybe Teddy really was a kids' kind of dog.

"My dad and I figure he gets bored with us. He wants more active companions," Zeke said, hanging on to the leash as Art got closer. "Right, Dad?"

"Yep. Teddy sort of wandered into our lives. Maybe he had kid friends in his puppyhood and now he wishes we had a girl like you around." Art came closer to the stern. "I'm Art. You must be the one Teddy's been waiting for. What's your name?"

"Brooke." She stared at the dog. He was

still jumping and straining to get free. "Are you sure the dog—Teddy—likes kids?"

"Sit, Teddy, sit," Zeke ordered. "He's just all worked up now. He didn't know company was coming today."

Andi watched as the dog obeyed and sat, but his tail thumped on the dock. Seeing Teddy get this excited over Brooke, Andi couldn't help but be a little apprehensive herself. Zeke was holding him back, though.

"He'll settle down in a minute," Zeke said, as if reading her mind.

Andi waved to Art. "I'm Andi. I haven't had the pleasure of meeting you yet."

Smiling, Art said, "It's nice to see this place looking alive." He elbowed Zeke. "It gets kind of dull around here with just the two of us."

Andi could have planted a big kiss on Art's cheek. In spite of herself, Brooke was focused on the dog and Art. Distractions, Andi thought. Maybe the initial knee-jerk negativity would soften.

"Mind if I come aboard and have a look around?" Art asked. "Zeke has had all the fun out here getting her ready for you. I've been so busy in the store I haven't had but one quick peek inside."

"Of course." Andi swept her arm in a welcoming gesture. "Come aboard."

Zeke stayed behind with the dog, and Brooke stood still and kept her eyes on Teddy, while Andi led Art into the cabin.

"Zeke is bringing me supplies to help fix the leaks," she said. "Brooke and I will move aboard in a couple of days, and provided we don't get more rain, I ought to be able to fill the cracks on the cabin top."

Art nodded. "Zeke will get that done for you. Right away. We don't want you and Brooke living with towels and buckets all over the place." He opened some locker doors in the galley, nodded in approval and then looked into the bigger stateroom in the stern. "She was built to be a luxury yacht. That much is clear."

Andi heard Teddy on the deck and Zeke's voice warning him not to jump. "Sounds like Brooke and Teddy are being introduced."

Art grinned. "He's a good little critter all around. As soon as he showed up, I knew that unless his owners claimed him, ol' Teddy would know he'd found himself a couple of suckers to give him a new home."

"Oh, yeah, I can tell he's been such a burden," Andi teased.

Art's brown eyes were full of fun. "Ah, you're on to us already."

Looking out to the deck, Andi could see Brooke had crouched down next to the sitting dog and was petting him, starting at the top of his head and running her hand all the way down his furry back. "You're a cute dog, Teddy," she said. "Lots of my friends in Green Bay have dogs, so I'm used to them. As long as they don't jump on me."

Zeke stood nearby keeping an eye on Brooke and Teddy. Art continued looking around—opened notched drawers, checked hinges and hardware on the lockers. Andi took her own inventory of all the hardware and wood she'd remove, repair and restore. The storage behind the curved seat at the table had sliding doors that dragged in their tracks when Art tried to open them.

"These can all be taken out," Art said. "A little sanding will get 'em riding in the grooves."

"That's the plan," she said, feeling lighter

now that she was engaged in talking about her work plan—her strategy to make real progress. Maybe the worst was over? At least Brooke could see they wouldn't be isolated on the waterfront. They'd even have a dog coming around to say hello.

With Zeke staying with him, Teddy came down into the cabin and began his rounds sniffing in the corners and disappearing into the cabin in the bow. Brooke's room, Andi thought. Pretending she hadn't noticed, Andi turned her attention to sliding some locker doors back and forth with Art to see what they'd need. She didn't comment when Brooke followed Teddy.

Andi soon heard Brooke's voice coming from the cabin. "What are you smelling, Teddy? Something good?"

Zeke caught her eye and they connected as if she'd known him for years. Art kept at his project of opening every one of the dozens of storage drawers and cabinets, exclaiming over the space.

"Zeke? Art?" Brooke called out. "Is it okay if Teddy sits on the bunk? He jumped up here."

Zeke held out his hand to his dad to keep

him from blurting an answer. Instead, he said, "It's your cabin, Brooke. It's up to you and your mom."

"It's fine with me," Andi said.

"Okay," Brooke called out. "You can stay, Teddy."

Putting her palms flat on the dining table, Andi rested her weight on them and exhaled as if she'd been holding her breath for hours. Relieved at last, Andi picked up her coffee and pulled off a piece of the muffin, moist with blueberries. She could savor it now.

"It's just like that dog to make himself at home," Art said, chuckling. "Right, Zeke?"

Andi quickly ate her half of the muffin in silence, while Zeke checked the towels and Art poked around in the lockers.

Suddenly, Art smacked his hands together. "Uh-oh, I just remembered. I've got to get back and finish repacking up all that foul-weather gear that got dumped at our front door."

Zeke spun around. "What? That shipment that came in yesterday was our new rain jackets and boots and pants."

"Nah, it was the wrong kind," Art said,

swatting the air. "We'd never order the stuff that's in those boxes."

Zeke gave Andi a pointed look. "I'll come with you, Dad. We can get it all sorted out."

"Did you say rain gear?" Andi asked, hoping her instincts were right and she was following Zeke's lead.

Nodding, Zeke said, "It's a new brand we're trying out. The first order arrived yesterday."

"I was just thinking that Brooke needs a raincoat. For the summer. She outgrew her old one."

"We have some in children's sizes." Zeke followed Art to the deck and off the boat.

"Why don't I get Brooke and we'll be right along," Andi suggested. "We'll bring Teddy with us."

Although clearly distracted, Zeke said, "Okay, that's good."

Sensing something was going on between Art and Zeke she didn't understand, Andi went back inside the cabin to get Brooke and the dog. Wow, in a split second, the atmosphere had changed. Or, more to the point, Zeke's mood had changed. Worry had changed his eyes, darkened his expression. Over raincoats?

THE RACK ZEKE had cleared for the new rain gear stood empty. Only the old hanging display held the same brand of heavy—some called it stiff and uncomfortable—rain jackets and pants they'd sold for years. "There's nothing wrong with the old foul-weather gear, Dad," Zeke said, keeping his hand on top of the pile of new jackets, "but we need to offer the lighter-weight type. I've done the research. People like it. Not everyone needs to be dressed for a gale, not when they're out for an afternoon in their runabout."

Agitated, Art slapped the side of the box. "Did you see the price on those pieces? They might be lightweight, but that doesn't make them any good. Could be just the opposite."

Zeke made his case about quality and customers asking for the newer gear. "You and I talked about this before I put the order in."

Such a small thing, but it was the kind of incident that triggered Zeke's growing fear about his dad. They'd been over and over the need to update merchandise, including a line of upscale marine clothing perfect for the cold, damp Midwest days. "Remember what we talked about, Dad. It's not only about what the customers need, it's about what they *want*, what they *ask* for."

"Maybe so, but I don't remember ordering any of this," Art said, his voice rising with every word. "Our regular rain gear has served this store and our customers for over fifty years."

Back to where they started. If he didn't stop it in its tracks, they'd repeat the whole circle of thought. He didn't like strong-arming his dad about decisions affecting the store, but Zeke found himself forced into it more and more. The squeak of the screen door opening came as a relief. Andi and Brooke might distract Dad and put the brakes on the argument. Teddy came in so fast, he slid across the floor. "Well, Teddy, you're having the best day ever," Zeke said. *Like I was...until now.*

"We hear you have rain jackets here. Did we come to the right place?" Andi's tone was so cheery it hurt. She was nobody's fool. She'd read the situation well enough to know something wasn't quite right.

He watched her study the piles of yellow raincoats. Maybe later, he'd have a chance to pull her aside and tell her what he'd uncovered about *Drifting Dreamer.* It wasn't all that much, but it was something.

"We stick with the standard yellow," Art said to Brooke. "Any other color and you'll look like a *landlubber.*"

Brooke giggled. At times like this, when his dad was funny and entertaining, it seemed a shame he'd never had a grandchild to dote on. But the next minute, his dad's face seemed to cloud over. Befuddled, he turned to Zeke. "So, what were you saying? You want me to box all this up?"

Zeke lifted a handful of folded jackets out of the carton. "Nope, we're going to stack some and hang up the rest." His arms loaded with jackets, Zeke went across the store and put them on a display table.

"I wish you'd told me about this order," Art said, his tone accusatory and plaintive.

Forcing a reassuring, soothing tone of voice, Zeke said, "No big deal." He turned to Andi, whose now solemn gaze was focused on his dad. Zeke's chest was heavy with raw impatience. No excuses, no weaseling out of the reality that irritation with his dad had nearly gotten the better of him. And over a shipment of raincoats.

So often the what's-next? question loomed in Zeke's mind. His fears of what was ahead were a constant presence, part of being vigilant, always on guard. What if his dad had managed to pack that merchandise and send it back? When he played the question out, all the way to the end, he relaxed long enough to see it could have been written off as a simple mistake and quickly corrected. But what was happening to his dad wasn't so easily fixed.

Since he'd brought Andi into their small world, he'd need to give her a heads-up. Regret lodged in his chest. Maybe he'd made a big mistake. Scrapping *Drifting Dreamer* would have been a whole lot easier.

Brooke's voice interrupted his thoughts. "Where did Teddy go?"

"He's probably flopped down in his bed next to the file cabinets," Art said, grinning. "You probably tuckered him out. He's not used to having a lively kid around." Art pointed to the open door to the office. "Why don't we go see what he's up to?"

"Maybe he needs water or something," Brooke said, following Art.

Andi smiled as she moved closer to the counter. "You should have seen Brooke just now. She caught a little of the excitement about living on the boat, discovering how many cubbyholes and shelves she has in her cabin."

Zeke nodded, but then gestured around him. "Sorry I had to run off so fast, but real life intruded around here."

"No problem," Andi said, patting one of the boxes. "Since I'm already here, why don't I help you finish unpacking this carton? You said it has the kids' jackets? I can pick out the size for Brooke and let her try it on."

Zeke responded forcefully. "You don't need to do that."

"But I *want* to." She held his gaze, almost challenging him. "I insist."

"Well, okay, follow me." He carried the carton to the display table in their clothing section and explained the process of getting them displayed and ready to sell.

"Sounds straightforward enough. And I'm sure I'll find a new jacket for Brooke." She leaned toward him. "Is everything okay—with Art, I mean?"

Zeke shook his head, grateful for the opening handed to him. "Something's off. It's not your imagination. I'll explain later when we're alone. But Art's fine most of the time."

When we're alone...an appealing idea, so much so, a surge of energy shot through him.

Andi glanced toward the office, where Art leaned against the doorjamb, one foot crossed over the other as he told Brooke stories about Teddy. "He seems like himself now, huh?"

"That's how it works," Zeke whispered. "It's why these episodes he has are confusing."

"I'm sorry, Zeke." She paused. "Obviously, I won't be far away. Come around anytime and fill me in. I have something I want to tell you, too. It's about the boat." She looked into the open box, then reached in and pulled out the plastic packages of rain gear in various sizes and colors.

Reluctantly, Zeke left her side and waited on a customer, and two more who arrived one right behind the other. The delivery truck pulled up and picked up packed orders, and then the store was empty. During the lull, he glanced over his shoulder and saw his dad still leaning in the office doorway.

"I've never seen a dog that could use his paw to get hold of a door and open it," Art said. "But Teddy can. Our back door wasn't closed all the way, and this little mutt used his paw, or maybe his nose, to pull it open," Art said. "He strolled inside just as proud as you please and before Zeke and I knew it, he flopped down on the floor in the office and took a nap."

Zeke smiled at the way his dad told the story, puffing his chest out and then letting his shoulders slump to show the way Teddy flopped down and made himself at home. Amused by his dad's show, Zeke kept eavesdropping. He glanced at Andi and saw her tilting her head toward Art as she worked.

"Wasn't he hungry?" Brooke said.

"Oh, yeah," Art said, going on to paint a picture of Zeke hurrying down the street to get dog food. "But once we fed him, he took another nap." Art's hearty laugh got Brooke giggling, too. "We didn't have time to take care of a dog, so Zeke said if no one claimed him, he would haul him over to Paws and Claws, that shelter on the other side of town. Let them find him a home."

"Really?" Brooke squealed.

Great, Zeke thought. Now the girl would think he had no heart. He glanced at Andi, who looked like she was trying not to laugh.

"Yep, we never got even one call about the dog," Art said, "so Zeke headed for the shelter."

There it was. Oh, how his dad loved telling this part of the story.

"But what happened?" Brooke asked.

"Zeke got to the place, but didn't even get out of the truck. Instead, he turned around and headed home."

Brooke laughed. Zeke didn't mind. He looked at Andi, who was opening another bag of jackets. But when she looked up, he rolled his eyes at her. She grinned and kept on working.

Zeke chuckled to himself, remembering his dad's razzing him when he came back home with the dog.

"I called him a softy," Art said. "But you know what? I never tried to talk him out of going to the shelter. You know why?"

"Uh, no," Brooke answered, her tone tentative.

"Because I knew Zeke would *never* leave that dog behind."

Zeke stole a glance at Andi, who shook her head and smiled.

"He picked a good home. He must have wandered around a long time until he found you," Brooke pointed out, as if showing proof that the dog knew what he what doing when he managed to open the screen door.

This was his dad at his best. A born storyteller, he retold the tale of Teddy as if he had a roomful of kids for an audience, not just one little girl. Lost in the story and aware he had Brooke's attention, his dad had probably forgotten all about the earlier troubles.

It seemed Teddy saved the day, for the second time. And it wasn't even noon.

Zeke glanced to his right and saw Andi's long dark hair hanging loose down her back as she smoothed out the folds of a rain jacket with her long fingers. Three days ago he'd never met this woman, but they'd already settled a joint living-and-business arrangement. And a boat he didn't know existed was getting a new life. Now ten-year-old Brooke had brought some fun into his dad's life. Not to mention Teddy's.

"You and the dog will have a great time this summer," Art said. "For a long time, I think he's been hoping someone new would come along to hang out with."

Zeke sputtered a laugh. *You and me both, Teddy.*

CHAPTER FOUR

SWIPING HER FOREARM across her brow, Andi groaned softly. One more door to go in this batch she'd removed. Even with the workshop fan on high, the small space trapped the stifling heat. Determined to push on to finish the task at hand, she ignored the buzz of her phone. Whoever it was could wait.

With the last door propped up on the workbench, Andi twisted the cap off a bottle of water and sat on the stool, ready to check her messages. One call, and not from Miles. Andi might have known her mom would respond fast to Andi's update about her whereabouts. She hadn't gone into too much detail, though. To say she and Brooke were living at the dock at Donovan's Marine Supply wouldn't come across well in a quick email.

She swallowed back half the bottle of water before hitting the redial button. The phone rang once, twice, three times.

"Hel-lo, Andi," her mom's voice chirped. "Got your message. Very mysterious. So, tell me where you and Brooke have landed."

"It's a long story, Mom, and came as a perk with my new summer job."

"*Summer* job? Not a real one?"

Andi glanced at the mahogany doors she'd just removed, along with the brass hinges. She scanned the assortment of tools and boat hardware on rows of shelving in the workshop. How much more hands-on could a real job get? "Okay, let's compromise. It's a real summer job doing what I love and getting my hands dirty, absolutely filthy, as a matter of fact."

Once Andi finished the story of coming upon *Drifting Dreamer*, her mother was all set to hop in the car and drive down from the family cottage in northern Wisconsin to rescue them. "We'll make room for you up here. And I suppose we could find a stable here, so Brooke can have her riding lessons."

Andi laughed. "Oh, please, Brooke would tie herself to her cabin door before she'd miss this riding camp." In her mind's eye, she could almost see her mother pursing her lips in disapproval.

"It sounds kind of harebrained to me. Are you saying you couldn't find anything else there? You should have started searching earlier."

Typical Mom. But even if her dad had been on the phone, it would have been the same message. Only Dad wouldn't sound like he was scolding her.

"What does Miles think of this scheme?"

"He's fine with it, Mom. He's Miles. As long as Brooke is happy, he's happy. Besides, he knows the two guys who own the boat."

A few seconds passed. "Mom?"

Her mother's heavy sigh came through the phone like a gust of wind. "Don't mind me. I'm thinking about Miles and how—"

"Let's stop that before it goes to old places…really old, ancient and rotting."

"I know, I know. But he loved you, Andi."

Not like he loves Lark. "We've been through this a million times."

She could almost hear her mother's echoing voice: *Divorcing Miles was the biggest mistake you ever made.*

Second biggest, as it turned out, Andi thought.

"I know you mean well, Mom, but at this

moment I'm content. My muscles ache from doing hard physical work and I feel like I accomplished something today. Everything came together for this temp job. We're *happy* here." How wonderful to say those words and mean them.

Wanting to turn a corner and change the subject, she added, "For me, the best part is bringing something that's in bad shape back to life. You know, like I did with the house."

"I suppose," her mom said. "You sound as determined now as you were when you insisted you could restore that old wreck of a place. I took it as a sign you were finally settling down."

Finally. Not the first time her mom used that word. She bit back reminders that she was in her twenties when she married Miles, not exactly past her prime. But why argue? At their core, she and her mother were two very different women. Andi believed in the importance of family. Her mother believed in family, end of story. Nothing else in life counted. If you couldn't create a marriage that went the distance, you failed at the only valuable thing in life. Plain and simple.

When she looked back over her past, Andi

couldn't blame anyone else for her mistakes, but neither would she deny her parents' pressuring her to marry Miles. Settle down, start a family. And so she did.

Eager to change the subject, Andi steered the conversation to Brooke's camp.

Not taking the bait, her mom asked, "But what about the future?"

"Uh, Mom, if we're talking about tomorrow, my plan is to throw on my denim cutoffs and slather nontoxic varnish remover on huge swaths of wood." Chuckling, she added, "I'll send you before-and-after pictures of the boat and the dock and Brooke's cabin. *Drifting Dreamer* was a beauty in her day." No exaggeration. The next sound was a stifled giggle.

"Was that you trying not to react to my lighthearted attitude?"

"Maybe," her mom said coyly.

Adding a little humor about whatever was going on was Andi's best weapon to deescalate a conflict with Mom. "Let's quit while we're ahead. I meant what I said about being content. Brooke is happy, and so is Miles. It's easier for him to see Brooke now."

She paused to take a deep breath. “Please, trust me on this.”

The light laugh coming through the phone was music to Andi’s ears.

“Oh, Andi, what choice do I have, anyway?”

Her mother’s mock exasperation meant they’d put things right between them. At least for the moment. They ended the call with a promise to stay in touch.

Andi sat on the stool in the open doorway of the workshop. Crossing her legs, she rested her elbow on her knee and her chin in her palm. Beyond the lingering disapproval, the worst thing about most conversations with her mother was the way they almost always led Andi into dark thoughts about her awful history with men and marriage, especially her foolish second marriage. Andi took a mouthful of water and rubbed her hand across her breastbone as she swallowed it. If only that would make the pain vanish.

Needing a change of scene, Andi gathered up supplies for a different job. She put the Shop-Vac, a spray bottle of cleaner, a scrubber sponge and a bunch of rags and paper towels into the shop's cart and pushed it across the grass to the boat. Better to attack the grime inside the boat than dwell on the past. She'd like to wipe Roger out of her past the same way she got rid of the dirt, but no such luck.

Only after shedding endless tears in a counselor's office had Andi linked her parents' views with her hasty marriage to Roger. To Mom and Dad, divorcing Miles had seemed incredibly stupid, so much so, she was diminished in their eyes. Marrying only six months after her divorce was final meant she'd done the right thing and created another family. Wouldn't that restore her parents' approval?

Kneeling on the cabin floor, Andi swiped the towel deep inside the last locker in the row she'd cleaned. Satisfied it was clean and dry, she smoothed shelf liner over the bottom, then unloaded a box of extra plates and bowls she probably wouldn't need.

With that job done, she put away stacks of Brooke's summer clothes in a few drawers she'd already scrubbed out. She could keep her hands busy, but her mind drifted back to how quickly she'd realized she'd fallen for a con man. A retail store manager when they met, Roger was a confident big talker, and had claimed he had to quit that loser job to free himself to launch a campaign to find a new and better one. The hours and hours he spent online weren't wasted, he insisted. He was networking and looking for what he called "a real opportunity."

Only weeks after they were married, she came home from work to find him shouting angry words at the computer screen. He finally admitted he'd been day-trading stocks. Poorly. But maybe he'd hit it big. Then he'd be a winner. At long last.

Andi left Brooke's room and stowed the empty duffels in a wheelhouse cabin.

When she slammed the cabinet door closed, Andi startled herself with the force of her disgust. She might actually have endured Roger a little longer. Maybe she'd have dragged him into marriage counseling. Financial stupidity was forgivable after all.

But she couldn't overlook the way Roger ignored Andi's funny and lively three-year-old.

"Ahoy, *Drifting Dreamer*."

Saved by the familiar low, smooth voice.

She hollered back for him to come aboard and hurried to the deck to greet him.

Zeke carried two canvas tool bags with him and passed one to her before boarding. "I thought I'd bring more supplies by."

"Good. I'm bringing the last of our things over in the morning, so we can be one-hundred-percent moved in by tomorrow." She pointed to the deck chair. "Have a seat." She expected him to beg off, perhaps claim he had to get back to the store, but she was pleased when he took her up on her offer.

They sat on the deck chairs with the tools between them. "I'm glad you stopped by. There's something I wanted to tell you, but there hasn't been a good time," she said, her eye catching a plastic jug in one of the bags. "Too much going on in the store the other day." She absently pulled out a tin of varnish remover. "More of the natural stuff, huh?"

"We don't even bother carrying the old brands anymore. Way too toxic."

Andi fished around inside the bag and pulled out the sanders and scrapers, and a supply of masks and gloves. "I'm good to go."

He nodded. "I'm available now. Be happy to help."

"You have time?"

"Depends on the day, of course." He looked away, as if troubled by something. Lowering his voice, he added, "I'd rather be doing this, anyway."

"That sounded a lot like a confession," she teased.

"Maybe a little. But really, I wanted to tell you what I found out about *Drifting Dreamer*."

"You, too?"

"You look shocked," Zeke said.

"Just surprised, because I looked her up, too." She pointed to him. "You first."

Zeke grinned. "Did you see the article about the launch in the Duluth newspaper, September 30, 1939?"

"I did," she whispered, reveling in the feeling they were sharing a secret. "Charles Peterson. Now we know who named her. And no one changed it in all these years." Andi's heart raced along. For no reason she could pinpoint.

"From what the article said, it was quite a launch party," Zeke said. "Peterson had guests and all three Metzger brothers were there, and the building crew, too."

“Peterson looks so young in the photo,” Andi observed. “Just in his thirties. I don’t know why, but I expected him to be older.”

Zeke agreed and reached out to touch the cabin housing. “Maybe because of what it cost to build a boat like this. The article leads to more questions about the history of the boat. Why build it at all?”

“Especially during such difficult times,” Andi added.

Zeke frowned and glanced at his phone and then down into the cabin. “I’ll have to get going soon, but let me help you take apart some of the cabinets and get the doors off.”

Happy for the company, *his* company, she led the way below into the cabin and pointed to a row of storage bins behind the sink and stove. “I started with those. I’m not using all of them, anyway, so I made them part of my warm-up act.”

Zeke snorted a laugh. “Warm-up act? Now that’s a new phrase to describe how I’ve started lots of projects. I’m going to remember that.”

“Yup. That’s me, I’m a real comedian. You haven’t seen my stand-up routine.”

Zeke's subtle frown prompted her to set the record straight. "Just kidding."

"Hey, I just met you a couple of days ago. For all I know..."

"What a hoot," she said, laughing. "Especially because I'm such a chicken when it comes to even being on a panel at a conference." She gave him a sidelong glance. An intimate glance, she realized. She had to watch it or she'd soon be flirting wildly with this man, who happened to have the most attractive brown eyes she'd ever seen.

Zeke's phone pinged again. He glanced at the screen. "Just a text. I can deal with it later."

His expression had dimmed, though.

Turning back to business, they worked side by side to dismantle a whole section of the mahogany lockers without damaging the wood in the cause of saving it. Falling into an easy silence, they tossed the hinges into small plastic buckets, producing the clang of metal hitting metal as the hardware piled up.

"Any second thoughts about taking on this behemoth?" Zeke asked.

"Not even close," she responded so sharply she surprised herself.

"Whoa. The lady has spoken." Zeke raised his arms as if warding off a blow. "I won't ask that again."

In the few times she'd been in Zeke's company, she'd felt lighter, as if some invisible burden had been lifted. Brooke was the only other person in her world who could so effortlessly lift her spirits. But Zeke wasn't just anyone. He was a man, and she was hyperaware of his breathing in the small space. She stole glances at his hands skillfully using the tools. It wasn't just the strength of his grip. He was confident, sure.

They continued to work in comfortable silence until they were ready to move the doors.

"I'll go get the cart," Zeke said, leaving the boat.

Andi examined the doors as she carried them to the deck. The yellowing varnish looked even worse under the sun, but her mood transformed that ugly reality into an exciting challenge. She might not have a *regular* job, but this project meant something to her, even if she couldn't define it yet.

It had certainly diverted her thoughts away from Roger. It annoyed her that he'd come to mind again. She hadn't seen him, not even once, since the day she'd made him leave. Their divorce was handled through lawyers. Well, mostly her lawyer pestering his. All she wanted was for him to sign the papers and be on his way. She had no idea where he was and didn't care.

As Andi spotted Zeke pulling the cart to the dock, a sense of pleasure raced through her and drove out the dark thoughts from the past. Her new summer gig sure came with an important benefit—some good company.

THE NEXT MORNING Zeke spotted Andi standing on the bow in khaki shorts and a stained yellow T-shirt. She turned to face the gray lake, flat that day without a hint of breeze. She lifted her arms over her head, clasped her hands and bent to the side, first to the right and then to the left. She repeated those moves a couple of times before leaning forward to touch the deck before slowly rolling up and letting her arms swing free. Must be yoga, he thought, to help her get the kinks out. He remembered achy shoulders and a sore back from sanding and scraping all day long, not to mention climbing up and down ladders and hauling around tools and supplies. But he couldn't imagine himself ever making it look easy. Not like Andi did.

"Is that helping?" he called out to make her aware he was coming up behind her.

She pivoted around to face him, her smile welcoming. "I think so." She rolled her shoulders once forward and once back. "I don't need to tell you the prep work takes a lot longer than the finish. And it works more muscles, too. I've put in a long morning already."

Zeke looked around the dock and gestured to the boat. "Where's Brooke?"

"I dropped her off at Miles's house to spend the day. She's kind of bummed. Lark and Miles are going to Philadelphia for the Fourth of July weekend. Miles has a presentation at a speakers' conference there." She shrugged. "She feels a little left out."

"Well, maybe she'd like to come to the marina party," he said, getting to the reason he'd decided to wander down to the boat in the first place. "Nelson has a barbecue every year and then people gather on their boats and the docks to watch the fireworks."

"That sounds fun." Andi paused and frowned. "But don't I need an invitation?"

"Yeah, you do." He chuckled. "You just got it. I'd like you and Brooke to tag along with me and my dad. So, you ready for a break from the sander? Could I tempt you away with a giant Bean Grinder donut, maybe the kind with frosting?"

She looked down at herself and pulled at the hem of her shorts. He laughed. "You only have a little grit on your clothes, maybe some wood dust sticking to your arms. You look like a hardworking woman." With a smile, he added, "I promise we'll sit at one of the outside tables and you won't leave any varnish flecks behind."

She gave him a long look as she appeared to consider his offer. Finally, she said, "How did you know I can't resist anything with a thick layer of frosting, preferably chocolate? But give me one second."

Zeke stayed put on the grass while she hurried into the cabin. A few minutes later, she stepped onto the dock, the yellow shirt replaced with a blue one. She'd pulled her hair back in a twist of some kind. Each time he saw Andi, she'd fixed her hair in some new way, surprising him all over again. Her beauty took him aback whenever she smiled or her curious eyes focused on something she hadn't seen before.

She shook her hands at her sides. "I splashed some water over my face and arms. I'll dry off in the sun on the walk over," she said. "What about Art?"

He patted his pocket. "Dad has a phone in case he needs me. I'm on his speed dial."

Side by side, they took off down the winding path that led through the park to the edge of downtown. Suddenly, Andi took the big clip out of her hair and gathered it in a knot before sticking the clip back in. "On days like this I dream about cutting off all this hair. Having it short would be a lot easier."

"But, it's so..." He kept quiet, afraid of crossing some line that would sound way too personal.

"What?"

"Oh, nothing. I was only thinking your hair is, you know, distinctive." What a weasel. Her hair was beautiful, like the rest of her. But it was more than that. Sometimes it made him think of silk, luxurious black silk.

"That's exactly what everyone says whenever I declare I'm getting a buzz cut." She patted the back of her head. "Well, maybe not that drastic."

Zeke opened his mouth, stopping himself before he could vote down any notion of chopping off her hair. He quickly changed the subject to Art's favorite cherry strudel. A pretty lame topic. But he wasn't used to anyone making it hard for him to talk, or even think.

A few minutes later, they crossed the stretch of grass to the outside patio of the coffeehouse and claimed one of the small molded concrete tables and benches.

"Ready to take your order, ma'am."

"Coffee and one those super-sticky donuts you tempted me with."

He tapped the table with his knuckles. "Your wish is my command." Walking to the entrance, it struck Zeke that not only did he like Andi, but he also realized when he was with her, like now, he wasn't worried about a thing. Despite his usual concerns about his dad or the business or missing the restoration work he liked so much, his life was looking good. A few minutes later, he carried away their order.

When he approached the table, Andi was staring at her outstretched hand. Amused, Zeke took the coffees and pastries out of the cardboard carrier, placed them on their table. "Am I interrupting?"

She looked up and he noted a light shade of pink traveling up her neck and face. Oops, he'd embarrassed her.

"You took me by surprise, that's all." She held out her hand and wiggled her fingers. "I was pondering the very serious question of what color nail polish for the manicure I'll get when your boat is back to its shining and elegant self. I'm leaning toward dark red."

Had he ever had a conversation with a woman about nail polish? Nope. He couldn't say he had.

"By the way, I'm already going to take you up on your offer to use the tub in the apartment over the shop. A good soak is exactly what I need."

"It's all yours," he said before adding the first of three creamers to his coffee. He liked his coffee to be a light tan. Otherwise, he'd skip it.

"When did your dad move out of the apartment?" she asked.

"About five years ago. I have a big house down the street. Four bedrooms and a finished basement. Lots of room, plenty of privacy."

"Was he okay with moving out of his apartment? Even with all the stock stored there, when I went up to check out the tub I could see it was a nice place."

He grimaced as he blended the cream with the wooden stirrer. "No, he wasn't happy to move. I more or less had to threaten to lock him out of it."

"I used to work for a medical practice, Zeke," she said, keeping her voice low. "I'm not a medical expert, but I've seen things. Talked to families in all kinds of situations. Listened mostly."

"I wish you were an expert," Zeke said. "It's been just the two of us most of my life. My mom died when I was young. My granddad started the store and Dad loves the business and has kept it going to pass it on to me." But did he want it? That was a more complicated—and unresolved—question, and he had no intention of bringing it up now.

"From what I can tell, Donovan Marine Supply is practically an institution around here." She shrugged. "Granted, that's based on only a couple of weeks of observation."

"Speaking of observation, I know you've seen my dad act a little odd. He has a type of postconcussion syndrome—PCS. They call it atypical, because most people recover from PCS. My dad didn't."

Andi frowned. "I've heard of symptoms lingering after a concussion, maybe taking months for headaches and insomnia to go away. I recall a patient telling me he felt like himself again. So, Art's situation is different?"

It was different all right, and since no one knew why, they reached back into his father's past. "When my dad was a young teenager, he and other guys played hockey games on the river when it froze over in the winter. Like pickup basketball games over in the park. They organized them on their own and didn't have the protective gear kids wear today. From what he says, Dad lost consciousness after a collision with another player."

Andi's eyes opened wide. "That sounds bad. Some people, even my own father, to be honest with you, talk about those as the 'good ol' days, before anyone worried about kids' safety and adults didn't interfere.'"

He found it charming that she'd lowered her voice to imitate a dad tone. He said, "I hear people say that all the time. You can bet I take it with a grain of salt."

"Does he know how long he was out?"

"No one can remember for sure," Zeke said. "My dad tells me it was only a couple of minutes, but years later, one of his friends said it was more like ten, maybe even fifteen minutes."

"That's a long time," Andi said, her expression one of alarm.

"It is. And he didn't go to the hospital or even the general practitioner when it happened. He's always claimed that back then a bump on the head was just something you took in stride. The blurry vision and headaches didn't go away, though, so weeks later, he went to the doctor in town. He didn't receive any kind of treatment. The doctor said he'd probably had a concussion and would be okay. Eventually."

"And he was, right? More or less. Art seems fine most of the time."

"Exactly." Zeke stared into the cup, and

then gulped back a mouthful of coffee. "I don't repeat this much because it makes him sound old, but I was there when he told the neurologist that what happens to him is almost like what his grandmother used to call a spell. He knows that's an old word for certain kinds of mental lapses. Funny thing, though, that doctor nodded along, like he understood. It's also a bit more complicated than that because my dad didn't just have the one concussion…he had two, possibly three."

"Three?"

Zeke made his way through the second injury, a fall off a ladder. "That happened when I was a little kid. I heard him talk about it later as the reason he's afraid of ladders. He made a funny story out of it, but it's not so amusing now."

"No, it's not."

"I got him to move in with me when he had a couple of scary episodes. He lost track of time and left the water running upstairs and it leaked through the ceiling and down the wall into the store. Another time, maybe the worst, was when he got food poisoning, and I had to take him to the hospital. I traced it back to some spoiled food in his fridge.

He'd forgotten how old it was, but he didn't know it had gone bad because he's lost much of his sense of smell."

"That's common with lots of conditions."

Zeke nodded. "He was tested for several. He doesn't have Alzheimer's disease."

"For some reason I didn't think so," Andi said, "but that's not based on any specific knowledge."

"It was good news, but no one doctor so far can tell us he won't develop many of the same symptoms. Down the road. But the food poisoning gave me the shove I needed to force the issue about his living on his own. I hated doing it, *hated it*, but I had to."

The sadness filling Andi's eyes disarmed Zeke. He saw his own hurt reflected back at him in her eyes. He had to look away.

"Whatever else is going on," she said slowly, "Brooke took to Art immediately. She says he's really nice—and funny. Naturally, I'm grateful to him—" she flashed a closed-mouth smile "—and to Teddy, of course, for helping me make this boat escapade seem like an adventure."

Back in familiar territory and with Andi's warm eyes amused, Zeke felt as if he'd returned from a faraway place. Not nearly as pleasant a place as where he'd landed now. "I'm glad to hear that. As a matter of fact, Dad's got something in common with Teddy. He likes kids, and they like him. Even babies seem to light up around him."

"What a gift," Andi said. Then she took a big bite out of her donut. "Mmm…thanks for the treat."

"Anytime." He shifted his weight on the bench and gulped back more coffee. "To be honest, though, when I first saw *Drifting Dreamer* at the dock, I was angry. At my dad. And not just because he forgot the boat was being delivered. He'd forgotten to even tell me anything about it." He paused, but then added, "Now I'm not so sure about that idea. If Smyth had settled his bill all those years ago, the boat, and you, wouldn't be here."

Was she blushing? It sure looked that way. With a laugh in her voice, she said, "Well, maybe you aren't sure, but I am. The boat drifted—pun intended—right into my life and became my personal live-in summer job. I'm loving every minute of the work, too, especially now that we know a little more about *Drifting Dreamer*."

And to think, he'd thought it was going to be a routine summer. Not even the Fourth of July celebration would be the same old thing.

"How lucky can you get? You even get a day off for good behavior to go to the Fourth of July party at the marina."

"I've heard it's a big deal in Two Moon Bay."

He wasn't sure he'd go that far, but it would be special for him, because of her. "You'll see and judge for yourself."

"With your dad along, Brooke will have a good time."

She was right. But it worked both ways. Everything, it seemed, came back to his dad.

CHAPTER FIVE

ANDI STRETCHED HER arm to get deep inside a hard-to-reach cubbyhole behind the navigation table to check for damaged wood. Her hand hit a divider with a finger grip, but the first tug didn't budge it. The second and third tries didn't move it, either. Determined now, she took a breath and gave it one more hard pull. *Bam*…she captured the graying piece of wood, but jerked backward with the force of the movement.

When she righted herself, she shone her flashlight inside to have a look inside the narrow space. The beam caught the corner of something that looked like paper.

"Well, well, what's this all about?" she said to herself, curious and excited. Secret papers? That could be an overstatement, but these pages weren't left out in the open. Someone had stashed them out of sight.

Papers in hand, she scooted back and stepped from the table to the cabin floor.

Riffling through the pages, she saw a couple of handwritten notes. They looked like they'd been torn out of an old-fashioned bookkeepers' ledger. Andi smiled. It was like holding artifacts from an era long over. Looking more closely, one yellowed sheet had a list of mundane items, like hinges and various wood screws, and a list of fabric colors. No mention of a name anywhere or, specifically, the *Drifting Dreamer.*

Andi pulled out a ledger page that showed what appeared to be scribbled phrases, at least a dozen of them. *Paradise Bound, Fly Away, Serenity Seeker...*all two-word names. *Names.* And beside each one, someone, maybe the owner, had neatly written "No." Andi smiled to herself. Zeke would get a kick out that list. The name *Drifting Dreamer* wasn't even on it.

Wanting to be certain she'd left nothing behind, Andi stuck her hand in the locker and fished around, startling when her fingertips touched what at first felt like tissue paper. She gently pulled the paper forward and saw it was folded in thirds. The paper was fragile, so Andi gingerly spread it flat.

"Ah…a letter," she murmured, conscious of the increased beating of her heart.

She scanned the page. Wow. She went back and read the letter again. She reached for her phone to call Zeke. Where would his imagination take him when he saw this? He'd already called the yacht's past a mystery to be solved.

Andi smiled to herself as she pulled her phone out of her handbag and sent Zeke a text: Found something interesting on DD—really intriguing—stop in tonight if u can—anytime.

ZEKE DEBATED IF he should text Andi to tell her he'd take a rain check on her invitation. Naturally, he was curious—an understatement—about what she'd found. Instead of definitely putting off the visit, he'd texted her back saying he'd try to get over to see her, but it could be late. He was frustrated he couldn't be two places at once.

His dad had had a tough day all around, and by closing time, Art was restless and agitated. Days like this puzzled Art himself. It was as if he was wired with energy, but at the same time tired and craving sleep.

When they closed the store, Zeke suggested a walk through the woods with Teddy down to an out-of-the-way point on the shore that was one of his dad's favorite places. Art reluctantly agreed, and the three of them had taken off. That hadn't stopped Andi's message from being on Zeke's mind all evening. He mentioned in passing that Andi needed to talk to him. An issue with the boat, Zeke said, leaving it at that. When they got back from the point, Zeke heated up leftovers. By the time they finished dinner Art had run out of steam and was ready to climb into bed and watch a baseball game on TV until he fell asleep.

"Are you going to see Andi now?" he asked from the doorway to his room.

"I suppose I will."

"It's kind of late, though. Maybe Andi doesn't know how early in the morning we start working."

"It isn't even nine o'clock, Dad." Zeke didn't get into the reason it was important he see Andi that night. "Besides, she gets an early start herself. As long as you're okay here, I'll go on down and see what she needs."

His dad opened his bedroom door wider to let in Teddy. "Teddy and I need our sleep, so be quiet when you come in."

"I will, Dad." *It's like I'm sixteen.* His dad's gruffer-than-usual tone was puzzling. Art liked Andi well enough, although he seemed annoyed when Zeke was busy with the boat. He hadn't mentioned it to Andi, but the texts that interrupted him on the boat the other day had all been from his dad. They were pestering questions that didn't need immediate answers. Something new was going on.

Writing off his dad's negative tone to a bad day, Zeke headed out the door and back to the boat. Cabin lights were on, but the deck was dark. He stayed on the dock to call out to let her know he was there. "Ahoy, *Drifting Dreamer.*"

Andi appeared on deck. "Hey, glad to see you." She waved him aboard. "I've got something fun to show you."

He followed her into the main cabin, again impressed with how livable it appeared, even in the midst of the renovation. She had the cabinets stocked with food and fresh fruit filled a bowl on the work-space counter, such as it was, in the galley. “Looks like you’ve been to the farmers market.”

“I have, and it’s great. Have a seat. Let me get you a beer or a glass of local wine—direct from a booth at the farmers market.”

“A cold one sounds good. It’s humid like a rain forest out there.”

“I happen to have a couple of bottles of the local brew, Two Moon.” She pulled two bottles out of the fridge and twisted them open. She handed him one and he slid along the seat of the large booth-style dining table.

“We could turn this into a party boat,” he joked. “Between the deck and this cabin, plus the wheelhouse, the boat already looks like an ad for a luxury yacht in the tropics.”

“Wait ’til it’s done.” She glanced around, pride showing in her face even in the dim light. “You and your dad will be so glad the boat showed up.”

“I’m already happy about that.” The words spilled out of Zeke mouth, surprising him.

Before sitting across from him, she held her bottle out for a proposed toast.

“To?” he asked.

"To *Drifting Dreamer*," she said, tilting her bottle and tapping his. Then she handed him some loose pages, holding back only one. "Take a look at what I found."

"It's about time something turned up on this old boat." He scanned the top page. "An original list of hardware and boat cushions, and other gear."

"I think that's exactly what it is."

He held up the papers. "Where did you find these?"

She pointed across the cabin to the storage bins. "They weren't easy to get to, but I persevered."

"So these pages weren't exactly hiding in plain sight."

"Not at all. Take a look at the bottom two pages."

Zeke scanned the sheets and laughed out loud. "Looks like old-fashioned brainstorming for names." He went down the list. "*Paradise Bound?* What was Peterson, or whoever, thinking? That's awful."

"I don't know," Andi said slyly. "When you read the letter, it might make a little more sense."

"Letter?"

She picked up the folded sheet and waved it in front of him. "You wanted clues about the rest of the boat's history? You got 'em. We may have a glimpse into at least one adventure *Drifting Dreamer* had as a new boat. Well, probably had."

She unfolded the page and handed it to him. "Go ahead, read it out loud."

"Okay." He glanced at the signature first, Charles, and then at the greeting, Mary. Self-consciously, he said, "Here goes.

"January 9, 1941
Dearest Mary,
It's been a whole week since I held you in my arms and kissed you at the station. I wish it had been a kiss hello rather than goodbye. I watched your train pull away and am missing you already. But now I cheer myself up by remembering our first Christmas. Most of all, I remember your beautiful smile when you told your parents I asked you to marry me and you accepted. I was glad your parents looked pleased. I want them to trust me to be a good husband and love you forever and give you a happy life.

Wasn't it fun to dance at the Odyssey Ballroom? Let's go back to the Odyssey next year to celebrate 1942 and dance all night again? For now I'm forcing myself to be content with counting the months until our wedding in June. Have you given any thought to my idea about spending the summer on Drifting Dreamer, knocking about Lake Superior, port-hopping and doing exactly as we please? Just the two of us for our first summer together. I got the boat in hopes I would one day share my dreams with a special woman. And then I met you.

So, Mary, I'll close for now. I'm due in court and can't be late. It wouldn't look good if my father fired me from the family firm, now would it? I know you're studying hard for your exams—I'm proud of you for working so hard to become a nurse, but you have only a few months of training ahead. I wish I could be with you down in Milwaukee, but since I can't, do imagine me by your side, loving you more every day.

I check the post every morning and again in the afternoon and my spirit lifts

when I see an envelope addressed in your hand. Waiting impatiently to take you in my arms my love, and cover your face with kisses.
Yours always,
Charles"

Zeke continued to stare at the letter in front of him. The silence in the cabin covered them like a cloak. Not even the dim background noise from the marina intruded.

Andi got a faraway look in her eyes when she mused, "I can't stop thinking that this happened in 1941. All this happiness and talk of the future in January, and then by the end of the year, the war. We don't know if they went back to that ballroom or not."

"Maybe he joined up?" Zeke swallowed hard. Maybe it was the talk of dreams in the letter that touched him. "Even if he did, they could have had the boat for a long time after the war. Maybe they picked up their lives where they left off?"

"Maybe so," Andi said. "This is a big yacht with a lot of hiding places." She gestured around her at the partially dismantled cabin. "Who knows what I might uncover next."

Zeke threw his head back. "Oh, no. Now every day I'll wonder if something new has turned up."

"I'll keep you guessing, section by section," she said, cocking her head. "We can hope I find other things to fill in the Petersons' story." She shook her head, thoughtfully. "But, oh, that letter."

"It's okay to keep the suspense going a while," he said. More reasons to visit the boat, more chances to share a few minutes with her alone.

"My imagination travels all over the place," she said, "but when it comes right down to it, I want to pull together the real story. We have the whole summer to fill in the details of your mystery boat being launched."

A long, low roll of thunder distracted them both. A quick flash lit up the outside. Without exchanging a word, they simultaneously slid out of the booth and moved to the deck. The wind had picked up, sending *Drifting Dreamer* rocking, and pushing the bow against the dock. The fenders groaned as they dragged across the pilings and did their job of protecting the hull from scrapes and scratches.

Zeke hurried to check the lines and the position of the boat. For the next few minutes they stood side by side under the afterdeck canopy listening to the continuous rumble of thunder and watching the unbroken flashes of lightning. As fast as the wind had picked up, it died down and then the rain let go, buckets of it coming down in a steady stream.

"What a racket," Andi said. "Between the thunder and the rain, it's like a train coming through the waterfront."

"We've had so many of these hot, sticky days and late thunderstorms," Zeke remarked.

"I love these sounds, though." Andi sat in one of the deck chairs. "If the rain turns horizontal on us, we can go inside the wheelhouse."

"The wheelhouse? I almost forget there is one," Zeke said.

"You'll want to take the boat for a spin or two before selling her, won't you?" Andi asked softly.

Andi was thinking too small. A spin? Out a few miles and back? Somehow, he pictured being with Andi, like now, talking and laughing, leaving the store behind. "Oh, yeah, we'll definitely give *Drifting Dreamer* the so-called maiden voyage for her new and revived life."

Another long roll of thunder sounded in the distance, but the lightning was dimmer now. Andi smiled faintly.

Seeing her expression, he was drawn to the faraway look that had come over Andi when she'd talked about the surprises she'd found. He wondered what was going on behind those blue eyes that dominated her face. He laughed at himself. His feelings weren't as complicated as all that. He just wanted to be closer to her.

CHAPTER SIX

"I HOPE IT stops dumping buckets of rain on us soon," Art said, tilting his head back to look at the sky and grinning as his face got wet. "What do you think, Brooke? If we stare at the sky long enough, will it stop?"

"I don't *think* so."

Brooke's lilting tone playfully mocked Art, but that's what he was going after, Andi thought. Her daughter and Art had developed an understanding. He thought she was an amusing little kid and a pal for Teddy. She treated him like a funny grandpa, even if he wasn't her real one. Sometimes, though, Art could be a little standoffish with Andi herself, as if sizing her up.

"It's a good thing you have your brand-new raincoat, huh?" For Art's benefit, Andi added, "In yellow, too. No landlubber blue or pink for you."

"The boat isn't full of leaks anymore, either," Brooke added.

"What? You didn't like a little water drip-dripping on you? And what's a boat without rain filling up a few pails?" Art spoke in a serious tone, but he couldn't hide his teasing brown eyes.

Brooke made a face at Art to let him know she was onto his joke. "I like the boat much better now. Zeke and Mom finally dried it out."

Andi caught Zeke's eye, and from his expression, she could tell he was getting a kick out of Art and Brooke's banter. With her three companions appearing content, Andi tried to coax her spirits to match theirs. She wanted to join in wholeheartedly. The annoying rain was only an excuse for wishing she'd planned a different kind of day. Not that she dreaded this Fourth of July event. That was way too strong a word. But she had a nagging urge to hide out alone on *Drifting Dreamer.*

"Since the storm is supposed to pass through and head north in a little bit, I have a hunch we'll see the fireworks later after all," Zeke said, glancing at Brooke. "For now, it's a good thing Jerrod offered to move the marina party to his office and the *Lucy Bee.*"

"Brooke has been out on *Lucy Bee,*" Andi remarked.

"Is that so?" Art said. "When did you get so lucky?"

"Last summer I got to go on one of Jerrod's tours. We went to Sturgeon Bay. It was fun," Brooke said. "Lark called it a 'girls only day.'"

Brooke had come back from that visit with Miles filled with stories about Jerrod and his little daughter, Carrie. She'd also met Dawn and her son, Gordon, and Jerrod's crew. Everybody seemed to know everybody, and somehow Lark and Dawn were at the center of it all.

Most of the time it was a point of pride that she and Miles worked out their time with Brooke with a minimum of trouble. Miles once joked that Brooke was a conflict-free zone in their lives. Andi also liked how she and Miles treated each other. When she'd been notified that her job was being eliminated, Miles jumped in to offer financial help if she needed. Hadn't she encouraged Miles to pursue Lark?

But on a day like this, when she'd climbed out of her bunk wincing from the deep aches in every muscle in her body, she caught a case of the blues. She didn't like admitting she harbored petty resentment over the need to enter Miles's world or, more to the point, Lark's circle. Andi often felt like the ex-wife who seemed to have nothing going for her except a delightful daughter these people already knew. No real job or home, and no romance. Putting it that way, of course, she couldn't measure up. But that's the feeling her morning musings had left her with.

"Dawn and Jerrod got married on *Lucy Bee*," Zeke said, breaking the silence. "They threw quite a party. Anyone who happened to be on the waterfront was invited to stop by for cake and champagne."

"I heard all about it." Brooke cast an accusing look at Andi from under her umbrella. "But I *missed* it. My dad saved me a piece of cake, though."

"We had a family thing...my family," Andi explained defensively. Her mother's sixtieth birthday bash. Her dad had gone all out with catered food and a singer performing a lineup of classic 1970s songs, nudging into the '80s. As far as Andi was concerned, there was no question that Brooke's grandma's birthday party would take precedence over a stepmother's best friend's wedding. Miles had agreed and that was that.

She glanced at Zeke and saw his puzzled frown. Andi willed her lips to curl up in a smile, hoping it didn't look too phony. Memories of her disappointment with Brooke's attitude at her grandma's party had lingered too long as it was. Even in the midst of their family and friends, Brooke had continued to gripe about missing the wedding. To her, birthdays came around every year, but a wedding was a onetime event. Not an easy claim to counter.

When they got to the dock, Zeke led the way to the *Lucy Bee*, where Dawn greeted them from a couple of feet back from the rail and out of the rain.

"Hey—happy to see you." She pointed to a corner where the bins of life jackets were stored. "Raincoats and umbrellas over there, please." Dawn extended her hand. "And you must be Andi."

A cloud of strawberry blond hair framed

Dawn's bright face. Andi shook her hand and felt a little better in spite of her herself.

"Carrie has been waiting for you, Brooke," Dawn said. "She's up at the office with Gordon right now. Gordon is playing chess with a friend, but they're letting Carrie hang out with them."

Brooke looked up at Andi. "Can I go find them?"

"Of course. I know you want to see them." She and Dawn watched Brooke scramble off the boat and pull her hood over her head as she took off at a run down the dock toward the office for Adventure Dives & Water Tours.

"I think I have all the kids and their parents straight," Andi said. "I've heard only great things about Carrie and your boy, Gordon."

"That figures, since Lark's son, Evan, and Gordon have been friends for years." Dawn led Andi deeper into the boat. "I plan to put my son to work pretty soon."

"I've seen Evan a few times. But the only thing I know for sure is that he's been really good to Brooke," Andi said. "She adores him."

Dawn wiped her hand across her brow in

pretend relief. "It helps when the families merging worked out, huh?"

Andi nodded, amused by Dawn's good humor. "This is my day to put some faces with names." Andi nervously gnawed the inside of her cheek. She glanced around to locate Zeke and Art. They were with a dark-haired man she assumed was Jerrod.

As if reading Andi's mind, Dawn said, "Come on back and I'll introduce you to Jerrod."

"A man I've heard a whole lot about," Andi said, exaggerating only a little. "Zeke and Art are big fans."

"I've been meaning to come down to the boat to see *you*," Dawn said, maneuvering around a couple of benches. "That boat is a huge undertaking."

"I can't say what the boat will be worth when it's restored, but it seems she'll get another life." Her spirits lifted as she expressed that thought. "That yacht has had quite a few lives already. We just don't know what they were."

We? How chummy. She liked the sound of it.

They passed another row of bolted seats

and benches and joined a group in the relatively large space aft of the wheelhouse. Zeke stepped aside to make room for her and Dawn.

Before anyone started a formal introduction, Jerrod waved. "So you're the boat lady. Glad you could join us, Andi."

"Thanks." Andi gestured behind her. "I need to sign up for a day tour—and soon."

Jerrod lowered his head in a single nod. "We'd be happy to have you."

Out of the corner of her eye, Andi saw Dawn frown and put her hand across her midriff. Then she stepped out of the cluster of people.

"Are you okay?" Andi asked in a low voice.

"Not this second. But overall, I'm terrific. This will pass." Dawn took in a deep breath.

It was obvious Dawn didn't feel well, and Andi thought she knew why.

"I bet you already guessed I'm pregnant." Dawn managed a weak smile. "I don't have much morning sickness, though. I can get queasy any ol' time of day."

"Congratulations," Andi whispered. "Are

you keeping the news to yourself, or do most of the people here know?"

She swatted the air. "Oh, I can keep a secret if I have to, but what's the point? I get this green look on my face, anyway, so we started telling people a couple of weeks ago." In a flash, Dawn beamed with happiness. "I don't even care that I'm sick half the day. Like the saying goes, I'm 'over the moon.'"

Chuckling, Andi added, "And living on cloud nine no doubt. You sure look happy. The queasy wave has passed, I take it?" Speaking of waves, Andi thought, some odd emotions were washing over her and rapidly draining what upbeat energy she'd managed to muster in the last few minutes. It wasn't jealousy, though. Two failed marriages had cured her of any romantic notion of family, despite her parents' attitudes.

But the mix of feelings bringing her down hovered, anyway. Suddenly conscious of the heat and the noisy conversations around her, Andi struggled to focus on Dawn's declaration that she was feeling fine again.

Dawn zipped her jacket and pointed ahead to the dock. "Let's get off the boat. I'll show you the way we set up Jerrod's office for this rainy party."

They hurried to the grassy shore and past the marina office to a small building added to the back.

"Nelson set up a canopy over by the gas grill," Dawn said, pointing to a relatively protected spot on the grass, where the white canopy tent wobbled in the wind but stayed up on its four legs to keep the grill dry. "Jerrod's crew took on that job. But I'm going to get Gordon to set up tables inside the office."

"I'll help you," she said, irrationally feeling out of place walking next to Dawn, who called out to people who looked only vaguely familiar to Andi. At moments like these, the needless social awkwardness Andi tried to hide was also tinged with fear. Why else did it even cross her mind that Jerrod and Dawn would be predisposed to dislike her? Did she assume they thought Miles was better off without her? Nothing Miles or Lark had said or done even hinted at that kind of backbiting. Knowing she was creating the drama in her own mind only made it worse.

"Last year was my first time at one of Nelson's famous fireworks parties," Dawn said.

"It was great fun. He provides the brats and burgers, and the rest of us bring everything else, from chips to cake."

"I met Nelson the other day when Zeke brought *Drifting Dreamer* to the dock to fill the water tanks," Andi said. "I'd walked through the marina a few times when I was finding my way around. That's how I discovered the old boat in the first place."

Dawn smiled. "You're a brave woman to take on that job."

Ah, but that was the easy part. If only Dawn knew how she relished picking up her tools at the start of each day. She'd felt the same way years before when she'd open her eyes every Saturday morning knowing the weekend had arrived and she was free to devote two whole days to fixing up the house. When she had a sander or scraper in her hand, whatever ruffled her thoughts usually drifted away.

Grinning at Dawn, she said, "Here's my secret. I'm never happier than when I'm getting my hands dirty bringing back the original beauty of something. And right before my eyes." It was so different from the other nine-to-five desk work that had taken up so much of her life.

Dawn's eyes opened wide. Then she laughed. "And here I am—I think 'sander' and all that comes to mind are backaches."

Andi wasn't surprised. Most people she knew felt that way. It was rare for a kindred spirit like Zeke to cross her path.

She followed Dawn inside the office, where Gordon and a young woman were carrying a large wooden desk across the floor. They set it down in front of a row of shelves loaded with diving supplies. A tiny girl with yellow bows tied to the end of dark brown braids hopped in a circle in the empty but dusty space where the desk had been.

Brooke stood midway between Gordon and the little girl. "Hi, Mom." She pointed to the girl and then to the boy. "That's Carrie and he's Gordon."

Andi reached out to put her arm around Brooke and squeezed her shoulder. "So I see. Nice to meet you both."

Without a break in her hopping, Carrie jiggled her hand in a distracted wave.

Gordon nodded and introduced the young woman, Wyatt, one of Jerrod's crew.

"Look, Dawn, the floor is all dirty here." Carrie jumped and landed with both feet that sent wispy dust bunnies flying in all directions.

"Right you are, honey," Dawn said with a laugh. "I guess your daddy didn't clean under his desk."

Wyatt said she'd grab the vacuum and disappeared through the doorway to what looked like a storage room in the back. Gordon followed her after saying he'd see to the card tables and chairs. Carrie and Brooke ran behind him.

"So that's your Gordon," Andi said with a sidelong glance at Dawn. "Brooke has told me all about him."

"Carrie is like a little puppy the way she follows her stepbrother around," Dawn said with a contented sigh, "but he doesn't mind." She rolled her eyes. "Well, to be honest he doesn't mind too much."

Andi understood. Brooke had adjusted well to her complicated blended family, but she griped some, too. Missing trips away with Miles and Lark, especially if Evan came along, always left Brooke feeling a little abandoned.

"We can set up some of the food there." Dawn pointed to the wooden desk. "Speaking of beautiful wood, that's an old schoolteacher's desk. Nelson ended up with it when the town closed the old grammar school and auctioned off some items before they opened the new building. He stuck it in here when Jerrod rented the space. Both guys talk about refinishing it or getting a new desk, but it's not a priority."

Dawn moved closer to have a look at the heavy oak desk and couldn't stop herself from using her index finger to trace a deep groove in the desktop. The only permanent scar on the surface. Dark spots and circular stains, probably from water or coffee, marred its beauty, but a slash in the wood could be taken care of easily. She rubbed her palms together. "Ooh, just looking at it makes my heart beat a little faster."

"Hmm…come fall when the season's over, we'll talk," Dawn said.

Not a bad side project, Andi supposed. She yanked her thoughts back, though. Other priorities jumped ahead in line. "It's tempting, I admit. But I need a regular job. Working on the boat is my summer gig. You know, what

I'm doing before I have to get a grown-up job again."

Andi glanced down at her slim jeans and gauzy tunic in her favorite deep shade of turquoise. So different from her usual work clothes. "I managed medical offices for years. I've polished up my résumé and regularly send it out, but so far haven't found anything." She paused. "At least nothing I'd call a good fit."

"Miles mentioned that," Dawn said, her expression thoughtful. "I have lots of contacts around here. Lark, too. Between the two..." Dawn cut off her sentence and shrugged, but her cheeks turned an embarrassed pink. "I'm sorry. I suppose I shouldn't—"

"Please, don't apologize," Andi interrupted, lightly touching Dawn's arm. The discomfort Dawn showed was exactly the reason Andi had been anxious about this party. "Miles and I were divorced when Brooke was still a toddler. We've been on friendly terms for years. I'm happy for him, and my dealings with Lark are fine, too." That was her pat speech and she stopped there. Any more than that and she'd sound like a woman protesting a little too much.

"You mean I don't have to trip over Lark's name?" Dawn teased. "Or, try not to mention her, you know, *ever*?"

Andi shook her head. "Are you kidding? That's the last thing I want, especially from you. I know you and Lark are best friends."

Dawn stared down at the desk, absently thrumming her fingers over a large water stain darkening the grain. "I've been through the dealing-with-an-ex routine. I had to adjust to his new family. I was bitter and early on in a rage half the time. I have instant admiration for anyone who can keep divorce—and remarriage—civil."

When Dawn glanced up, Andi saw hurt in the woman's eyes. "That aside, I meant what I said about lending a hand. My PR business keeps me in touch with all kinds of people in the area. It's a pretty big network."

"And I'd appreciate any and all leads." Andi gently tapped the desk. "And I wouldn't mind a little moonlighting later on. This oak can gleam again."

"Good to know." Dawn patted her stomach. "*I* sure won't be refinishing furniture anytime soon."

When Gordon came back, Dawn directed

the placement of the tables. Andi started setting up the chairs and scanning the shelves lining the walls as she worked. The equipment was well organized, which probably inspired confidence in the divers Jerrod and his crew took out. A painting of men escaping a burning ship dominated one wall. Brooke had mentioned it once because it depicted a ship that had sunk to the bottom of the lake. Jerrod took divers out to see the wreckage.

Zeke liked Donovan's to have this same orderly look, she thought, and he had an eye for arranging stock to draw a customer's eye. It hadn't surprised her when he'd mentioned working on historical restoration projects in years past. That work required caring about details and his eye for precision carried over to Donovan's.

They were just about finished setting up the room when a steady line of people from boats in the marina started bringing in bowls and platters of salads and rolls and everything else typical of Fourth of July barbecues. At one point, Andi put her jacket hood over her head and held the door open for a line of people to come in and out. She caught Zeke's eye and waved to him as he stood under the canopy by the gas grill, tongs in hand. If she was Dawn's assistant, Zeke was Nelson's.

With the downpour easing and turning into a steady drizzle, and daylight turning to dusk, Dawn started spreading the word that the buffet was open. She shouted to Nelson and Zeke to bring platters of brats, burgers and chicken to the office.

Andi propped the door open with a chair, while Dawn went off with Gordon to round up marina guests and the group that had gathered on *Lucy Bee*. Andi positioned herself behind the buffet table and arranged the containers and platters of food while overseeing Carrie and Brooke.

With Andi's help, the girls soon took their full plates to a card table in the corner.

Andi tried using logic to quiet the shakiness rising inside her again, for no good reason, especially since Dawn had welcomed her like an old friend and Miles and Lark weren't even around. True, despite appearances she'd always been a bit of an introvert, but that didn't fully explain her feelings.

In between introducing herself to sailors coming in from their boats in the marina, and engaging in the typical social chatter about the weather, Andi kept up an internal debate about her ability to get along with people. She'd spent years dealing with patients and their families at the medical practice. Hadn't she gotten along fine with the staff she managed? Part of that job involved keeping track of birthdays and work anniversaries and remembering to ask after a sick child or someone's elderly parents. She put out weekly memos that usually included newsy items about employees' children and grandkids and their graduations and weddings.

Granted, those office interactions were lighthearted, but even those predictable social routines had gone out the door when her job went away. Even when she'd snapped up opportunities to take every kind of management seminar available, in person, she preferred those she could attend online rather than in a classroom. Taking the advice she picked up over the years, she'd drawn boundaries separating work and friendship. That had suited her, anyway. She hadn't made many friends among the families of Brooke's friends. Time constraints had defined Andi's life, or so she told herself. Preparing to move to Two Moon Bay brought home the sad reality that she'd made no close friends in recent years. Her world had become smaller and everything—people, places, events—was all about Brooke.

"We should all wear name tags," a white-haired man in the line remarked as he plopped a spoonful of potato salad on his plate.

Andi mentally yanked herself out of the rundown of her past and quickly introduced herself.

"I'm Ian," the man said. "I believe I've seen you over at the dock at Donovan's. My wife and I are staying on our boat here at the marina. Been spending summers down here for years."

"I'm Andi, from *Drifting Dreamer*." She explained how she happened to be living and working on the boat.

He nodded knowingly. "I figured you were the woman. From what I saw, that boat needs all the attention it can get. When was she built?"

Grinning, Andi filled in the details, always happy to talk about *Drifting Dreamer*.

"But it does my heart good to see a classic boat spruced up."

"Please, stop by anytime to check the progress." She didn't think Zeke would mind some casual visits. Couldn't hurt his business. Besides, she was proud of how even small pieces of the refurbishment were coming together. It's what left her with a sense of satisfaction at the end of each day.

When Ian nodded enthusiastically, Andi guessed she'd see him soon. She passed the next couple of hours schmoozing with several local people who kept their boats at Nelson's all summer and in his storage yard all winter. She also chatted with sailors whose home ports were in coastal towns in Michigan or Illinois. Two Moon Bay was one stop on their annual summer cruise. A few had chartered boats for a week or two of sailing on Lake Michigan. Some had standing reservations at Nelson's for the Fourth of July every year.

"I never knew Two Moon Bay was so famous for its fireworks," Andi said when Zeke came in to switch out a load of brats for an empty platter.

"What? How could that be? It's one of our major claims to fame," he joked. "And it looks like the legend has been salvaged for another year. The rain has stopped."

"I guess so," she said. She hadn't seen Brooke or Carrie since they'd finished eating and had run off. "I should check on Brooke."

Zeke shook his head. "Nah, she's fine. I just saw her on *Lucy Bee* hanging out with some other kids. Eating cookies, I think."

Andi let out a self-deprecating scoff. "Don't mind me. I forget she's not Carrie's age and I can't let her out of my sight." She swept her hand above the messy plates and dishes. "I suppose I better start cleaning up."

"I'll give you a hand," Zeke said. "Not many leftovers, anyway. Just these few brats Nelson took off the grill. That's it for this year."

"Where's Art?" Andi asked.

"When the rain stopped he went to get Teddy. He figured the dog would want to play in the grass with the younger kids," he explained. "Now that most of the food is gone, the mutt won't embarrass us with his begging. He's not above making the rounds to wait for crumbs to drop in the grass."

"I'm sure he does quite well," Andi said with a light laugh. "With that cute little face."

"He does have some bad habits." Zeke winced, but then his eyes went soft. "Truth is, he acts like a dog that probably wasn't given enough to eat, to be honest. We think that's why he tends to overreact around food. We can't say for sure."

Watching Zeke's eyes, Andi's imagination formed dark images about the condition that little dog must have been in when the two men took him in. From the first day she'd met Zeke, his eyes told her a lot about him. They were a gentle brown when speculating about Teddy's past and Art's injuries, sometimes appearing a little darker, filled with impatience or dread when he went over Art's work or fixed a mistake. Mostly, though, they were observant eyes, always quietly paying attention to what was going on around him.

Together, they finished cleaning up and refolding the tables and chairs.

Suddenly, the door flew open and Dawn stepped inside. "Hey, thanks, guys."

"My pleasure," Andi said. "I had the best spot of all. I got to meet quite a few people going through the line." She glanced at Zeke. "One guy, Ian, will likely wander down to the boat to have a look."

He gave her an amused look and said, "Glad to hear it. You can show off your handiwork."

Before Andi could respond, Dawn gestured for them to follow her. "Come on down to *Wind Spray* and watch the fireworks from there. It's a great location."

Remembering *Wind Spray* was Jerrod's dive boat and likely to be less crowded than the larger tour boat, the invitation was appealing.

"It turned into a nice evening after all," Andi said as they left the office. The sky had changed in the time she'd been behind the buffet table and now only a few dramatic reddish-orange streaks were left of the sunset in the western sky.

Tied up behind Jerrod's tour boat, *Wind Spray* had an open cockpit and diving platform that made Andi think of adventure and challenge. According to Zeke, the tours on *Lucy Bee* and Jerrod's diving excursions had turned out to be important additions to Two Moon Bay's waterfront and drew even more people to town.

Andi spotted Brooke and called out to her. "I need to make sure she knows where I'll be," she explained.

"And here she comes," Zeke said, "with Carrie tagging along."

Brooke waved and ran toward her, but reached *Wind Spray* first and went aboard with Carrie.

"I still sometimes forget my daughter knows many more people here than I do," she said. "She feels right at home with Dawn and Jerrod and their crew."

"I hope the same is happening for you."

Zeke's gentle tone sent a buzz through Andi. She hadn't expected that comment and didn't know how to respond. Maybe her heart knew she was right at home here on the waterfront with Zeke and Art, and even Dawn and the others, but her head needed time to adjust to such an unfamiliar feeling.

Wanting to keep her emotions about Zeke uncomplicated, she said, "That boat seems like a real home to me now, odd as that might sound. Until I walked over this way on a night not too long ago, it never occurred to me that living on a yacht would be one of my choices—the best choice."

"Hadn't occurred to me, either," he said, grinning. "I was spending my time wondering how soon we'd be able to get the broken-down thing off our hands. But seeing your effort spent on her every day, ol' *Drifting Dreamer* looks like she's found herself a new home port in Two Moon Bay."

“Even Brooke admits it’s kind of cool, you know, living on the boat.”

“Teddy might have had a little something to do with that.”

“You think so?” Andi said with a laugh.

When they got to the dive boat, Zeke stepped aboard, then quickly turned and offered his hand.

He no doubt knew she didn’t need his help, but she took his hand, anyway. His fingers were cool, his hold firm. This was the first time she’d touched him except for their initial handshake, or when they’d accidentally brushed past each other. Suddenly flustered by the tingling in her arms, she stole a glance at him, but when she saw him staring at her, she instantly lowered her eyes. The touch was a matter of seconds, but she liked it. It was one thing to make a new friend, a good friend, but it was another to get all tingly over taking Zeke’s offered hand. She couldn’t indulge those kinds of feelings over something so trivial.

“Glad you could join us.” Jerrod lifted his hand in greeting. “I heard Dawn put you to work.”

Jerrod's words broke through the odd fog that had descended over her.

"You give me too much credit, Jerrod," she said, chuckling. "Stationed at the buffet table was part of my master plan to stay out of the rain. I enjoyed every minute of it."

"Dawn said we could go sit up on the bow," Brooke said, coming to her side. "It's where we can get a good view of the fireworks."

"If Dawn says it's okay, then it's fine with me." Andi smoothed her thumb across Brooke's cheek. "You've been busy all day, haven't you? I've hardly seen you."

Brooke shrugged. "I guess so. Gordon said he'd come later."

Andi caught Dawn's amused eye. "He has a couple of friends from school here, Andi, but I'm sure Gordon will stop by and listen to the girls tell him all about their day."

"Uh, Brooke, did Art say anything to you about taking Teddy back home?" Zeke asked.

"Nope. He just said Teddy needed a walk on the beach."

Frowning, Zeke said, "I think I'll go rescue my dad. He'll be tethered to Teddy all night if the dog has his way." He quickly got off the boat and hurried down the dock.

He's worried, Andi thought. But Art had seemed fine. So far, there had been one incident over the raincoat delivery in the store and another Zeke mentioned about an order that was mixed up, but he'd caught it in time. Although, in both cases, Zeke seemed unnecessarily concerned more than either incident warranted, out of proportion to what had actually happened. She couldn't help but think he was overreacting now. On the other hand, who was she to second-guess him?

Accepting Jerrod's offer of a glass of chilled white wine, Andi settled in the cockpit and chatted with Wyatt until the first crack of fireworks left bursts of red and white lights cascading in the sky to the sound of Sousa marches. Yellow sunbursts filled the sky over the lake, followed by a flurry of star shapes twinkling in the night. In a lull of a couple of seconds, Andi craned her neck to search behind the dock to the row of folks in canvas chairs set up on the grass watching the fireworks. No sign of Zeke or Art.

The minutes passed, ten, then twenty. After thirty minutes, the show was over. Zeke never came back.

CHAPTER SEVEN

SEEING THE LIGHT coming from the cabin, Zeke decided to take a chance. Since Brooke was probably sleeping, he barely raised his voice when he called out Andi's name from the dock.

She appeared on the deck almost immediately. "I was just thinking about you," she said in a stage whisper. "Is everything okay?"

He shifted his weight from one foot to the other. "Uh, it's fine now. Dad's asleep."

She gestured to the deck table. "Can you sit a minute?"

"Sure. I stopped by because I wanted to tell you why I left." He paused, but came aboard. "Well, why I didn't come back."

She put her hand on his upper arm. "You don't have to explain."

"Maybe not, but I want to." He gripped the

back of his neck, stiff and sore now from the stress of the night.

"Okay. I'll get us some sparkling water." She went into the cabin and seconds later he heard the sounds of ice clinking in glasses.

"It's such a muggy night," Andi said, coming back to join him. "I couldn't concentrate on the movie I was watching on my tablet and was going to come up here and sit for a while, anyway. Brooke wore herself out today. She's sleeping like a rock."

Zeke gulped back half the tumbler of lemony water. "I found my dad and Teddy in a kind of hidden place on the other side of the yacht club. They were okay."

"What a relief," Andi said.

"I think I overreacted."

Andi turned her head and waved toward the yacht club down the shore. "You mean Art was lost over that way?"

"Not exactly lost. I mean, he knew where he was." He shook his head at his own tentative answer. "But I don't really know if he intended to go to that spot or just ended up there. I had a hunch he might wander down to a spit of land that's at the end of the public waterfront. You have to go along a path in the woods before you get to it. There's one picnic table there and that's where I found him."

"No one else was around?"

"A few people were sitting on blankets in the grass closer to the water. Watching the fireworks, I suppose." Almost tongue-tied, he had trouble finding the right words to explain his concern. "I'm having a hard time pinpointing what's bothering me about how he wandered off."

"Take your time, Zeke. I'm not going anywhere."

The sound of her soothing voice saying those words loosened something inside him. Tension, maybe. Half the time he didn't realize how on edge he was. But seeing his dad through her eyes, a stranger's eyes, made every incident bigger and even more worrisome. It was habit now, Zeke thought, the easy way he wrote off his dad's mental blips. *Blips.* He used that weak word sometimes, even afraid to call a lapse a lapse. Andi's presence made it harder to ignore his dad taking off on his own with Teddy.

"He'd been around people he knew all day," Zeke said, "so when he left for the beach with the dog I assumed he'd be back for the fireworks. He looks forward to it every year."

"Did Art forget the two of you were invited aboard *Wind Spray*?"

Even in the dim dock light, he saw concern in Andi's eyes. Just from the focus and attention she fixed on him, he knew she was struggling to understand the situation with his dad. And why not? He even had trouble defining the problem.

"That's the thing. Honestly, I'm not sure. I asked why he'd gone so far away from the marina party. He had to detour to the street to get back down to the beach—it's not a straight shot from here to the yacht club." That's one of the things that stumped Zeke about this odd wandering.

"Maybe he needed to get away from the crowd." Andi's hands moved in a rolling gesture as she spoke. "At the medical practice, I'd hear stories about older people avoiding crowds. A neurologist once told me people's brains tire out more easily as they age, not that Art is that old."

"No need to sugarcoat anything, Andi. The doctor is all smiles when he says Dad's heart is young. Then he changes his tune when he warns that his brain has aged faster than the rest of him." Zeke scoffed. "He was trying to tell me not to 'fret over'—his words—my dad's health. I don't know why he thought that would help."

Andi sighed. "No. It sounded like a clumsy way to say there's nothing they can do for him."

"Well put." Zeke met Andi's gaze. He struggled not to stare at her hair piled in a loose bun on top of her head. Earlier at the barbecue she'd put it in a high ponytail that hung down her back. He shifted in his chair to distract himself.

"I think my dad was cheated." For a long time Zeke had wanted to be that blunt about his dad's situation.

"Uh, cheated how?"

Her question came out as a challenge and he took it.

"Cheated out of recovering from those concussions. Not having them diagnosed, not being followed by a doctor who knew what happened to him." Zeke rested his elbows on his knees. "It makes me mad, that's all."

"I'm sorry," she said, her tone filled with sympathy that threw him off his center. He wasn't used to talking this way. Even Nelson, who knew what Art was dealing with, rarely mentioned it, as if the subject was off-limits.

"It must be even harder," she said, "because Art is fine most of the time. He's such a great guy. You remember how Brooke took to him the very first day she saw him again. They'd only met once or twice, but they've become fast friends."

Zeke nodded. "That's the hardest part." He knew missing pieces of the story hung in the air between them, like real, tangible things. "It's been just the two of us for most of my life. I mentioned my mother died a long time ago."

"I see... I think." Andi leaned toward Zeke. "I was curious about your mother. I'm glad you said something."

"It's not as if I'm blaming my dad's problems on my mother's death. Dad got over that loss better than I did, at least, at first." Flashes of his dad's attempts to explain why his mom left them still touched Zeke after all these years. But he wasn't ready to reveal that. "He was more concerned about me than he was about himself."

Wanting to change the subject, Zeke

pointed to the quarter moon, high in the sky now. A few stars were visible, but the ambient light of the marina blocked most. "You have to get out into the lake a ways before you see a true starry sky."

Andi tilted her head and looked where he was pointing. "Stars. Imagine that. It's been ages since I've seen more than a few of the brightest ones."

Zeke exaggerated a sweeping gesture to take in the boat. "So happens we have a boat. I guess when we get her put back together some, she could take us far enough out to see some stars, huh? This fall, before it gets too cold."

Andi responded with a quick slap of her palms. "See? You inherited a floating stargazer. She's only slightly torn apart."

Zeke laughed. *Drifting Dreamer* wasn't exactly ready for even a short cruise. It wouldn't be long, though. Andi was making progress. "We'll let her loose from the dock one day soon."

"It's back to work, tomorrow," Andi said. "I won't be slathering on the varnish just yet, not in this humid weather. Tomorrow, with Brooke off to her riding camp, though, I'll get these portholes off and that wood sanded down and bleached."

Andi's updates were good, but he appreciated the lilt in her voice and the energy she exuded even more. She hadn't lost a drop of enthusiasm for the project, even for jobs that were drudgery. Still early in the process, it was going to get a whole lot messier before it all came together. "You're coming along at a fast clip."

"And enjoying every minute of it. And you know, I might come across some other tidbits on the boat. You never know."

"The letter makes me all the more curious because of how little information we really have about this boat."

"True—so much love and hope in the air between Charles and Mary. A new boat, a summer wedding and honeymoon, but then, so much neglect at the end."

Zeke nodded. "When you put it that way, it sounds dark." He drained his glass and stood. "I should get back. I hope everything's back to usual with my dad tomorrow."

"Who knows? Maybe I'll find more lists. Or, with any luck, I'll come across another letter."

"Another chance to snoop," he said, laughing.

"Hey, you know what I meant." She laughed with him.

"You just happen to be very easy to tease." Surprised by how familiar, even intimate, he'd sounded even to his own ears, he said a quick good-night.

"Sleep well. I hope Art's okay."

He stepped off the boat and headed toward the street filled with the satisfaction of knowing she'd be on the boat tomorrow. And for the days and weeks ahead. He'd been so wrong when he'd seen *Drifting Dreamer* as a big headache. But the boat had brought something—someone—new into his life. When he reached the corner of the building, he pivoted to take a last look at the boat.

She was standing on the stern. He hadn't expected to see her there, and it felt as if he'd been caught at something. But she'd been watching him. Smiling to himself, he lifted his arm in a goodbye gesture at the exact same time she waved at him.

CHAPTER EIGHT

"YOU CAN'T EVEN sit still," Andi teased, glancing at Brooke in the passenger seat. "Look at you bouncing all over the place."

"I *finally* get to ride a horse." Brooke clapped her hands. "Not my own horse yet, but still."

"You've ridden before," Andi said, recalling the treks to the riding school at a large stable a few miles west of Green Bay.

"Not *every day*. Not all summer. Not like now."

Andi laughed at Brooke's singsong tone. "Okay, okay, I get it." This riding camp was one more step leading to the day when Brooke would have a horse of her own. This fascination had started with an attachment to the horses in the picture books she and Miles read to Brooke before she could even talk. Later, from the perch of her car seat, she'd spotted a mare and her colt through the window as they passed a farm outside of Green Bay. Her first horse sighting, Andi liked to call it. Now, at age ten, Brooke rearranged her shelf of ceramic and wooden horses on the boat almost every day.

"I don't know anyone at the camp," Brooke said, out of the blue.

A quick change of subject, but Brooke's nervousness about camp surfaced now and then, and no amount of reassurance that she'd meet other kids soothed her worries. Of course not, Andi mused. Understanding words weren't enough anymore. She said them, anyway. "Not for long, Brooke. You don't know what could happen. You could even make a new friend today."

Brooke nodded. As Andi made the right turn onto the road to the stable, she smiled to herself, glad Brooke took her words to heart.

Over the last few months the promise of riding and learning how to take care of horses had kept Brooke's enthusiasm alive and stronger than her fears. Afternoon swimming hadn't hurt, either, or lunches served on picnic tables set up outside of a snack shop next to the pool.

Grassy Shore Stables and Riding School

was only a few miles out of Two Moon Bay on a side road that ended at the lakefront. The camp sat on several hundred acres of woods and fields crisscrossed with trails outside of the fenced training corrals. The owners lived in a sprawling house—*estate* might be a more fitting word—set back from the entrance at the end of a birch- and oak-lined drive.

Andi found a parking place in the already half-full lot. Even before getting out of the car, Brooke spotted the arrow pointing to the small red-and-white clapboard building marked Riding Camp. Other arrows led to the east and west stables and corrals filled with horses. Still others led to the riding trails. Andi breathed a little easier when Brooke ran ahead to the building. On their first visit they'd taken a tour in a surrey-topped truck along with other parents and kids checking out the camp. It was more like a complex than what Andi's mom had casually referred to as a horse farm in a phone conversation with Brooke, who'd jumped right on it. "Stables, Grandma, stables," she'd said.

They were greeted by a couple of cheerful young women in bright red T-shirts with Come Ride With Me printed in black in an arc above a horse's head. Brooke probably knew exactly what kind of horse it was, Andi mused.

Brooke claimed their place in line behind a girl with almost white-blond hair, cut short and with little spikes that seemed more natural than styled. Andi assumed the woman with her was likely her mother because she had the same short blond hair, only a little tamer. Andi smiled at the look-alike pair, especially at the girl. She rocked back and forth on the balls of her feet, raring to go.

Andi caught the woman's eye. "I'm Andi, and this is Brooke. The big day finally arrived, huh?"

A smile tugged at the corners of the woman's mouth. "At long last, if you know what I mean. I'm Joy Lindberg, and this is my daughter, Florey."

Brooke smiled broadly at Florey, all traces of shyness gone. "Have you ever been on a horse before?"

"Couple of times," Florey said shyly, "but this is my first camp."

Brooke nodded. "Me, too." As if holding

a grooming comb, she moved her arm in a long sideways motion. "I want to learn how to keep the horses looking nice."

"I read in a book that horses have their own special shampoo," Florey said.

Brooke giggled. "It must come in really big bottles."

Andi exchanged an amused look with Joy as they moved up a couple of steps in line. When Florey's turn came, she told Brooke she'd wait for her, and a few minutes later, the two girls had their name tags and camp bags and took off with a counselor for their orientation session.

"Whew," Andi said with a laugh. "We're new to Two Moon Bay, so Brooke was nervous about not knowing anyone here. I'm glad we ended up in line behind you and Florey."

"We're just the opposite. I've lived around here my whole life. Florey saw some kids she recognized from school, but none were close friends. I could tell she was happy to meet someone new." Joy checked her watch. "Do you have time for coffee at the snack bar? It's just up the hill."

Andi thought about the portholes and the

hatches and all the other work on the boat waiting for attention. Her first impulse was to say no and retreat into herself. But would a quick cup of coffee and a friendly conversation throw off her schedule that much? She'd just work a little later in the day. "Sure, and maybe one of those outdoor tables will be free."

She and Joy meandered up the hill on the red-cedar-chip path to the point it split, with the house off to the left and the stables, the pool and other outbuildings on the right. The sun shone brightly, but it wasn't too hot, at least not yet.

"We're not the only ones who had coffee on the brain this morning," Joy said, waving to a couple who hurried past.

"And you probably know them all."

Joy pointed to the couple now ahead. "Parents whose kids go to Florey's school."

"By any chance is it the Lincoln School in Two Moon Bay?" Andi asked.

"Matter of fact, it is."

"That's where Brooke starts in the fall."

"Great. She'll know at least a few kids there. When did you move to town? And why?"

Andi did a quick rundown about Miles's

move and the demise of her career, which made this a perfect time to move. She left out the major loose ends—a real home and a real job.

It didn't take long to get a cup of coffee at the take-out window of the snack bar with the tantalizing name Rich & Sweet Corral, but all the tables on the patio were full. Joy pointed to a low stone wall, where they could sit and look down the hill at horses grazing in fields or inside a corral. Groups of kids sat in circles on the grass. "Orientation, I suppose," Joy said. "I hope Florey doesn't spot me. She made it clear this was her thing."

"Sounds familiar. Brooke gives me some attitude, too."

After a couple minutes of small talk, Andi learned about Joy's deep roots in Two Moon Bay. "I'm a third-grade teacher in Sturgeon Bay, so I have the summer off. A good thing, too, because all Florey has talked about is this camp." Her expression curious, Joy asked, "Where did you wind up living?"

Andi laughed. "On a boat, actually. *Drifting Dreamer*." She explained how she was spending the summer, ending her story by brushing the air with an imaginary paintbrush. "It will take all summer to get it done."

"That sounds a lot different than office management," Joy observed, her expression frankly puzzled. "You sound pretty excited about it."

She described the feeling she had restoring her house. "It's taking something apart and repairing it and then putting it all back together."

"Now that's what I call a summer adventure!" Joy exclaimed. "Where is it docked?"

"Down at Donovan Marine Supply. Zeke Donovan and his dad, Art—"

"Zeke?" Joy's eyes opened wide in surprise. "I know him. We went to school together."

"Small town, small world," Andi said. "Then you know he runs the marine store with his dad."

Joy's subtle frown wasn't lost on Andi.

"I run in to him once in a blue moon," she said, her expression thoughtful. "Years ago, I saw that he'd been part of a team restoring a building in a town up the coast, a stone building called Settlers Hall. But the last time I saw him he was mostly working full-time in the store with his dad."

"Yes, Zeke mentioned doing that historic restoration. In the past, though."

"I suppose it's in the past," Joy said, "but restoring the octagonal building, which you now know as the Bean Grinder, left his mark on Two Moon Bay."

"Really? I had no idea," Andi said. She drained the last of her coffee and stood to leave. Something about the way Joy talked gave her a sense Zeke's old friend knew a lot about him. Much more than Andi did. It put her on guard against saying too much. Especially about Art.

"Why don't we carpool?" Joy suggested, getting to her feet. "We're not far from Donovan's. We live on Night Beach Road."

"I'm familiar with that street," Andi said, leaving out the part about staying in Lark's cottage. Joy probably knew Lark, anyway. And Dawn, too, and maybe even Nelson and the whole crowd. "Carpooling is a great idea."

"Why don't I pick them up today to start," Joy offered.

Andi agreed and jotted down Joy's address. She knew exactly where it was. "I pass your house on my way to the bike trails in the state park. Lovely homes on that street," she said, knowing that with the exception of Lark's cottage and two more just like it, the rest of the houses were newer and bigger.

Their pick-up and drop-off arrangements set up, Andi followed Joy's car out to the road and back to town. Soon, she pulled into an available spot in the Donovan's lot. And there weren't many. The gravel lot was unusually full.

She walked past the building on the way to the dock, but something felt off. It wouldn't hurt to peek inside and see if they were as busy as they looked.

Opening the back door, Teddy trotted toward her. "Hey, boy," she said, leaning over to scratch the fur on his neck. "What's up around here, huh?"

When she saw the line at the counter, and no Zeke or Art in sight, she had her answer.

Spotting Zeke standing in front of a row of bins filled with stainless-steel fittings, she called out, "Hey, you need some help?"

Immediately, Zeke's face registered relief. He hustled back to the register. "Can you bag a dozen of those fittings for an order and then look around to see if other customers need some help?"

"No problem," Andi said, grabbing a bag with the Dovovan logo off the counter. She kept one eye on Zeke, who quickly started a credit-card transaction at the checkout. After helping a woman carry an armload of stainless-steel deck hardware to the counter, Andi hurried to a couple standing at the display of kayaks and canoes. She'd overheard Art quip that these small boats and trolling motors were "impulse buys." The couple seemed eager to fulfill the prediction Art had joked about. But no sign of Art himself.

Approaching the couple, she said, "I'm only filling in today, and I'm no expert on kayaks, but perhaps I can help you."

The woman flashed a bright smile. "We talked to someone—an older man—right before the Fourth about getting a couple of kayaks. We're standing here pretending to consider this, but really, we've made up our minds."

The man laughed. "Oh, yeah, we're down to the big decision now. Yellow or blue? We have a truck, so we'll pile them in the back."

"Let's get this done," the woman said. "I say we go for the blue ones."

"Well, then," Andi said, eyeing the kayaks. "I'll take you to the counter and we'll tell Zeke which ones you're buying." She looked at the shrinking line and saw he was folding a pile of sweatshirts and T-shirts of various sizes for a family of five.

"I can fold those items." She gestured behind her. "Why don't you help this couple with the kayaks they just picked out."

Zeke didn't protest, but pushed the pile to the side. "That would be great."

Andi bagged and boxed the clothing and chatted with the family that had come in for one pair of oarlocks, but left with two shopping bags of stuff. Not long after, Zeke assisted the couple with loading the kayaks into their truck, along with their two complimentary Donovan Marine Supply T-shirts. The design on the shirts showed variations of the two moons of Two Moon Bay.

"Where's Art?" Andi asked when Zeke came back and they'd cleared the checkout line.

Zeke tightened his mouth. "He wasn't feeling so well this morning. He slept later than usual and I told him to stay home until he felt well enough to come in."

"Do you want me to go check on him or stay around here?" Andi asked.

He waved her off. "No, Art said he'd be fine. Go ahead and get on with your day."

"Okay, but you have my cell number, so call if you need help."

Odd, but she didn't like leaving Zeke alone. Ridiculous, really. Zeke had handled the unpredictable nature of life with Art just fine without her. But she'd felt so at home in the store she'd have been happy hanging around longer.

Stop it... I'm here for only a few weeks. It's like being a temp in an office. That's all.

APPROACHING THE BOAT, Zeke heard the grind of the hand sander start and stop, start and stop. Zeke stood at the stern and waited for a break in the noise from the cabin before calling out to Andi.

A minute later, she appeared on the deck. "Is Art okay?"

"He's fine. He's in the office. I just came by to let you know he felt good enough to come in."

"Good. Come on aboard," she said. "I need a break before Brooke comes back full of stories about her first day at camp."

He'd hoped for an invitation more than he cared to admit. He stepped on board and commented on her progress.

She took him on a quick tour to show him that she'd repaired some damaged wood. "The old varnish is almost falling off," she said.

He nodded, but he was much too distracted just looking at her to actually follow her commentary. Since her hair was hidden under her baseball cap, that left him staring into her dark blue eyes. Flashing a smile before she went off to get bottles of water, she looked remarkably happy.

"You seem like you're enjoying yourself amidst the dust and grime," he said when she came back.

She leaned over and brushed sand and varnish flecks off her knees. "The time of my life," she said, laughing. "I think only you believe me when I say that." She took several long swallows of water.

"You were that thirsty?" he teased.

"I guess so." She glanced around her.

"When Brooke gets back from camp, she can bring her tablet or some art supplies up here on the deck. I'll keep going for a while."

"Here she comes now," Zeke said, gesturing to the drive next to the store, where Brooke had appeared with another little girl at her side.

"And Florey is with her." Andi waved to the girls. "And her mother. I think you know her."

Zeke kept his eyes on the woman coming toward them. Tall like Andi, but with short blond hair. He knew exactly who she was. "Joy Goodrich, or rather, Lindberg. I haven't run in to her in a while." He wasn't especially pleased to see her now.

"Joy and I worked out a carpool. I'm doing the picking up and dropping off tomorrow," Andi said.

Andi had no idea he and Joy had a history, Zeke thought. Well, to say it was a history gave it more weight than it deserved. They were only kids when Joy had been an unwitting witness to his really bad family drama. He hadn't planned to share any of that ancient history with Andi.

Zeke raised his hand to greet Joy as she approached and Andi invited her on board.

"Haven't seen you in ages, Zeke," Joy said, leaning in and planting a quick kiss on his cheek.

"Not since some fund-raiser or another, I guess," he said with an awkward laugh. He sounded vague to match her words, but he recalled they'd spoken briefly at the yacht club only last summer.

Joy and Andi turned their attention to the two excited girls full of stories about their day. Brooke had ridden a Morgan horse named Maple, because she was the color of maple syrup. Florey's horse, Jasper, was an Appaloosa, Brooke explained, and when she drew out the *loosa*, they all laughed.

"They went swimming and they watched some older girls groom their horses," Joy said.

"We'll do that again tomorrow." Brooke spoke like she meant business.

"Sounds like a good time," Zeke said, glancing at Andi. "But I better leave you all to it and get back work."

"How is your dad these days?" Joy asked.

"Doing well," Zeke answered, stepping off the dock. "We're keeping the store going."

"So I hear," she said. "You tell him one of your old friends said hi."

"I'll do that. Stop in and say hello sometime." He pointed to Florey and Brooke. "Looks like you might be in the neighborhood now and again this summer."

Grinning at Andi, Joy said, "Florey and I both made a new friend at camp."

Zeke saw Andi looking back and forth between him and Joy. Probably curious. "See you later," he called out.

He got back into the store in time to accept a couple deliveries, and admitted to himself he was bothered that Joy had shown up out of the blue.

"Hey, Zeke," Art asked, "is this really a life raft?" He was looking at the oversize box delivered by a small freight company and stored out of the way in the office.

"It is. Nelson is working on fitting a sailboat for a retired couple from Green Bay." He repeated the couple's ambitious plan to take their sailboat to the Mississippi River, then to the Gulf Coast, and from there it was off to the Virgin Islands.

"That's a big plan," Art said.

"I know," Zeke said, "a dream that takes some work to carry out." Thoughts of *Drifting Dreamer* came to him, along with the letter. The yacht's name hadn't been lost on Andi, either. Somehow, it seemed important that the next owners wouldn't let that restored classic beauty deteriorate again. It deserved a dream.

"Do you remember Joy Goodrich, a girl I went to school with?" Zeke asked, as much to change the subject as anything else. Thinking about *Drifting Dreamer* drying out in a boatyard for years made him sadder than he cared to admit.

"Sure I do. That awkward little girl turned into a pretty blonde, huh?"

Zeke laughed. "She wasn't *that* awkward, Dad."

"Yeah she was," his dad said thoughtfully "Had a nice family. I remember her mother well. A teacher."

"So is Joy," he said. "Let's start cleaning up, so we're ready to close up on time. Then we'll go to the Bean Grinder and get some coffee."

Taking out his phone, he sent Nelson a text

about the life-raft delivery. Then, starting at the front of the store, he straightened out the rack of boating magazines and a shelf of cruising guides and charts, along with their fairly extensive collection of books on boat handling and maintenance. He looked up when the minivan passed through the lot and turned left onto the street. He watched as Joy and the little girl drove away.

A part of him wished he'd told Andi the whole story of what happened to his mother. He wondered what Joy might have told her. But what difference did it make now, anyway? It all happened decades ago.

CHAPTER NINE

STANDING ON THE deck, Andi asked—demanded—that Brooke repeat the story one more time. Andi wasn't taken by complete surprise. Since the first day of camp, over two weeks ago now, she'd been trying not to think too much about the possibility of Brooke taking a fall.

"No big deal, Mom. I don't even have a bump."

"What's up?" Art called out as he followed Teddy closer to the *Drifting Dreamer.*

"I fell off Maple. But I got right back on him." Brooke's beaming smile was smug and self-satisfied.

Andi struggled to keep her tone neutral, but why did Art have to show up and jump into the conversation? She didn't want to undermine Brooke's confidence, and the riding instructor had given her a fairly detailed account of Brooke's spill. It wasn't unusual for new riders to fall off a horse, and Brooke never mounted Maple or any horse without her protective helmet in place. One voice in Andi's head told her to let it go, accept the tumble from Maple was, as Brooke described, "no big deal."

Another voice told her to probe a little deeper. But not with Art standing right there.

Changing the subject, Andi said, "Is it a slow day in the store?" She'd seen only one car parked in the lot, so she knew that's why Art was free to visit with Teddy.

"Nope. Uh, we're real busy. Matter of fact, we could use some help if you got a little time."

"Did Zeke send you down here?"

"Not exactly. But I saw you pull in and figured I'd come ask you myself. Zeke's on the phone with a customer."

Andi glanced at Brooke. She was on the ground rubbing Teddy's jowls and looking none the worse for wear after an eventful day at camp. "Okay, I'll be glad to help out."

"Good. We need you." Art spoke with conviction. Then he turned to Brooke. "Will you walk Teddy right around here, Brooke? You can bring him inside if he scratches at the screen door."

"Come on, Teddy." Brooke stood and broke into a run. With his ears flopping, Teddy ran ahead and led her in a circle around the expanse of grass between the dock and the store.

When Andi followed Art into the store, she spotted a couple of customers, one browsing the magazine rack and another loading deck stanchions into a shopping cart. Zeke was in the office in front of the computer.

"So, what can I do?" Andi asked Zeke. "I hear you could use a hand."

Zeke frowned and glanced at his dad.

A setup. Something had seemed off about it. "Maybe you need me to do a Bean Grinder run?" She eyed Art and kept her tone light.

"Later," Art said. "I want to know about Brooke's fall. Did she hit her head?"

Andi's heart softened at Art's ruse. He just wanted to get Zeke in on the conversation about Brooke. Too often, Andi herself forgot how painful these mental lapses must be for Art, especially because most of the time his mind clicked along fine as he went about his business.

"It wasn't a hard fall, Art. And Brooke wears a helmet when she rides—all these kids do," Andi pointed out. "Just like when they ride bikes."

"Did she lose consciousness?" Zeke asked, his features set in concern.

"No, no. This is getting overblown." She paused to figure out how she really felt. At first she'd been like Art, demanding answers. But she trusted Brooke—and the riding instructor. *Mostly.* "I mean, no one suggested her head even hit the ground. She claims she fell on her backside and hip."

"You sure?" Art demanded, his arms tightly folded across his chest.

"As sure as I can be."

Art abruptly turned around and left the office, and with a complete change of tone chatted with a customer as he ran a credit-card sale of books and magazines.

The man with the stanchions pushed his cart to the counter. "I'll be right back," Zeke said.

Andi had helped out often enough to understand that a packing job was involved in the substantial sale of deck hardware. She followed Zeke and asked if she should start wrapping the stainless-steel stanchions in packing paper.

"If you don't mind," he said tersely, keeping his eyes on the register.

Who was he annoyed with? Her? Art? Or maybe a perceived problem of Brooke's interrupting his work?

From the back-and-forth of the conversation, it was clear the customer had a vendor account with Donovan Marine and Zeke knew him well and spoke in a kind of shorthand. As Andi rolled and taped each piece, she found her thoughts drifting back to Art and why he'd come down to the boat in the first place. It certainly wasn't to ask for help in the store. That came later, after he'd heard about Brooke's tumble off Maple.

While Art waited on other customers, Andi watched Zeke load the two cartons into the customer's truck. Zeke watched the guy drive off and came in through the front door at the same time Nelson White came through the back, with Brooke and Teddy following.

"This is quite a little family you got going," Nelson joked, glancing down at Brooke and Teddy.

Self-conscious, Andi's cheeks warmed up.

"You got that right," Art said. "Now you guys handle your business, and I'm going to have a little talk with Brooke."

"Dad…what's going on?" Zeke looked perplexed.

"I just want to know if anything hurts," Art said, tapping the top of Brooke's head. "Any bumps on that smart head of yours?"

"Nothing hurts, Art. I already *said…*"

Andi hurried to Brooke and cupped her chin in her palm. "He just wants us all to be really careful, honey."

As if needing a new person to tell, Brooke looked up at Zeke and Nelson, and said she'd turned a corner going a little fast. "Then all of a sudden, oops," she said, bumping the heels of her hands together and grinning. "I fell right here." She patted her hip. "I keep telling them my head never hit the ground. I had a helmet on, anyway."

She'd never changed even one detail of her story, Andi thought. She was now inclined to drop the whole thing. Joy had gone through the same thing with Florey on their second day at the camp.

"Okay, enough," she said, glancing at Zeke. "I better get back to the *Dreamer*."

"What was that you said about a Bean Grinder run?" Zeke blurted.

That was fast. She glanced at Brooke. "Do you think you can carry a bag of muffins?"

Dropping her shoulders in an exaggerated slump, Brooke teased back. "I don't know, I'm so tired from riding horses and swimming all day."

Art snorted. "I'll have the blueberry kind, young lady. Pick out a good one with lots of purple spots."

Saying he'd only stopped by to pick up an order of supplies, Nelson declined the offer of a Bean Grinder treat, but everyone else was all in. Andi had been craving a double-chocolate-chip muffin all day.

Given the odd frenzy in the store, mostly because of Art and how he'd flipped the subject back to Brooke's fall, it was a relief to take Brooke and start down the path to the Bean Grinder. Andi understood Art's concern, but she couldn't help but resent his interference. Obviously, Zeke wished Art had never started grilling Brooke and not taking any hints about backing off. It had thrown off his day.

"Nelson said we're like a family," Brooke

said, swinging her arms and doing a little skip every few steps.

"I guess we sort of are," Andi said, "but just for the summer. When we live in an apartment or a house again, we probably won't see much of Art and Zeke."

Brooke shrugged. "I don't see much of Grandma and Grandpa, either. But they're still my family."

"Right." She couldn't argue with that logic. "But you know I was talking about our real family. There's a difference." She had no choice but to push that point, even if the difference wasn't always so clear to her, either. But in only a couple of months, she and Brooke would be moving on. New job, new house. But she didn't want to think about that yet and darken her mood. Yikes, a new job wasn't supposed to bring her down. A couple of evenings ago, she'd forced herself to polish her résumé one more time and make sure she had interview clothes—and shoes—ready to go.

"I'm glad you're enjoying your summer here, sweetheart." Andi put her arm around Brooke and gave her shoulder a quick squeeze. "I'm happy working on the boat.

Living there, too. But we'll need to move on to our next adventure soon."

Brooke looked up and purposely scrunched her face into an unhappy expression. "It won't be this fun."

Andi bit her tongue to stop herself from contradicting Brooke. She wasn't in the mood for a useless war of words. Who would she be trying to convince, anyway? "Speaking of fun, when would you like Florey to spend the night?"

"Soon. But first she's sleeping over with me at Dad's this weekend."

"She is? You didn't mention that," Andi said, trying to sound neutral. "What does your dad have planned?" This was annoying, but she couldn't put her finger on why.

"Nothing special. Just Florey sleeping over." She took a leap over a dip in the path, where earlier rain had left mud behind. "Lark likes to grill in the yard a lot. Florey's mom and dad are coming, too. Then they'll go home and Florey will stay."

How cozy. Two couples and their little girls. *Wow, how petty can you get?* But wasn't the overnight on the boat supposed to be the special occasion? Whether he knew it or not, Miles had stepped on something she'd wanted for herself. *Right. As if anyone owned the idea.*

The aroma of coffee at the Bean Grinder drew her out of her agitation, at least a little. She focused on what she needed to order—the three coffees—and reminded herself to order extra cream for Zeke. Brooke ordered lemonade and pointed to a particular blueberry muffin she wanted for Art.

A few minutes later they were on their way back to the store.

Miles's plans for Brooke's weekend left dull dissatisfaction lingering in her chest. It wasn't her ex-husband's appealing family life that gnawed at her. It was her life that brought on gloom. Oh, she was finding herself getting comfortable in Two Moon Bay, especially because it was a friendly place. The baristas at the Bean Grinder even greeted her and Brooke by name. This wave of dark emotions welled up from a much deeper place.

"Let's hurry," Brooke said. "I'm hungry."

"And I need to work," Andi said, realizing that even with aching muscles and her neck stiff from maneuvering in tight spaces, measuring how far she'd come with transforming *Drifting Dreamer* was the best part of her day.

THE NEXT AFTERNOON, on the drive from Grassy Shore to Joy's house, the girls' voices and plans held her attention. They were full of talk about Appaloosas, Morgans and Arabians. But mostly they loved Maple and Jasper. Andi was learning more than she ever wanted to know about the care and feeding of horses.

She pulled up in front of Joy and buzzed down the passenger window when her friend approached to meet them.

"Why don't you come in for a few minutes?" Joy asked. "I've just made a pitcher of lemonade."

Eager for a close-up look at the huge older home, with its wraparound porch and side yard, Andi accepted.

"We can sit out on the back porch, where screens keep the bugs out," Joy said, leading the way along a stone walkway to a gate. "We can keep an eye on the girls in the yard."

"I could even walk to my dad's house

later," Brooke said to Florey as they ran through the yard to a gazebo at the back.

"Doesn't take much to make them happy, does it?" Joy said as she pointed to chairs around the glass table. "Somehow, Florey thinks it's so cool that Brooke's dad is right down the street."

No matter how many years had passed, a low-level hum of embarrassment traveled through her. Once again, she was a single parent in a sea of couples. At moments like this, she didn't need her parents' tight-mouthed disapproval. She did that all by herself. "You're a teacher, so you're probably used to kids in two households living the reality of that term *blended families*."

That seemed to amuse Joy. "You bet. And not-so-blended. Lots of single moms are doing it without much help from the dads."

"Fortunately, that's not the case for me, or I should say, for Brooke. Miles and I agree on the important stuff."

Joy looked at her closely, as if deep in thought. "I don't know Lark McGee well, but in a town this small, we cross paths with other parents all the time. I remember when we bought this place, Lark still lived in the cottage on the corner."

"Brooke and I stayed in the cottage a few days before the boat gig came up."

"Boat gig? When you put it that way, it sounds exotic."

"And messy," Andi said with a laugh.

The girls ran back to the porch while Joy went to get their drinks. The two plunked themselves down in wicker chairs and propped their feet up on the porch rail. Despite what she'd said about her summer, Andi was caught off guard by a strong pang of envy over what seemed like a perfectly settled life. Part of it was as simple as recalling how much she enjoyed the homey porch at her house in Green Bay. Watching the girls chatting about their day at camp, maybe it came back to family.

Deep in thought, she was startled when Joy appeared with a tray of glasses. "I was admiring your setup back here. I had something similar in the house I just sold. It was great expanding the living space to the outdoors. I was recalling how Brooke and I used to have dinner out there on days like this."

"Like that deck on the boat," Joy said,

grinning. "It's more private over by Donovan's than it would be at the marina. It's like you have your own backyard, too."

"And here I was feeling envious," Andi joked. "But you're right. My front yard is pretty special, too. I watch all the changing moods of the lake and on a clear night there's almost always a reflection of the moon that seems to glow in the water."

"Have at it," Joy said wryly. "Now, my husband is a water guy. He's going out diving with Jerrod and that gang next week. I can handle the big tour boat, but I leave the diving to others. I go way back with Jerrod's wife, Dawn."

That news brought on an irrational disheartened thud inside her. Andi was hit with a bout of shyness. She missed—for the moment—her old anonymous life.

Joy took a long gulp of her lemonade and then shifted in her chair to face Andi. "I'm not sure how to ask this without being nosy, but I'm wondering how Zeke and his dad are doing these days."

A warning bell went off in Andi's head.

"They seem fine. The boat wasn't part of any plan. It just showed up one day," Andi explained, adding the story about settling the debt. She shrugged in a humorous way. "And the next day, I wandered by and asked Zeke what he'd charge me to live on it."

Joy laughed along with her, but then her face quickly turned serious. "I guess I've always had a soft spot for Zeke. It's been just him and his dad for almost as long as I can remember."

Almost? "Uh, then you knew Zeke's mother before she died?"

"No, I didn't know her, but Zeke and I went to school together. I was a year behind him."

Had they been childhood sweethearts? Maybe so, but Andi thought better of asking right out. "It's not easy for a young boy to lose his mother," she said as noncommittally as possible. "It's got to be such a painful loss to get past."

Joy opened her mouth to say something, but then apparently changed her mind. Not until the girls left the yard and took off for Florey's bedroom did she pick up the conversation.

"I'm probably speaking out of turn," Joy

said, grimacing, "but I had a peculiar kind of bond with Zeke because of his mother."

"Oh?" Andi's heart pounded as she waited for the information. She was impatient for it, whether she'd like what she learned or not.

"My mom was a teacher, too," Joy said. "One afternoon I was waiting outside for her after school. Zeke was there, too. I remember how he was kicking a stone around the gravel schoolyard while he waited for his mom to pick him up."

Call it intuition or simply picking up Joy's somber tone, but Andi began to feel a little queasy. "This story ends badly, doesn't it, Joy?"

"Yes." Joy paused, but Andi didn't fill the silence.

"My mom came out and told Zeke she was going to take him to our house for a little while." Joy sighed. "I could fill in all the little details, but they're not important now. Zeke came home with us and then Mom made some calls to a couple of the Donovans' neighbors. Mom turned the TV on, not something she typically did after school. She brought out a plate of brownies and Zeke and I watched some kids' program."

"What did Zeke think was happening?" Andi asked, her throat tightening from anxiety.

Joy stared off into the distance, as if trying to focus on the hedges at the back of the yard. Finally, she shook her head. "I don't know. It's funny what stands out about an incident, especially in childhood. But I recall my mother's low, reassuring voice when she talked to Zeke. He was pretty quick for a nine-year-old, so it stuck with me that he seemed to sense something was up."

Andi winced, thinking of a young boy losing his mother and learning about it from his teacher. "So eventually did someone—or Art—come to tell him his mother died?"

Joy shook her head. "That's not the way it happened, Andi. It wasn't that clear-cut."

Andi put her hand over her churning stomach. She hardly knew Zeke, but she couldn't stop the heavy dread taking over her body. Even her heart thumped hard in her chest.

"Mom kept making calls and then put out dinner for Zeke and me."

"How *did* his mother die?" Andi laced her fingers tight and held her hands under her chin to keep them still.

Joy gave Andi a curious look, but after a second of hesitation, she answered. “She had liver cancer, I believe. She died about a year after that night.”

“That’s awful,” Andi said, exhaling air she’d been holding in her lungs.

“But there’s more, and I might as well finish filling it in,” Joy said glumly. “The day Zeke was at my house, his mom—her name was Natalie—ran away with a man. She left Zeke behind, and when Art saw her note on the kitchen table, he took off after her.”

“But where did she go?”

“She and the guy ended up somewhere in Michigan.”

Andi closed her eyes in a futile attempt to block the image of a woman running away from her child. “Did Art assume he’d find her or that he’d be back in time to pick up Zeke at school?”

“No, not exactly. He left a message for a neighbor, but she didn’t get it in time, so no one showed up for Zeke. It took a few more hours and a police officer intervening to connect Art and my mother,” Joy explained. “It was almost midnight when Art came to our house to get Zeke.”

"So, by chance, really, your family accidentally was entangled with Art and Zeke," Andi said, running the story through her mind again.

"That's right," Joy said, "but we were kids, so I thought I had a secret that I shouldn't have. Zeke stayed home the next day, and Art closed up Donovan's for a couple of weeks to regroup—get himself together, I suppose. My dad stopped in a couple of times to see how he was doing. My mom called him every few days for a while."

"So Zeke's mom never came back? Did she call Zeke, write to him? *Something?*"

Joy lifted her hands in a helpless I-don't-know gesture. "We didn't talk other than to say hi. But then one day he came up to me when I was alone at my locker in our school and told me his mom had died. It was a whole year later." Joy shook her head. "It was always so strange."

Now that she knew the story, Andi's eyes burned as she fought back tears. She'd known them for such a short time, but already she'd developed a place in her heart for Zeke and Art, especially because of the odd mental lapses Art suffered and Zeke's fierce loyalty to his dad.

"Why did you tell me this?" Andi asked, finding it hard to get the words out.

"Hmm… To be perfectly honest, I'm not sure," Joy said, shaking her head. "It's just that Zeke seems like this regular guy—attractive, really smart, a talented restoration contractor, successful businessman—"

"Really good son," Andi interrupted, suddenly amused by the rundown of all the positive things about Zeke.

"And single," Joy said, her face suddenly brightening. "Maybe that's why I said something. You two seem to have connected."

Reflexively, Andi raised her hands to stop that assumption. "I'm not sure I'd go that far." She couldn't deny being pleased with Joy's words, though. "Like I said, it was serendipity. The boat showed up one day, and so did I."

"Maybe so," Joy said, her blue-gray eyes sparkling, "but I have a nose for these things."

"You took to Zeke yourself, didn't you?" Andi asked.

"It's hard to forget a vulnerable nine-year-old trying to be brave," Joy said softly. "My parents always gave Art credit for getting himself together and being a good dad to Zeke. It's not Art's fault Zeke's been a bit gun-shy when it comes to women."

Gun-shy. Like her. Just as Zeke had said his mother died and left it at that, she hadn't told her whole story, either. No need. "Oh, I'm a bit gun-shy myself," Andi blurted for no particular reason, "so I understand."

Changing the subject once again, Andi described the work she'd done on *Drifting Dreamer.* "By the end of the day, the combination of wood dust and grime and sweat makes me socially unacceptable. The boat may be a cosmetic nightmare, but it has hot water and a shower. I can even soak in the tub in the apartment above the store."

"Believe me, I've all heard about it," Joy said, casting Andi a pointed look. "Apparently, Brooke described the exotic half-moon shower on the boat." Laughing, she added, "With a curved sliding door and *everything.* Much better than hers. Mind you, this ten-year-old has a bathroom all to herself."

Reluctantly, Andi stood, knowing it was time to get Brooke. "Don't complain to me. I got an earful about Florey's *suite* the other day. The biggest closet she's ever seen. Speaking of suites, I better get her over to her dad's. She has a lovely setup in the new house. By the way, I hear Florey is staying over there tonight."

"That's the plan. We're having dinner there and then leaving Florey with them for the night." Joy said. "I'll call them down." Joy disappeared into the house. A couple of minutes later Brooke and Florey arrived on the porch skipping and bouncing in their exuberant way.

"Full of energy, I see," Andi said.

"See ya later," Brooke said, hopping down the porch stairs.

"She's already thinking about her dad now," Andi said to Joy, following her out. "She can switch her focus so fast sometimes my head spins."

"Hey, I teach kids around their age—my head is always spinning."

Seeing Brooke and her new friend running to the car lightened Andi's heart. But she was soon on her way after dropping off Brooke. Alone and still reeling from what Joy had told her. Odd, though, that the story confirmed the hunch she'd had that Zeke's mother hadn't simply died young. It was more complicated than that.

Andi pulled into her parking place and didn't see either Art or Zeke through the store windows, so she kept walking to the dock and boarded *Drifting Dreamer*. In the wheelhouse, where she'd been working earlier, she downed half a bottle of water before turning to the other side of the electronics panel. Someone had installed radar, but not satellite navigation, and relied on old-fashioned paper charts stored in shallow drawers. When she'd first moved aboard, she'd noted the drawers were empty.

Now she stared at the row of drawers with a surge of optimism. It couldn't hurt to take a closer look. Andi started by pulling the top drawer all the way open and felt around the whole surface. Nothing but one folded chart of the Duluth Harbor. The second drawer was completely empty, but when she reached to the back of the third drawer, her fingers touched something firm. She tried to pull it toward her but it was stuck on the metal shelf bottom. She pushed at it—once, twice, three times—until she freed it and she could inch it toward her.

It was a notebook. Its faded, water-stained green cloth cover had a sewn binding, and only a few pages remained in what was likely a ship's log. Jagged edges were left behind where someone had torn out most of the pages. The writing on the few remaining pieces was faded and, in some cases, damaged by water.

Just holding the notebook set off a pleasant buzz in her fingertips. She perched on the captain's stool and began reading. "Well, well, another clue," she murmured.

CHAPTER TEN

ZEKE HEARD THE back door close and by process of elimination figured it had to be Andi. Nelson had already stopped by once and his dad had just gone home. That completed the list of people who used the back door. He came out of the office and met her at the counter. Holding a clear plastic bag with what looked like a green book inside, she seemed pleased with herself. Smug, actually.

"Good news?" he asked, glancing at the bag.

She held up the bag. "Very good. A notebook...well, I should call it a log. That's what it is, sort of."

"Was it hidden?"

She bobbed her head from side to side, as if considering her answer. "More or less. It was in the back of a chart drawer. I might have missed it if I didn't have finding more information on my mind. Either way, they tell us a little more about people I'm assuming are Charles and Mary. The pages could be from the summer cruise Charles wrote about in the letter."

Andi's first find had fed his curiosity, which had started on the day the boat arrived. And now they had another hint about what happened to the yacht over the years. Zeke held out his hand. "Let's have a look."

"The notebook is kind of fragile," she said, giving him the bag. "That's why I stuck it in a plastic bag."

Zeke went into the office and gently let the notebook slide out of the bag onto the desk. When he opened it, he was surprised to see the jagged edges of the pages, as if they'd been torn out. "Why would someone preserve these few pages, and throw away the rest?"

Andi lifted her hands, palms up. "I don't know." She pointed to slightly smeared lines, but the town name was clear—Grand Marais, a port town in Minnesota. "I couldn't decipher it completely, but the date looks to be September 19, 1941."

"Getting toward the end of the boating season up there," Zeke said.

Andi tapped the date. "And three months later, we were at war." She rested her palms on the desk. "It could be the log from the honeymoon cruise, assuming they had one. But why didn't he leave in more about it?" She ran her finger over the ragged edges left behind. "The missing pages came before these. If it's a log, it's the end of the cruise."

Zeke turned the remaining handful of pages until he reached the last one. He knew a to-do list when he saw one. "This list is about closing up the boat for the winter. Maybe they were headed home."

Andi turned the page back and pointed to another entry. "Look at this one. 'Worrying charcoal clouds passed by, no rain today. Heading back tomorrow. I can't describe…' And then nothing. The rest is water-smudged."

Zeke groaned. "What a shame. We'll never know what she can't describe."

"She? You think Mary wrote that?"

He couldn't say. Why did he assume a woman had written these words? "It just seems like it somehow, maybe it's the section about the clouds… 'Worrying charcoal clouds.'"

"That phrase conjures so much in my imagination. If only we could read the other words! The handwriting is different, though, so two people wrote entries."

Andi reached over and flipped to another page, which had a few lines listing course headings, speed and nautical miles. "This handwriting matches the first pages we found, the one with the list of possible names. The entry about the clouds doesn't match."

Maybe because the war had so quickly followed, or even because of how the boat had come to his dock, the reality of that early history brought up feelings he couldn't sort out. Not yet. "But we know that in September of 1941, at least two people were aboard. Let's assume they were Charles and Mary."

"Aboard a boat they named *Drifting Dreamer*. A romantic honeymoon on their sleek new yacht."

Zeke tapped the page. "Maybe we'll learn how long they owned it. I'll always wonder how it ended up derelict decades later in a boatyard in Kenosha."

"Ah, but with updated refrigeration and a newish stove and modern equipment,"

Andi added. "Charles and Mary weren't the only people to spin dreams about *Drifting Dreamer*. When I first opened the notebook it seemed like those two people were by themselves, as if no one else existed." She smiled wistfully. "But that's my active imagination at work."

The energy in the room changed, as if no else existed except the two of them. He liked the feeling. Abruptly changing the subject, he asked, "Uh, are you waiting for Brooke?"

She looked up, surprise in her expression. "No, no, it's the start of her weekend with Miles. He'll do the carpool with Florey on Monday."

"Okay, then, come have dinner at my house, and then we can go out for a drink. Dad believes in charcoal grilling, none of those fancy gas grills for him. This morning he said he's making his famous barbecued chicken." Leaning in, he said, "He does a mean job of it."

Andi's face brightened. "Are you sure Art won't mind a last-minute guest."

"Not in the least. When it comes to grilling, he's kind of a show-off," Zeke said, overstating what his dad might think. Oh, he'd be friendly enough. But he seemed to run hot and cold about Andi. The other day after Andi and Brooke went to get them all coffee, his dad had been critical of Andi, acting like she wasn't concerned enough about Brooke's fall. He kept on it even after they'd gone home for the day. Zeke had brushed him off, but Art hadn't stopped until the baseball game started later in the evening.

"Well, then, how can I refuse to try his famous chicken?"

He reached for the notebook. "Let's store that bit of treasure with the other things."

She smiled slyly. "I wonder what I'll find next. I have a feeling this isn't the end of the discoveries."

Zeke nodded, struck again by how much he looked forward to seeing Andi every day. His usual reaction was to ignore how he felt, but it was different this time.

It took only a few minutes to finish the routine to close up the store for the night and be on their way down the block.

When they got to the house, he led them to the back door, where his dad was in his red-striped grilling apron turning chicken pieces.

"The only thing missing is the chef's hat,

Art," Andi said. "I hope you don't mind me showing up without warning, but Zeke tempted me with tales of your to-die-for chicken."

Art beamed. "The best there is, if I say so myself."

Zeke laughed. "Brag a little, Dad, that's okay."

"What a beautiful day, huh? Look at those flowers." With tongs in his hand, he pointed to the lilies blooming along the fence.

"Gorgeous," Andi said.

"Where are your manners?" Art said, now waving the tongs at Zeke. "Take Andi on a little tour of the house. You did the hard work. Go on, show it off."

"Please," Andi said with a snicker, "show off a little."

Taking the bait, he gestured for her to follow him inside.

"Wow, this kitchen is like something I've seen featured in magazines," Andi exclaimed the minute she entered the room.

"It's probably my favorite room in the house," he said.

"Is this the original floor?" she asked, running the toe of her shoe across the wide pine planks.

"It is. But there was nothing unusual or special about it back when the house was built in the 1880s." He pointed to the stone fireplace. "My dad likes to have his morning coffee there on winter mornings. A kitchen fireplace is considered a luxury nowadays."

"A fireplace always adds something besides warmth," Andi said. "They're like silent invitations to sit down and relax."

He hadn't thought about it quite like that, but she was right. "Originally, the house sat by itself on several acres, but by the 1920s or so, this was a residential street. Sidewalks and everything. That's what probably saved this house, that and a family that owned it for seventy years."

Zeke walked her through the house, pointing out the original scrollwork and built-in hutches in a couple of the rooms. But Andi noticed everything on her own, even the cedar closets.

"What a restful room," Andi said, when he opened to the door to his dad's bedroom and gave her a chance to peek inside.

"I used the tan and forest green on purpose." He paused. "Sometimes my dad gets a little anxious. This room helps." He left it at that. *Anxious* was a mild word for what sometimes happened to his dad. Agitation was closer to it. If they hadn't stopped the conversation about Brooke's fall, his dad might have become agitated over that.

"Even Teddy has his own bed," Andi said, gesturing at a green dog bed.

"Dad jokes about what a softy I was about keeping Teddy," Zeke said, "but if I hadn't brought him back, he'd have walked the five miles to the shelter to bring him back."

"It's a beautiful room, Zeke." She drew her hand down the side of the chest of drawers he'd refinished many years ago.

Zeke's heart suddenly starting pounding. Probably because Andi's eyes were filling with tears. From the start she'd seemed concerned about Art in a gentle sort of way.

Changing the subject, he talked about the attic he could redo one day, and then he led Andi around the corner back to the living room that he'd joined in an open space with the dining room and kitchen. There was also a small office and the place his dad liked to watch his sports.

In the kitchen, Zeke stopped her before they went back outside. "I grew up with my dad in the apartment above the store. It's a nice place. No complaints. My dad did a good job. He took great care of me. But when I bought this house, I had a different vision. It wasn't just about restoring one of the oldest houses in town, but having a place for my dad. I always knew I'd eventually need him to be where I could keep an eye on him."

She stared into his eyes, as if she'd had an emotional reaction to what he'd said.

"It was a little different for me when I took on the old house Miles and I bought," Andi said. "In my case, I was mimicking the kind of home I'd grown up with. The kind I thought I was supposed to have."

Not sure what she meant exactly, he couldn't think of anything more to say.

"Turned out I didn't do home and family very well," she said, with a wry smile.

"Ah, don't be so hard on yourself." Knowing he sounded too dismissive, he steered her toward the door. "Let's go eat my dad's chicken. He'll be hollering for us any minute." He awkwardly rubbed his palms together as if suddenly enthusiastic about dinner.

Zeke took salads out of the fridge and handed Andi a basket of sesame rolls fresh from the bakery. Out on the patio, Art exclaimed, “There you are. I thought you got lost. I’m taking these babies off the grill right now.”

“Anything I can do?” Andi asked.

“Now you ask?” Art teased. “Everything’s done.”

Andi returned Art’s teasing with an amused sidelong glance. “Hey, I’ve been working my fingers to the bone on that old boat of yours all day.”

“I like a woman with a sense of humor.” He passed a bowl of chips to Andi. “Try these. I’m supposed to watch salt, but you don’t need to worry.”

Zeke looked on, and watched Andi’s sparkling eyes. He liked her spunky manner. She teased Brooke that way, and he’d been on the receiving end a few times. He also saw a side to her that was like him in a way. She had a hard time explaining her life, and so did he.

“Great chicken, Art,” Andi said.

“Natalie liked this barbecue sauce, too,”

Art said. "She was Zeke's mom. I suppose he told you about her. You know, how she died after she left us. Ran off with a man."

Andi dropped her fork on her plate. He quickly glimpsed a flash of recognition in her eyes. He'd told her his mom had died. But he'd never mentioned her leaving them. "I doubt Andi needs to hear our life story, Dad."

"Why not? Everyone else in town knows your mother walked out. Andi's camped out in our backyard, more or less. She's our new friend." Art cast a sharp look Zeke's way. It matched the edge in his voice.

"Sure, Dad, but still."

Andi didn't meet his eyes, but concentrated on buttering a roll.

"Don't get me wrong. Natalie and I were real happy when Zeke came along," Art said.

"I'm sure you were," Andi agreed, still not looking at Zeke.

"I should have told you more of the story," Zeke said, sliding his hand across the table toward her. "I'm sorry."

Closing her eyes, she gave her head a little shake, as if telling him not to worry.

"That's true, Zeke. Don't know why you

were hiding it. Things like this happen all the time." Leaning toward Andi, Art added, "You wouldn't believe some of the stories I could tell about the people in this town."

"Hey, Dad, let's not get into other people's business." Something was happening to his dad right now. He'd soon lapse into one of his looping series of thoughts.

"Nobody cares about privacy anymore, Zeke, just like nobody cares that your mom left us."

I care... Why did Dad need to do this?

"That's probably true, Art," Andi said, her expression neutral.

Art shrugged and helped himself to another spoonful of potato salad.

Only the sound of Teddy gnawing on a chew toy by the flower beds broke the silence cloaking the table. Even a slight uptick in the light breeze was welcome. Zeke fought his discomfort and tried to come up with something new to say.

"I didn't so much mind her leaving me." Art pointed his fork toward Zeke. "It was you, son, I worried about. I mean, who leaves her little boy for some other guy?"

"I'll explain all this later," Zeke said, seeing the uneasy look cross Andi's face. She probably wondered why he wasn't speaking up. Only he knew that would make it worse.

Suddenly, Art looked up, a deep frown distorting his features. "Oops. What was I going on about that for?"

"It's okay, Dad." It was as if a hypnotist had snapped his fingers and Art came out of a trance.

"You're right, Zeke, who here in town even remembers?" Art picked up the bowl of chips. "Help yourself, Andi."

"Yes, sir." She plopped another handful on her plate.

Art slapped the tabletop. "Atta girl, enjoying good food is enjoying life. Including the key lime pie we have for dessert."

Andi's light laugh seemed to say "all is well." It was then Zeke realized the burning in his gut had stopped. Hungry now, he looked down at his barely touched plate of food and lifted his fork.

Andi quickly steered the conversation to baseball. His dad beamed.

"You found yourself another baseball fan, Dad." Zeke could have kissed her, he thought, which sounded like a great idea. But he pushed aside that thought notion. Andi wasn't about to entangle herself with his complicated family situation.

"I ran in to Dawn Larsen at the grocery store the other day," Andi said. "She looks well and happy. I enjoyed meeting her on the Fourth."

"She went from blushing bride to glowing mom-to-be in about two weeks," Art said.

Zeke snickered. His dad sure could be funny sometimes. "Knowing Dawn, I think she'd get a big kick out of hearing you say that."

"I know. But it's a story. A stranger came to town and got one of Two Moon Bay's finest women." Art chuckled, looking like he was getting a big kick out of himself.

"It's hard to keep track of all the people Brooke knows that I'm just now getting acquainted with," Andi said.

"I guess you have your hands full," Art commented, his tone sharp. "A daughter to raise and all that. You must not have much time for socializing or having fun."

Zeke noticed Andi didn't respond right away, but looked at Art with a curious expression. "You're right. I haven't had a lot of time for other things."

"Like Zeke. For some of us, running a business takes all our attention. He wouldn't have been much of a family guy."

"Hey, Dad, leave it alone." Zeke gritted his teeth and pushed back his chair. This spur-of-the-moment barbecue dinner had turned into a strange night, thanks to his dad. Zeke could have predicted his dad's rambling conversation, but he hadn't thought it all out.

Still, he wasn't sorry he'd invited Andi to dinner. Unlike a lot of other people, Andi didn't walk on eggshells around his dad as if she was afraid to talk to him. A couple of women he'd dated had acted like his dad was nothing more than a problem to be solved.

Zeke got their dessert on the table and listened to Andi and his dad banter about everything from Bean Grinder cookies to the downtown farmers market. He tried to cast aside the way his dad had plunged into the subject of Zeke's mother. Andi hadn't looked surprised by his dad's story. Zeke scoffed to himself. Joy had no doubt already filled in all the dreary details about the night his mother left town.

Zeke waited, impatiently, for the moment he and Andi could leave, enduring the small talk about calories and pie and the Spanish ancestors who got the credit for Andi's hair.

Then, as if she'd had enough, Andi pushed her chair back and looked pointedly at Zeke. "Time to go, huh?"

"Yeah, let's be on our way."

Andi walked closer to Art and patted his shoulder. "Thanks, Art. I had a good time with you and your chicken."

Art nodded. "Hey, Zeke, why don't you get the leash and take Teddy along with you when you walk Andi home."

"I'll walk him later. Andi and I are going to the Silver Moon Winery. Going to have a glass of wine on the patio."

"Pretty fancy," Art said with a smirk. "Must be trying to impress somebody."

"Right, Dad. Andi's never seen a wine bar before."

Andi burst out laughing. "You two really are funny."

Art waved his hand, shooing them away. "Go on now. I need to watch the news. I like to be in the know."

He and Andi headed to the path that led through the park to the winery.

"Did Art just kick us out like a couple of kids?" Andi asked, a laugh in her voice.

Matching her light tone, he said, "Wouldn't be the first time he more or less told me to go away and leave him alone. I think he gets tired out and doesn't want to admit it."

He waited until they were seated at a table for two on the winery's patio and the waiter had brought them each a glass of cabernet before he brought up his dad's meandering talk.

"I should have told you about my mother, so you wouldn't be caught off guard."

"It's okay, Zeke," Andi said. "You didn't know your dad would go off on that tangent."

"But it wasn't a surprise, anyway, was it?" Zeke challenged. "Joy already told you what happened, didn't she?"

Andi shifted in her seat and took a quick sip of her wine. "Not in a gossipy way, Zeke. Not at all."

He'd been right. "I thought as much."

"Joy spoke well of you. Mostly, she talked about her mom's involvement that day."

He watched her frown, as if gathering her thoughts.

"Her recollections were mostly about his concern for you."

At one time Zeke might have been furious that Joy had talked about his past. She'd crossed a line. But he didn't have the energy for it, or maybe his heart wasn't in it anymore. His mother running away with another man had always seemed like a shameful secret, spoken of in whispers. But that fortress had been chipped away. Now, even when his dad talked about her, like he had at dinner, it was as if he was talking about a stranger.

"I used to get mad if I thought people were talking about my dad and me," he admitted, "but not so much anymore. When it comes to Joy, I get it. She was only a young girl herself, but she and her family know more about the day my mom left town than anyone else except my dad and me."

"It was surprising that Art brought it up for no particular reason," Andi said.

"It alarmed me that Dad didn't seem aware that he'd taken the conversation to that place. It was rambling and odd."

Andi kept her gaze down, as if the glass

table had captured her attention. He expected her to ask more questions—he was sure she would. Instead, she commented on the cool night and the nearly full moon lighting up the sky. The patio had strings of lights wrapped around the bushes and trunks of ash and birch trees, creating a romantic atmosphere. There were tea candles in silver holders on every table.

"It's festive, like a party is going on back here," she said. "Kind of like my summer."

"And…" He gestured as if expecting more of an explanation.

"Every day is fun for me, Zeke. I enjoy the work so much. And of all the people around, only you understand the satisfaction of repairing and restoring." She curled her fingers into fists and flexed her muscles. "And my body is already stronger than when I started. I don't even mind the occasional neck cramp or sore arms."

"I like watching you enjoy yourself, Andi," he said in a low voice. "You seem made for this."

She held up her glass. "I'll toast to that. It's flattering coming from you. A professional."

He touched her glass with his, thoughts of

his dad and the store receding, as they sipped wine and Zeke asked about her old job, and she made it clear she was ready for a change.

Later, they walked toward the store and boat in silence, but when they made the turn to head down the driveway toward the dock, she stopped abruptly, and in a light tone said, "I'm very curious about something, Zeke."

"Is that so?" he asked. "What's that?"

"Joy casually mentioned a building in Settlers Hall—and she also said you were involved in saving the building that became the Bean Grinder. A true landmark."

"Those old places?" he said in a mocking tone.

"Settlers Hall was one of my last major projects. It's a real landmark. I'm glad I was involved."

"I've passed Settlers Hall so many times, but never had a reason to stop and have a better look," Andi said, walking again.

He'd like to see it himself. Or, maybe a chance to show it off appealed to his vanity. "Let's go up there one day. I'd be happy to show it to you. We found the best stone masons around to repair the structure—we brought back the interior tile work, as well as the wood. It's a showy sort of place, inside and out. Like the way *Drifting Dreamer* used to be."

"Is it open to the public?"

"No, but I've got connections. We could go one day next week."

"How?" she asked. "What about the store? Art?"

"We can figure that out." He mentally ran over how he could get away for a few hours without closing the store. "It's supposed to be rainy toward the end of the week."

They'd reached the dock and Andi was ready to step aboard. But she stopped and gave him a quizzical look. "Uh, what does the rain have to do with leaving the store?"

"On a rainy day, the marina is slow," he explained. "Fewer boats leave and fewer boats come in. I can hire away one of Nelson's people for a few hours. Melody fills in now and again."

Andi tilted her head, and rolled her eyes. "The *entanglements* around here never quit," she said sarcastically, "but I know, I know, you're one big happy family."

Her tone jolted him more than her words. And rolling her eyes didn't help. "Are you mocking us? Like being friendly or helping each other out is a joke?"

"I suppose I was teasing a little." She looked away for a couple of seconds and then turned to him and flicked her hand. "You're like a little closed group."

"Has anyone ever made you feel *unwelcome* here? Have *I* acted like you were just one more stranger?"

"No, no, Zeke," she said, raising her hands in surrender. "It's just everyone seems to know so much about each other. And people I've met know someone to call on for every little thing."

She was grinning now, as if trying to lighten things up. But Zeke couldn't quite get past her tone. She made it seem like helping each other out was a negative thing. "I guess that's the way we *like* it around here." Wait a minute…he hadn't meant to be that cold.

With her back to him, she stepped aboard, turned halfway around and gave him a quick wave. "Tell Art I said thanks again for dinner."

"Andi, wait. You misunderstood—"

"I know, I know," she interrupted. "No need to explain. 'Night. I'll see you soon."

She disappeared into the cabin and a second later a light came through the porthole.

Should he call out? Apologize? But for what? His tone? Deciding against saying anything more, Zeke left the dock and walked away, leaving the boat behind him. He'd patch things up in the morning. But what was he sorry for, anyway? She seemed to make fun of people he counted on and who counted on him. He wasn't about to apologize for who he was.

CHAPTER ELEVEN

ANDI TOOK HER coffee to her favorite perch in the wheelhouse just as the sun peeked over the horizon against a pink and deep red sky. *Red sky at night, sailors delight; red sky at morn, sailor forlorn.* Not a good sign for the coming day. The dim dock light was still on, along with Nelson's brighter lights that rose high above the marina. Last night she'd fallen asleep to the low buzz of a typical Friday night at the marina, with an occasional burst of group laughter piercing the silence. More distant were the social sounds of activity at the yacht club.

Running her hand across the almost completely stripped console, it struck Andi that in her heyday, *Drifting Dreamer* would have been a standout at the yacht club, with many people strolling down the dock just to have a look. A throwback to a time when yachting was still a gentleman's game.

Gentleman. In old-fashioned terms, that would have described Zeke. Maybe that's why his frosty tone in response to what she thought of as teasing hit so hard. Well, mostly teasing. She didn't intend for her irrational resentment about the big-happy-family image to bleed through. But it had, and Zeke had picked up on it.

She sipped her coffee and swiveled the captain's chair a quarter way around so she could prop her feet on the seat of the mate's chair. She loved this spot on *Drifting Dreamer.* But what spot did she dislike? She couldn't name even one. Every day, even on rainy days like this, there was always a worthwhile task.

But a pall hung over her morning because of how she'd left things with Zeke. And it had all started innocently when she'd asked how he could manage a day off. If only she could start that conversation over again. The sun disappeared behind a thick bank of gray clouds covering the sky. Within minutes, the plop of fat drops obscured her view. She sighed as she refilled her cup and stayed in the cabin and tried to refocus on the work ahead. With any luck, rain or shine, she could spend her day making a dent in polishing the bronze pieces throughout the boat, from the portholes to the anchor chocks.

The rain slacked off to a drizzle, prompting her to grab her rain jacket and pull some cash from her pocket. Her lockers were bare except for the granola Brooke liked and some eggs she didn't feel like cooking. Peanut butter and crackers held no appeal. But the Bean Grinder called her name. A little rain and wind and a mild case of the blues couldn't stop her.

A few minutes later, she was walking fast on the path and almost there. The lake was the same color as the sky on this dark morning. Only an erratic pattern of whitecaps broke the mass of gray. It had the look of bad weather that would last all day.

Pushing back the hood of her rain jacket, she went inside the café. She scanned the room for a table. There he was. At a table for two. Alone. His raised hand greeted her.

Her pleasure at seeing him took her aback. Smiling sheepishly, she wove through a bunch of empty tables until she reached him. He got to his feet when she stopped.

But she hesitated to sit until she'd said her piece. "Look..."

"Uh, look," he said at the same moment.

They both let out embarrassed laughs, quick and short.

"You first," he said.

"Okay. Zeke, I'm sorry I sounded so snarky." She pulled out the chair and sat, and so did he. "That was all about me and my bad attitude, not about you."

"I'm sorry, too."

"What for? You didn't do anything."

He cocked his head. "I was cold. Worse, I shut down the conversation. You already feel a little like an outsider, what with Miles and Lark and all the people they know right under your nose."

"And everyone is so-o-o nice." Andi giggled self-consciously. "I'm teasing, I'm teasing."

"It's okay, Andi. I got that point." Zeke's eyebrows lifted in amusement as he stood.

She glanced at the half-eaten scone on his plate. "Are you leaving?"

He looked at her in disbelief. "No, of course not. I'm getting you some coffee and whatever else you want."

"Really?" She reached into her pocket. "I can certainly pay..."

He waved her off. "Put your money away. I can buy my woodworker-in-chief a cup of coffee." His mouth curled up in a wry smile. "I'm trying to change the tone here, Andi."

She took another look at the almond scone on his plate. "In that case, I'll have what you're having."

He gave the table one of his quick knuckle raps and went to the counter.

Andi cupped her cheeks. Another mood swing. Down in the dumps to buoyant in what...? Less than sixty seconds? For no particular reason, she turned sideways in the chair so she could watch Zeke at the counter placing his order to the teenage boy on duty. There was something special about bumping in to him like this. The chance to clear the air, the happy relief rushing through her once they were okay with each other again. And after something so minor in the first place. But maybe her happy state had to do with a quiet Saturday morning that wasn't all about Brooke, or the store and Art, or even *Drifting Dreamer*.

Shrugging out of her rain jacket, Andi

welcomed the food put in front of her. "Ah, thanks."

"You're welcome." Zeke's voice was warm when he said, "I had a great idea while I was waiting at the counter. Let's go today."

"Go? Go where?"

"To Settlers Hall. A little rain won't matter, so let's do it while we can. I'll text my contact. Well, he's more than that. Ward's an old friend. He oversees the use of the building. He lives around the corner from the place, so he probably won't mind opening it up for us."

This was all fine with her. Brooke was with Miles for the weekend, the boat work could wait and there was something special about these dark, rainy summer days.

"And you're sure Art won't mind?" She took a gulp of coffee, suddenly eager to be on her way to see one of Zeke's projects. With Zeke. Alone.

"I didn't say that." Zeke smirked. "He'll mind. He'll give me an earful, but mostly because I'm sending what he calls a babysitter to the store."

"Your dad doesn't mince words, I noticed."

"That didn't get by you, huh?" Zeke nodded. “Until he got off-track and started that conversation about my mother last night, his thinking and focus had been fine all day.”

What were those little stabs of guilt in her stomach all about? She still had her secret, that’s what bothered her. She understood the reason his dad’s well-being was critical to him. But he’d been a kid and had no responsibility for what had diminished their life. Unlike her. Her pride got in the way of telling him about failing at marriage, not once, but twice, and all before she’d turned thirty. Her mistake made her look bad in her own eyes. Maybe it would seem irrational and even insignificant to other people, but the shame of it lingered for her. It kept her from being honest, not just with Zeke, but with most everyone.

Andi pushed away those thoughts. She didn’t want anything to ruin her day with Zeke.

“These scones really do melt in your mouth,” Andi said. “No exaggeration.” There, she’d changed the subject. “When do you want to go?”

Zeke got out his phone and sent a text. “I bet I hear back from Ward within the hour.”

When Andi ate the last crumb of her scone and drained her cup, they pulled up their jacket hoods and left. The rain had slacked to a gentle drizzle when they hurried to the path leading back to the store.

"Mom—hey, Mom." The voice she'd know anywhere came from behind.

"That's my name," Andi joked, turning to see Brooke and Florey running toward her from the parking lot. Miles and Lark were walking arm in arm behind them under an oversize umbrella Miles held in place over them.

An umbrella built for two, Andi mused. An odd quivering started in her gut, like she'd been caught doing something wrong.

"Hi, sweetie." She opened her arms and Brooke came right in to them for a hug. "I didn't expect to run into you this morning."

"We're getting a little breakfast after the big night." Miles subtly rolled his eyes at her, and then nodded to Zeke.

Determined to at least appear nonchalant, despite being the opposite, Andi waved to Lark, who, friendly as always, called out a cheery hello.

Andi patted Brooke's cheek. "So, you girls had fun, huh? Did you get any sleep?"

Bouncy and energetic in her yellow raincoat, Brooke giggled. "A little. I told Florey she could stay over on the boat. Soon."

"I promise. I'll talk to your mom this week," Andi said to Florey.

The quivering got stronger as she made small talk. She'd come down with a stupid case of nerves. And not because of Lark. Andi had never been uneasy around her. This reaction was all about Zeke. Miles and Lark seeing her with him early on a rainy weekend morning.

"How's that boat project coming?" Miles asked, glancing from her to Zeke.

"Really well," Zeke said amicably. "Andi's got everything under control. The old yacht is looking better every day."

"I told you that, Dad," Brooke said.

Andi let out a quick laugh and squeezed Brooke's shoulder. No social small talk for her. Andi noticed Lark casting an amused look her way.

Miles opened his mouth as if to speak, but closed it again. Andi was certain he stopped himself from tossing out a casual comment about what she'd done to restore their house. Good thing he kept his mouth shut. He'd have made the already stilted moment even worse.

"We need to run," Andi said to Brooke, planting a kiss on her forehead. "Zeke's going to show me a building he restored up in Elmwood Pond. It's called Settlers Hall."

"One of my earlier projects," Zeke said, his phone pinging in his pocket. "That's probably Ward now."

"We'll be on our way, then," Lark said, turning around and taking Miles with her. "Enjoy Settlers Hall. It's a real showpiece."

"I will." She reached for Brooke and gave her a quick squeeze. "See you tomorrow after camp. You, too, Florey."

Miles began talking to Brooke as Andi fell in step next to Zeke, whose fingers were busy texting.

"I let Nelson know I'd need someone for a few hours. He's fine with that—he doesn't need everybody today. Ward texted he'll meet us there. I'll get back to him and tell him we're on our way. He's already opening up the place today to show it to a new wedding planner, and they're also setting up for a small ceremony this afternoon."

"And he was okay with us showing up?" Andi asked. "We don't want to be wedding crashers."

"We'll time it right," Zeke said, his expression amused. "Ward thought it would give you a sense of how the building is used today."

When they reached the store, they agreed to meet in the lot in thirty minutes. Back on the boat, Andi hurried to change into her best black linen pants and her favorite off-the-shoulder peasant blouse she'd stashed away in the hanging locker. She considered dragging out her favorite wedge sandals, too, but slipping around in the mud made that a bad idea and she stuck with her waterproof shoes.

As she put in silver hoop earrings, she mulled over the way she'd overreacted to bumping in to Miles and Lark. She was the one who'd made it awkward. Everyone else was fine. Being in Two Moon Bay now, she better get used to it. It was only natural they'd all cross paths once in a while.

Walking to the store, she took a few deep breaths to settle her jumble of emotions. Spotting Zeke in the parking lot, she was excited about the day ahead.

"So you got the store covered?"

"Yep, we're good. Nelson's there."

His breezy tone was a little much. It certainly didn't match the concern in his eyes. "Wait a minute, Zeke. Are you sure about this? We could cancel and go another time."

"*No.* Dad just got a little confused today. And he and Nelson are old friends. They'll be fine."

"Lots of convoluted arrangements, though."

Zeke opened the passenger door of the car. "This is something I'd really like to do."

"Okay, then, let's go." She climbed inside and grabbed the seat belt.

Once they were under way, Andi put her head back and relaxed in the seat. As they put miles behind them, she looked out the window at the orchards and dairy farms and felt a sense of peace on the drizzly day. They also passed several horse farms and stables. "I hadn't realized how many places we can choose from when we board Brooke's horse. Although that's still way off."

"I can think of at least three boarding stables near Two Moon Bay." Zeke tilted his head toward her and added, "She's a happy girl, Andi, that daughter of yours. Exuberant."

"Thanks." She chuckled at her own response. "I don't know why I'm thanking you, like her happiness is my doing."

"Don't be modest. You and Miles have done a great job."

Maybe it was the one part of her life she was truly proud of. Her job? That was just a skill she'd acquired. "Okay, I'll accept that as parents, Miles and I lucked out."

"Good, take a little credit."

"It's a deal." Being with Zeke and watching the landscape pass by on the nearly empty two-lane road, Andi felt like she was out on a date. A real grown-up date. Her first one in many years. Being with Zeke at the winery felt special, too. She hadn't allowed herself this kind of fun in years—seven years to be exact. No matter how appealing the man.

"We're almost there," Zeke said, turning right at the sign on the county road that would take them to Elmwood Pond.

A few turns later, the building came into view on her side. "Oh..." she breathed. "I've gone past this building at least a dozen times and never really noticed it."

Zeke nodded. The building sat between

rows of cedars that marked its boundaries. The garden near the street was English farmhouse-style with an abundance of dahlias, hollyhocks and gladiolas. Pots of impatiens and geraniums were clustered in front of the building.

But it was the gray stone that made the building stand out. That and the carved wooden door flanked by two small stained-glass windows, one designed to show a fishing boat, the other a plow in a field.

"It looks like a church," Zeke said. "But the windows remind me it was the first town hall in Elmwood Pond."

"It's no wonder couples book it for weddings," Andi said. "It's gorgeous."

"Ward is around here somewhere," Zeke said, pointing to a van parked closer to the entrance. "We can go on in."

"Maybe the bridal party arrived early for photos," she said.

Zeke opened the heavy door leading into the main room and pointed to an area he said had been added on. "To modernize and build indoor bathrooms."

The back two rows had curved oak benches, but the half dozen or so rows in front consisted of padded folding chairs. "A concession to modern life," she said, "those folding chairs."

"We kept these original curved benches with an aisle between them. The original settlers were from New England. They wanted to duplicate those town meetings here."

Andi went to the front, which was dominated by a long oak table, with an old-fashioned lectern in place.

"I refinished that table myself," Zeke said. "They use it for everything from workshops to big dinners. Of course, the room's set up for a wedding today."

Andi tapped her fingertips on the table. "I know exactly what went into bringing this back." She pointed to the wooden-slatted ceiling and beams. "Did you do that work, too?"

"The whole crew had a hand in that. We added track lighting. Stone masons brought back the fireplace and hearth."

Andi gestured around the room, from wooden ceiling to stone floor. There were more stained-glass windows on either side of the fireplace. "It's incredible. And you must have been so relieved you could give it another life."

"A team of us managed to get the funds. I wish you'd been here for the reopening reception. You'd have really liked it. We had a fire going and local artists were invited to add pieces for a display. Sometime I'll show you before-and-after photos from my portfolio. I still take on a job now and then."

Out of nowhere, Art intruded into Andi's thoughts. Looking at this building with Zeke's fingerprints all over it, she had to wonder how much he even cared about the store. "I bet not as many as you'd like."

"No, I wish..." He didn't finish the sentence. Instead, he pointed to the ceiling. "It was water-stained and blackened when we started," Zeke said. "Lots of leaks. Like *Drifting Dreamer*."

The sound of heels clicking on a wooden floor broke into their conversation. Led by a woman holding a tablet, what appeared to be a six-person wedding party filed in.

Zeke approached the planner and introduced himself as a friend of Ward's.

"He said you'd be stopping in," the woman said. "We just had some photos in the garden under a canopy. We'll do a few in here now."

"You look beautiful," Andi called out to

the bride, who was probably in her mid-to-late thirties. Her age, Andi thought. The woman was smoothing the front of a sophisticated strapless sheath the color of violets. "Love that dress. You can really pull it off."

The woman left her group and walked up to Andi. "Thanks. I did one of those fluffy white numbers the first time around." She snorted. "For all the good it did me. This time I was up for something modern."

"I hear you." Andi had gone for a small wedding both times. Just their families with Miles, and only her parents with Roger. She quickly refocused on the bride to keep herself from jumping into that ancient history. The style of the dresses and the size of the weddings were completely irrelevant to the failure of both marriages. She nodded at Zeke. "He's showing me the building. He was part of its restoration years ago."

Zeke stood chatting with the planner, his manly hand propped on one manly hip. Glancing at the bride, Andi was sure they were having similar thoughts. Zeke looked good in casual khakis and a light blue shirt. He'd left his navy blue blazer in the car. Seeing him standing there, it was easy to mentally dress Zeke in a dark suit with a crisp white shirt and tie. Or, like the groom, in a tux, perfectly cut to fit across his broad shoulders and narrow torso. He could wear anything and look good. Andi almost let out a hoot. What a train of thought. All of that because of a group of people looking sharp in their tasteful wedding clothes.

"Are you here to look at the venue, you know, for your wedding?" the bride asked, nodding toward Zeke.

Andi raised both palms. "No, no, nothing like that. I'm working for Zeke for the summer. I'm restoring an old motor yacht. Trying to bring her back to her glory days. The kind of work he did on this building."

"I see," she said, obviously surprised. She glanced at Zeke again.

Yes, he's really attractive. Andi laughed to herself and then went for a quick change of subject. "Are you having a reception somewhere else?"

"Cocktails and dinner at the Black Swan Hotel."

"Ooh, sounds fun," Andi said, pointing to the groom, who stood by the door frowning at the two of them. "Uh, I think your groom and more photos await."

The bride beamed and walked away, almost giddy, Andi thought. And why not? She gave the room a once-over again, suddenly filled with happiness for the woman in the violet dress.

"Let's go look at the garden in the back," Andi suggested when the wedding group moved to the fireplace.

As they walked down the hall, Zeke said, "The groom mentioned he found this place and knew the historic building would appeal to the bride. She's an American history professor at the university in Green Bay."

"She certainly glows," Andi said, recognizing wistful feelings coming over her. "And this is a good place to go back in time."

It had started raining again, but Andi didn't bother with her hood. A little rain wasn't going to ruin her hair.

Part of the back garden was a mass of black-eyed Susans and daisies on one side, and more formal white and pink climbing roses on trellises that would be a pretty backdrop for photos on the other.

A stone path led to a neat clapboard building set back from the hall and off to the side and hidden by a cedar border. "The kitchen, I presume," Andi said.

"That's right. It was added later, when the town decided to keep the building and use it for meetings and parties. Sometimes they put a canopy over the path."

Andi gestured around her. "It's all so beautiful. It must have been so interesting to work on."

"The architect turned the details over to me. It was great." He gazed into her eyes. "It was exhilarating. One of the best projects I was ever involved with."

"It's energized me to see it, Zeke. It makes bringing *Drifting Dreamer* back to life even more compelling. I can't say exactly why."

Zeke started to respond, but the phone interrupted. "A text. Let me get it."

Andi found the interruption annoying, as if it broke a spell. She moved away to take a last look at the garden, where it was easy for Andi to envision weddings with brides in special dresses. If *she* ever had another wedding, this setting would be her choice. Maybe a winter wedding, with a fire blazing and lots of candles to provide the light.

What are you talking about? You're not the woman in violet, in love and beaming.

"Andi?" Zeke waved his hand in front of her face.

"Oops... I got lost somewhere in the past." Not true. She was lost in some impossible vision of the future.

"That was Nelson. All's quiet on the waterfront. Too quiet today. He and my dad are in the office working crossword puzzles. He ordered pizzas to be delivered in an hour. We'll make it there just in time, and then Nelson can get back to his day."

"Sounds good." Andi gave herself a B+ for fake enthusiasm. She didn't feel like going back. She'd spent the last hours curiously light-headed, but now she was out of sorts. It was about Zeke, she thought. Even this short trip with him had been a time-out, a novelty to be with the man when it wasn't about the boat or the waterfront or his dad. She didn't want to go back to regular life just yet. Pizza had never seemed so mundane.

CHAPTER TWELVE

ZEKE RESTED HIS weight on one hip while keeping one eye on his dad sitting in the office with his head lowered. A moment ago, Art's chin almost hit his chest. Andi's phone rang once, twice, three times. But he was sure she was aboard the boat. He'd just seen her walk by with Brooke after camp.

Finally, she offered a cheery greeting. "I was going to call you later."

"Andi… I've got to get my dad to the ER. Can you come and watch the store?"

"Of course. What's happened?"

"Some bad dizziness. He's got a history of this, but I need to get him checked out."

"I'll be right there."

"I'm going to the house to get his car. I don't want to try to get him up in the truck."

"Use mine, Zeke. I'll be there in one minute with the key."

Zeke ended the call. "Come on, Dad. We're going to go now."

Art lifted his head. "You didn't call an ambulance, did you?"

"No. I can get your there just as fast," he said, taking his dad's elbow and helping him up. "I'm taking you in Andi's car."

"Haven't had this happen in a long time," Art said, jutting his chin as he tried to straighten his body into a full standing position. "I'm not some old man who needs to be carted down the road with lights flashing and sirens blaring."

"No, you're not, but you do need to let me hang on to you while we walk to the car."

"Clear down the block? You know my car's in our garage at home. I haven't driven it in years."

"We're going in Andi's car," he repeated.

"Right, right. You just said that." Art bumped the heel of his free hand on his forehead. "My mind's a sieve today."

Sometimes those little blips in short-term memory upset his dad, but not so much today. Not when the room was spinning.

Zeke got Art to the car just as Andi jogged up the drive, hair flying. The car locks clicked as she approached. Brooke was with her, Zeke noticed, but Andi turned around and held up her hand. Brooke stopped several feet back at the side of the building.

"Hey, that was fast," he said, taken aback by the intensity of her panicked expression.

The muscles in her face relaxed when she saw his dad standing next to the passenger door.

"Hey, Art." She moved closer and folded her long fingers around his shoulder as Zeke opened the car door.

"I've got another one of my spells. I feel like the world is spinning like a top," Art said, offering no resistance to Zeke gripping his elbow and easing him into the seat. "Don't worry about me. It's going to be okay."

"Sounds like you're trying to make *me* feel better." Andi beckoned Brooke, who ran to her side.

"We'll take care of Teddy," Brooke said.

"Good to know," Zeke said. "He's sitting right inside the front door. He'll be happy to see you, Brooke."

"Nice car," Art said, nodding in approval. "Newer than ours."

"I'm glad you approve," Andi teased.

Zeke tried not to laugh out loud at the small talk. His dad was pale, all the color had drained from his face and he couldn't stand up straight and keep his balance, but he noticed Andi's car. He helped his dad click the seat belt in place.

"You know what to do in the store, Andi. Nothing is critical." Zeke walked around to the driver's side and got into the car. Seconds later, the engine was on and he was pulling out into the street.

"Call me," Andi shouted, raising her hand.

He responded with a quick wave. His mind immediately took him back to Saturday, when they'd been out together. Now he wished she was sitting next to him in the car on their way somewhere fun. Instead, she was standing with her arm around Brooke. Smart of her to have Brooke stay back until she knew what was happening so Art wouldn't upset the ten-year-old.

"I suppose Andi will be moving on soon," Art suddenly said.

"She won't be going far," Zeke said. "She'll find an apartment in town, probably buy a house soon."

"Still, you won't be spending as much time with her. She'll be busy with a real job soon, too."

That sounded suspiciously like what his dad wanted. If they weren't on the way to the ER for what could turn out to be something serious, Zeke would have asked outright if he resented being left with Nelson on Saturday. His dad had had an edge to him ever since.

"By the way, Zeke, I'm sorry for spilling the beans about your mother the other night. Shouldn't have done that. It all happened so long ago."

"But it did happen, Dad. And neither one of us forgot about it." Far from it.

"I used to think about it a lot, Zeke, but—" Art shrugged "—it doesn't seem to matter much anymore."

It wasn't the right time to bring it up with his father, but Zeke was tired of his dad saying that what happened didn't matter. Maybe they didn't talk about it much, and Zeke no longer thought of his mother as a secret to keep, but that didn't mean her loss hadn't left a scar, particularly on a boy who loved his mom. Zeke had spent his twenties too terrified to commit to anything but his work.

His dad had never showed any interest in finding another woman, either. Zeke looked at their lives and could see that being abandoned mattered.

Zeke pulled into the half-circle driveway and let a nurse help his dad slide out of the front seat and into a wheelchair. Under protest. Of course, reacting against help was as natural to his dad as breathing. Through the open car door, Zeke saw his dad lurch to the side and fall into the nurse's steadying arm.

With a heavy sigh, he drove away to find a parking place.

When he went inside, he was directed to an exam cubicle, where his dad sat in a straight-backed chair with armrests. With a tablet in one hand, a doctor was listening to his dad describe when the dizziness started. "A couple of years back, my doc gave me a drug for it and said it was benign. You know, not serious."

"Yes, I see that in your records," the doctor said, glancing down at the screen.

"His neurologist prescribed it, Dr. Wright," Zeke explained, after glancing at her name tag. "He sees his neurologist, Sidney Kauffman, every six months. That's because he has some lingering symptoms likely linked to concussions."

"I just told her that, Zeke. I can speak for myself."

Zeke raised his hands in exaggerated surrender. "You're right, Dad. Sorry." The doctor didn't respond, but scrolled the screen of the tablet in her hand, apparently not amused by his exchange with his dad.

"I see you had scans, a neuro workup and blood work less than a year ago, Mr. Donovan. And two years ago, you were diagnosed with benign vertigo."

"Right. But he said not to worry."

"Was this episode any different from what happened a couple of years ago?" she asked Art, but then raised her eyes to cast a pointed look at Zeke.

Zeke held the eye contact and lowered his chin. A subtle nod that he hoped his dad wouldn't catch. This episode absolutely was different from others in the past. Worse. This time, Art was disoriented as well as dizzy. It hadn't lasted long, only a few seconds, but that was enough to scare Zeke.

Dr. Wright frowned. "Tell me about those old concussions, Mr. Donovan."

Art swatted the air. "You mean back when I was a kid playing hockey?"

"That's what I see written here. And one from a fall. That one was diagnosed at the time it occurred."

She still hadn't cracked a smile and was looking back at the screen.

"Like I said, I was just a kid. We didn't know a bump on the head could be so bad."

"It says here you lost consciousness."

"Yeah. With the first one for sure."

"Do you have reason to question the diagnosis?" Zeke asked. All his life it seemed everything with his dad came back to what happened long before he'd even met Zeke's mother.

"Not really," she said, addressing Zeke, "but your father has apparently experienced the aftereffects of postconcussion syndrome. Most people recover from mild to moderate concussions. He's had these lingering issues. For several decades, apparently."

"Hey, Doc, I'm right here. Talk to me." Art's back stiffened. "The dizziness is gone now. I'm thinking clearly. And my hearing is good."

Good for him, Zeke thought. They'd been

through this before. If Zeke was in the room, the doctor tended to ignore his dad and address him.

Dr. Wright finally smiled and shifted her gaze. "Got it, Mr. Donovan. And from what I see, I believe you've had a recurrence of the vertigo, maybe a little worse this time. They call it benign for a reason. It's not a tumor or a sign of a stroke. It's not serious in itself."

"Why didn't I know where I was?" Art demanded. "That never happened before. Well, not with the dizziness, anyway."

The doctor's frown returned, leaving deep creases across her forehead. "I can't tell you exactly why that happened."

Zeke caught the way his dad's face fell, his shoulders drooped. It was almost as if the doctor reminded him of something he'd momentarily forgotten about.

Zeke didn't like hearing that, either, but he needed a more precise answer. "So, it seems like you're saying the two things—the conditions—converged?"

"I believe that's our best answer at this time."

"Should I have one of those scan things?" Art said, pointing to his head.

Glancing at the tablet, Dr. Wright shook her head. "I don't think that's necessary at this juncture."

"If you say so. I just don't want to have a stroke or something."

"No indication of that. And your vitals are good—blood pressure is normal and your heart rate is perfect." She pulled a prescription pad and pen out of her coat pocket and scribbled for a couple of seconds before handing the form to his dad.

"Must be my heart's in good shape because I'm so active," Art said, stretching his arms out to the sides.

"Probably so," Dr. Wright said. "I wish more of our patients were active like you."

Zeke could see where this exam was going. They'd soon be sent home with the new prescription in hand.

"What's the new drug for?" Zeke asked.

She explained it was a slightly increased dosage of the drug Art already took.

Zeke wanted to ask if they could expect these episodes to occur more often as his dad got older. But he kept quiet. He could call the doctor later and get her opinion. Besides, when it came to his dad's health, no doctor had ever confidently predicted anything.

"What now?" Art asked.

"Go home and rest today and start the meds."

"Ha! Easy for you to say." Art scooted to the edge of the chair. "I've got a business to run."

Zeke put his hand on his dad's shoulder. "I can take over the store for the rest of the day, Dad. Tomorrow is soon enough to get back behind the counter." Feeling defensive about his dad, he turned to the doctor and said, "My dad works full-time in our family business, Donovan Marine Supply."

Her eyebrows lifted in surprise. "I see. That's good." She shook his dad's hand, and then Zeke's, and out she went.

"Let's go, son," Art said, gripping the armrest to give him a boost out of the chair.

Art insisted on walking—and at a good clip—alongside him to retrieve Andi's car and in a few minutes they were on their way. Given how his dad was behaving in that moment, Zeke could easily forget the reason he'd hustled him off to the ER.

Suddenly, Art rubbed his palms together

and said, "I'm hungry. I was so dizzy I missed lunch and now it's moving toward dinnertime."

"I'll make you a sandwich when we get home."

"No, you won't. You drop me off. I'll fix my own food." Art slapped his knee. "I feel real good now."

"No kidding?" Zeke joked.

"That's what happens when you find out you're not having a stroke. I can live with that concussion stuff. You don't remember but a stroke took my mother."

"I do remember, Dad." At the age of eighty, Zeke thought. On the other hand, his own mother wasn't much over thirty when she died of liver cancer.

Once they'd pulled into their driveway, his dad couldn't get out of the car fast enough. "Gotta make a sandwich."

"And rest," Zeke said.

He looked inside the car at Zeke. In a low voice he said, "I will, Zeke, I will…and thanks for, you know, getting me to the hospital. I know I'm not always the easiest guy."

"No, you're a real bear, Dad," Zeke said,

his heart softening right there in his chest. "But I love you, anyway."

"Lucky for me." He grinned and shut the car door.

The store was empty when he got back. Except for Andi, texting, and Brooke, reading. Both sat on stools behind the counter, and Teddy was snoozing in the office.

"How's Art?" they said simultaneously, and then chuckled.

"He's okay." He filled them in on the vertigo. "He's content right now. None the worse for wear and all that. When I dropped him off he planned to make himself a sandwich and rest."

Andi's face broke into a happy smile. "What a relief."

She means it, Zeke thought, aware of the warmth moving through his body.

"I bet Teddy will be glad to see him later," Brooke said, sticking a bookmark inside the book and hopping off the stool.

"We'll get out of your way. It's about closing time, anyway." Andi patted a notepad next to her. "I jotted down a couple of sales, just to update you, and took an anchor order over the phone."

"Thanks for helping on short notice. You, too, Brooke."

"We're just across the yard," Brooke said with a nonchalant shrug as she skipped and bounced her way to the back door.

"Such energy," Andi said, staying behind. "If you can stop by later, I want to show you something. I found some other things on the boat."

That news brought a pleasant jolt. It almost didn't matter what she'd found. It was sharing a secret with Andi that made him notice his rapid pulse. Zeke pointed with his chin to the back door, where Brooke waited. "Say around nine o'clock?"

"See you then."

Amused, the word *conspiracy* came to mind as he watched Andi leave.

"ARE YOU WORRIED about Art?" Brooke asked as she climbed into bed.

"A little, but apparently, he's had dizzy spells before and it isn't serious." She left it at that. "Art and Zeke wouldn't want you to worry."

"Art's funny, isn't he? Funnier than Grandpa Max."

Not a hard act to follow, Andi thought. Dried mud was funnier than her dad. A loving, sweet man all in all, he'd either been born without a humor gene or it had withered away from lack of use.

"Art likes you," Andi said, standing in the doorway to the cabin. "He's happy you and Teddy are pals."

"I'm Maple's pal, too."

"That's true. I'm so glad."

She and Miles had agreed to let Brooke ride on Saturdays through the fall and maybe on the snow trails when they were open in the winter. The riding camp had been even better for Brooke than basketball or soccer. Riding had given her body confidence, something Andi knew would serve her well. Her ability to relate to a flesh-and-blood animal had made her seem more mature, too. Riding year-round was her reward for being serious about learning to take care of a horse.

"Are you going to read your book a little while longer?"

"I think so. The girls almost figured out who tried to steal the Appaloosa horse from another kid's barn."

"Okay. When Zeke comes over, we'll

talk quietly up on deck. We won't keep you awake."

"Are you going to tell him about those pages you found?"

"Yep. They're pretty special. It's another clue in *our* mys-ter-y." She wiggled her fingers in the air to illustrate the intrigue.

Brooke tapped her knuckles on the bulkhead behind her. "Maybe you'll find out who slept in this bunk a long time ago."

"Could be. You never know."

Andi shut the cabin door and gathered the new pages. There was something different about this batch.

THE PIECES OF the boat's past were filling in, Zeke thought, as he glanced at the screen Andi pulled up on her tablet. The steady breeze had broken up the cloud of humidity that had hung in the air for days and gave them a cooler August evening.

"See here? So many Charles and Mary Petersons in Duluth and up in that other little town they were from, Ash River," she said. A notice in the newspaper showed the Petersons, a young couple, at their wedding. "We can be certain they're the Petersons we're looking for because of their wedding notice."

Zeke read through the copy until the last line.

> The Petersons will be relocating to Duluth, Minnesota, where they will honeymoon on their yacht, *Drifting Dreamer.* They will return to Ash River in October. Peterson will rejoin his family's law firm.

"It matches what Charles says in the letter. He got his summer on the boat with Mary."

"The summer of 1941," Andi said. "At least one of Charles's dreams for the yacht came true. They started out without a care in the world, but things changed. In these new log pages, Charles wrote—I believe it's his handwriting—about his brother, Quinn, spending a few days with them up in Ontario. Thunder Bay, specifically. They're dated in July."

Zeke was confused. "How do you know Quinn is Charles's brother?"

"So glad you asked." Andi picked up one of the log pages and pointed to an entry. "He mentions 'Mother' being concerned about Quinn and hopes the time on the boat will do him good. But Charles says her hopes usually lead to nothing."

"Why do I get the feeling this story doesn't have a happy ending?" Zeke asked.

"Because it doesn't," Andi said. "After reading that love letter, I almost feel like I know these people. It's like we lost friends of ours."

"Lost?" Zeke looked on as Andi pulled up another image of a newspaper article. A death notice for Mary Peterson, who was a casualty in the bombing of a transport ship in the Pacific in 1942. "She died in the war?"

"She was a nurse. The thing is, Zeke, it says here she was thirty-four, which means she was already in her thirties when they married. I went back to the wedding notice, and Charles was thirty-five."

Zeke leaned forward and rested his elbows on his knees. "And you're going to tell me he died, too?"

Andi nodded. "Right after the war, 1946. The death notice called it complications from wounds sustained in the war. I pulled it up."

Zeke tapped the deck table, scanned the wood on the canopy and cabin doors.

"I know," Andi said, "all summer we've been making the *Dreamer* look like it did back when Charles and Mary lived aboard that one summer."

"At least we know it was a good summer," Zeke said, with a cynical scoff. "Some comfort."

Andi turned her head and stared off in the distance. Even in the dim light, he could see her thoughtful expression. "Just think. Being out on Lake Superior, going up to Canada, port-hopping. They never thought they'd be involved in the war."

"But now, this is like an unexpected and great summer for me, Andi. Having you and Brooke here, seeing the boat transform. Even searching for some answers about this old yacht herself."

Andi smiled, but sadly. "When I read that Charles and Mary had both died in the war, I found myself feeling sad for *Drifting Dreamer*, as if the boat lost her champions. But now, here she is with two people who care about her."

The air held that electric charge again, like

what happened when he'd first met Andi. It was as if they had a secret of their own in uncovering at least a little of this boat's history. He covered her hand with his. "You're right about that. We care enough to make her shine again."

Andi wrapped her fingers around his hand.

"Do we know anything after that?" he asked. "Anything that tells us what happened later?"

Andi straightened up and released his hand while she checked the notes she'd made. "As a matter of fact, it keeps getting interesting. Not so many *Quinn* Petersons in Minnesota and Wisconsin. It's the only other name we have."

"Did you find him?"

Her voice rose as she shared her discovery. "He turned up in Ontario—Thunder Bay, to be exact. He lived in Canada after the war and kept the boat."

"Why? Do we know why he went there to live?"

Andi shook her head. "Sorry, no answer for you on that. But he had a son he named Quinn, who lived in Duluth."

"No kidding?"

"There's more. That Quinn had a son, also named Quinn Peterson, who's up in Ashland, right here in Wisconsin."

Zeke recalled the sight of the deteriorating yacht when the guys from Kenosha motored up to the dock. "Did Quinn Peterson let that deterioration happen? Did this Quinn guy sell the boat to Terrance Smyth."

"That's where the trail goes cold, Zeke. But I looked up Quinn in Ashland. I found him. Just him, though. No family is mentioned, at least according to his Facebook page, and there's almost nothing on his page. The thing is, we don't know that he ever heard of *Drifting Dreamer*. Family history can be tricky. Maybe Quinn and Charles weren't close. We're not even sure how he ended up with his grandfather's boat, or I should say, his great-uncle's boat."

Zeke chuckled. "To me, she will always be Charles and Mary's boat. But we could get in touch with Quinn if we wanted to."

"We could try." Andi leaned back and raised her palms. "I should say *you* could try. She's your boat, Zeke. It's *your* call, not mine."

Hands off, huh? Is that what she was saying? But he didn't feel that way. "I think of it as your boat, too, Andi." He'd almost said "our boat," but caught himself in time.

"That's sweet, Zeke. I can't deny feeling like I have a stake in what happens to *Drifting Dreamer*, but you're the one who has to make the decisions. Now that she's almost fixed up, you may want to sell her."

"Maybe so," he said noncommittally. "But I'd rather find out more about Quinn Peterson. Could be he'd hear the history of the boat and want it back in the family. We don't know what he knows. And I can't say how *I'll* feel if he does want it. But I think he should have a chance to at least find out what happened to the boat."

"How will you feel if you learn he was the one who let her go downhill?" Andi shifted in her seat. "I'm not discouraging you. Just putting it out there."

"Well, Andi, no telling how I'll feel if that's the case, but I want to know all the same. It might not affect what my dad'll do with the boat later, but just knowing *Drifting Dreamer* had a life gives me a lift somehow." He paused. "It's not that different from sanding those ceiling beams in Settlers Hall or watching the stone masons repair the fireplace. It's bringing something of value back to life."

"It's kind of like honoring them in some way," Andi said. "Two people who died when they were a little younger than the two of us."

Zeke was aware he'd need to leave soon. Even the nightly summertime noise from the marina had all but ended. But he'd rather stay right where he was.

Suddenly, Andi's voice broke the silence. "I've got an open bottle of white wine in the fridge. Want a glass?"

"Sure," he said quickly.

"Good. I'll be right back."

Smiling, he watched her go down into the cabin. These times with Andi were a lot like dates. To him, anyway. But what would she call their time together?

CHAPTER THIRTEEN

ANDI RECOGNIZED DAWN'S voice calling out from the dock, but Brooke got to the deck first and helped Carrie step aboard.

"Wait a second, Carrie," Dawn said. "We weren't invited yet."

"It's okay, I invited her to come on the boat," Brooke said.

Case closed, Andi thought, still wiping her hands on a towel when she got to the deck. She waved Dawn forward. "What brings you here this morning?"

"The summer is passing quickly, and I'm arranging the all-girls day on the tour boat."

"And you can come, Brooke," Carrie said, "and Lark and Wyatt are going to be there, and Lark's mom and—"

"Enough, little girl," Dawn said fondly. "Andi doesn't need to hear the whole guest list."

Especially since she wasn't on it, Andi

mused, her mood dropping fast. Dawn's and Lark's moms were even going along. Quite a little party.

"Brooke is free until the end of the week. Then she leaves for her trip with Miles," Andi said in a cool tone.

"We're going tomorrow," Carrie said.

"Yes, Miss Spokeswoman," Dawn said to Carrie, "the weather looks good for tomorrow."

"Sounds fine, huh, Brooke?"

"And don't forget Florey, too."

"And Florey," Dawn said, decisively. "I'll call Joy to see if she and Florey can both come."

Of course, Joy would be included. But Andi thought of Joy as *her* friend. Yikes, sometimes her own pettiness floored her.

"Hey, Brooke, I'm wondering if I could ask you a favor." Dawn spoke in a serious voice.

Brooke shrugged. "I guess, sure."

"Maybe you could teach Carrie how to do a cartwheel. She's almost there, but not quite. And yours are pretty impressive." Dawn gestured to the area beyond the dock. "Maybe out on the grass."

"I can try." Brooke's face showed reluctance. She glanced at Andi.

Since the request seemed to come out of the blue, Brooke was likely confused, Andi thought, but she nodded to encourage her. Did Dawn want to talk without being overheard?

With obvious resignation in her voice, Brooke said, "Okay, come on, Carrie, let's go."

The girls scrambled off the boat.

"I'm in no shape to bring out the cartwheels," Dawn said, giving her growing baby bump a pat. "Here's the thing. Correct me if I'm wrong, but you and Lark get along well, right?"

No problem answering that. "We do. We've always been on friendly terms. Right from the start." Andi shrugged. Dawn likely knew that already. "Lark's good to Brooke."

"Then, why don't *you* come out on *Lucy Bee* with us tomorrow?" Dawn asked. "Florey and Joy are likely coming, and you're not a stranger around here anymore. You know Wyatt and Melody, too."

The unexpected invitation touched Andi. Nevertheless, she blurted, "You already have your group. You don't need to feel obligated to invite me along. You all know each other."

She waited for Dawn to jump in and protest, but she surprised Andi again. The seconds ticked by in silence, and when Dawn spoke, her voice was low and serious. "I know Lark well. She's quieter than I am, you know, not in constant motion flitting around organizing this or that event. But she's talked to me—a lot—about how impressed she is with the way you and Miles share Brooke."

"Well, she gets credit for making it easy for this fairly complicated blended family to work." It was true, not a trivial attempt to deflect attention away from her and Miles.

"You're right about that," Dawn said, back to her animated self, "but, and I'm gossiping when I say, her situation with her son's father hasn't been nearly as smooth. In fact, her ex is openly hostile most of the time. That's why she admires you and Miles. Anyway, it comes down to this. I don't like having our girls' day out without you being a part of it. You're Brooke's mom, and you're a part of our waterfront crowd."

Feeling emboldened and needing one more push, Andi said, "I hope you're not insulted by this question, but do you really feel like that? You aren't just asking because you think you should?"

Dawn threw back her head and groaned. "Do I strike you as that kind of woman?"

Andi swallowed a big, loud hoot. Of course, Dawn, with her outgoing personality, struck her that way. Andi didn't think of her flitting about so much as being vibrant and lively. She kept her answer simple. "No, not exactly, Dawn, but even on the Fourth of July I could see you like to have a good time and want the same for everyone else."

Dawn lifted her palms to her sides. "I plead guilty. So will you come?"

Laughing, she said, "Yes, Dawn, I'll be happy to join you. I'll need to check with Zeke, though, just to be sure he doesn't need me in the store."

Dawn walked to the edge of the deck and took a look around before stepping off. "This boat is a jewel. Talk about a face-lift."

"Best summer job I've ever had," Andi said, sighing.

"How much longer will you be on the boat?"

"Moving day will come around the first of

October. I'm sure I'll find a house or apartment by then." In a joking tone, she added, "And maybe even a job. At some point I'll begin hunting for a home to buy. Then we'll be full-fledged residents of Two Moon Bay."

"I think of you that way now. I'm sure things will work themselves out. See you tomorrow. As Jerrod always says, 'We toss the lines' around nine o'clock."

Andi watched Carrie skip across the grass to catch up with Dawn and take her outstretched hand. Brooke followed behind doing a series of her nicely done head-over-heels cartwheels. Just watching Dawn and the two girls filled her with the kind of contentment she'd hoped a move to Two Moon Bay would bring. She'd gambled on the change, and despite the uncertainty ahead, the risk had been worth it.

"CARRIE IS SO enthusiastic about the trip," Andi remarked to Melody. "She seems that way about most everything."

Melody nodded. "I'm still Carrie's nanny, although more like a babysitter now that she has a new mom." She pointed to Brooke. "Your daughter is a real favorite of Carrie's."

Andi kept her gaze on Brooke and Florey leaning against the rail, with Carrie standing between them. Carrie's usual braids were tied with aqua bows to match the color of the flowers on her sundress. No dresses for Brooke and Florey, though. They'd decided to dress alike in white jeans and blue tank tops.

"I bet Brooke shot up a couple of inches this summer," Andi remarked, resting her elbows on the edge of the passenger rail behind the row of benches. *Lucy Bee* was filled with tourists with binoculars and cameras following Jerrod's hand as he pointed to landmarks on the shore.

The boat cut back its speed as Jerrod explained they were passing over an area where the bones of two sunken ships rested on the bottom. Andi had learned that Jerrod had run diving excursions and water tours mostly out of Florida and the Virgin Islands, but last year he'd decided to take a chance and set up a location on Lake Michigan. His shipwreck diving day trips had taken off in a big way in Two Moon Bay. He and Dawn had taken off, too.

"Will you be staying on to help with the new baby, Melody?" Andi asked.

Melody's face brightened as she ran down possible plans, all of which meant staying in town. "I'll help Dawn, but pick up jobs here in town. I love Two Moon Bay in the winter, too, so I'm staying no matter what. I worked a shift at the Bean Grinder last weekend—and that's like being in the middle of everything going on in town."

"Sounds perfect." Usually not a big believer in magic, Andi admitted to being a little awed by how life seemed to fall into place for people who found their way to Two Moon Bay. "Sometimes I think Two Moon Bay itself holds a secret recipe for happiness."

"Huh?" Melody's face looked puzzled, as if Andi had just said something really weird.

"What? You didn't catch on to my scientific analysis?" With a light laugh in her voice, Andi said. "Let's just say people I've encountered found what they needed in this town. Maybe what they were looking for all along." Andi extended her hand toward Melody. "Look at you."

"That's kind of true, I guess you've got a point," Melody agreed.

Still, Andi was perplexed by her own words. What had she been thinking? She had made Two Moon Bay sound like a fantasy town, not a real one with flesh-and-blood people with struggles. Like Zeke and Art. But that didn't mean it wasn't a little magical, too.

Her expression thoughtful, Melody said, "Now that you mention it, Two Moon Bay has given me much more than I expected." She looked around in every direction. "Yes, I'd even call it a magical place."

"Exactly. So you *do* get it."

Jerrod announced they'd be in Sturgeon Bay in fifteen minutes, and a quiet settled over the boat. A few passengers went to the rails to try for a good shot of a majestic schooner under full sail not far away. The girls waved at the sailors in the cockpit and Melody moved quickly to lift Carrie so people on the other boat could see her wave.

Andi got out her phone and took a couple of pictures of the three girls and Melody lined up next to each other. She shot a few from the back and when *Lucy Bee* pulled ahead of the schooner, she called out, "Turn around now. Big smiles."

She got the happy faces of the four of them and when Melody stepped out of the group, she took another of the three girls. Where was the tingling and pressure behind her eyes coming from? Contentment? Yes. A sense of loss? Yes. Over summer days that came and went too fast. This interlude in her life would soon come to an end. It had been unplanned, unforeseen, but she'd always think of it as part of the magic of Two Moon Bay.

Their group hung back when the boat was secured at the dock at Jacobson's Marina in Sturgeon Bay, and passengers filed off.

"Will we get to sit at the captain's table?" Florey asked in a comically formal tone.

"Of course," Dawn said. "You're special guests."

"Everybody sits together," Carrie said. "That's cuz all the passengers are special."

Andi stifled a giggle rising up from her chest and caught a glimpse of Lark standing next to Dawn doing the same thing. When Andi caught Lark's eye, she held her gaze as they smiled over the girls' antics. When they left the boat, Andi made a point to walk to the restaurant alongside her. Other than greeting each other at the boat earlier, Andi had hung back from Lark, as if avoiding her. That made no sense at all.

"Brooke seems pleased about school starting," Lark said.

Andi nodded. "Meeting Florey was a godsend. They're doing their sleepover on the boat tonight. Brooke won't feel like a total stranger on the first day. There were a couple of other girls from the school at riding camp."

Lark grinned. "Miles asked if she was nervous about her new school. She gave him one of those pointed looks, as if wondering why he'd ask such a dumb thing.

"She's grown up so much," Lark added. "The riding camp boosted her confidence."

"She walks a little taller, all right," Andi said, smiling. "She thinks Evan is the best, you know. And don't get me started on Perrie Lynn…the skating princess."

Lark grinned. "It can get complicated."

"But you made it work," Andi said, finding her voice to say what had been on her mind for a long time. It hadn't been easy for Lark and Miles to explain to Evan and Brooke they'd given a baby up for adoption when they were still kids in college. Then they found Perrie Lynn just as the eighteen-year-old was rising in the figure skating world. Brooke got to see her half sister at least once a year. And she watched her skate on TV every chance that came along. They'd see her skate next week on the family's summer trip.

"We don't talk often, Andi, but I'm always happy when we do. You and Miles and the way you share Brooke—I've been green with envy. I'm not sure when—if ever—my ex-husband's resentment will end, even now that Evan is a teenager."

"That must be hard." Andi was surprised by Lark's open attitude, considering how perfect her life looked from the outside. As usual, self-deprecating stories about the mess she'd created with Roger jumped into her mind.

The waitstaff at Jacobson's was evidently used to putting out big lunches for Jerrod's tours. They brought platters of fruit kebabs and hot dogs and bowls of chips and coleslaw to pass. Across the table, Dawn tended to Carrie, putting a kebab on her plate as if it was the most important task in the world.

Lark asked after Art, but Andi hedged. "It's hard to say. He's been okay lately." Zeke would probably prefer she not say anything.

Lark lowered her voice when she said, "I've told Zeke in passing that I come across new research about brain injuries. I'm always happy to let him in on what I find."

Andi nodded, but she suddenly felt protective of Art, and Zeke, and her impulse was to reassure Lark that everything was okay, but that wasn't true, either. Lark's research might come in handy one day.

The weather held for the cruise back to the dock in Two Moon Bay. Jerrod's presentation was old hat to Lark and Dawn. But Andi learned a lot from the images Jerrod projected on a mounted TV screen. The old newspaper articles about freighters and schooners sinking not far off the shore, the photos of ships in pieces at the bottom of the lake. Even Joy, who'd lived in Two Moon Bay all her life, said she'd known nothing about the shipwrecks they were passing over on *Lucy Bee*.

"Everything on land looks different, too," Joy remarked when they passed the beaches and cottages dotting the shore, along with bluffs and woods. "And here I thought it was just a few hours on the water. I didn't know I'd learn so much."

"Me, neither," Andi said, her mind in a dreamy haze as they approached Two Moon Bay.

She and Brooke and Florey said their goodbyes to Joy and they strolled back to *Drifting Dreamer.* All the while, Andi's mind was traveling down two tracks. One was about the pleasure of the day, of spending time with other women and the girls. The other took her to the pesky topic of what was next. A job. The résumés she'd sent in response to job postings. Wanting and not wanting a response. Admitting to herself she was doing nothing more than dutifully going through the motions.

When they boarded the boat, Andi stopped and pressed her hand against the freshly varnished deck rail, warm and almost velvety under her fingers. The oiled teak deck gleamed under the late-afternoon sun and could have been brand-new.

"Mom?"

She turned to look at Brooke standing behind her.

"What are you doing?"

Andi tapped the wood and smiled at Brooke. "Hmm…just admiring my work, I guess."

CHAPTER FOURTEEN

"YOU TAKE YOUR backpack, Brooke. I'll get your luggage across the grass." Andi bumped the wheels across the ground, and once in the parking lot the purple suitcase rolled a little easier toward Miles, who was waiting by the open hatchback of the minivan.

Last night, Brooke had been quiet, maybe a little sad. Camp was over, and she'd miss Florey, but by bedtime, after Andi had helped her pack the last shorts and shirts and a couple of dresses, Brooke started looking ahead, and had been almost too excited to sleep.

Like every year, Andi was a little down herself when she had to say goodbye to Brooke for her annual two-week vacation with Miles. This year the two weeks was a road trip that included visits to Andi's parents on the way to Minnesota, where they'd see Perrie Lynn skate in an exhibition.

Andi waved to Miles and then to Lark and Evan, who were in the car.

"So, this is it? You have everything?" Miles asked.

"Yep, let's get going, Dad." Brooke dropped her backpack in the trunk and rushed to open the rear door.

"Hey, my friend," Andi called out, opening her arms, "not so fast. One more hug."

"Oh, all right," Brooke said, pretending to drag her feet over to Andi.

Andi pulled Brooke to her, murmuring again about having a good time. "Send me texts and pictures. You can even stick a stamp on a postcard and put it in a mailbox."

"Your mom can be a little old-school, Brooke," Miles said. "We'll see what we can do."

"Okay, you're off." Andi dropped her arms and stepped back. She watched until Brooke was settled in the back seat and Miles drove down the street. She waved at the car one last time.

At the store, Andi peeked inside, but Zeke was busy at the counter, and there were several cars in the lot. Nothing to do but wander back to the boat and start the day's work.

Once on the boat, Andi swallowed half a mug of coffee and half-heartedly picked at a carton of yogurt. She was used to Brooke being gone a few days at a time, but two weeks always stretched a little too long.

Her breakfast, such as it was, over, Andi went topside carrying supplies in one of the canvas tool buckets Zeke had loaned her. Applying varnish had a mesmerizing effect, at least for her, and over the next couple of hours, she steadily applied another coat to the cabin house. She only stopped because she heard the signal of a text coming in from her phone on the deck table.

Ah, Brooke. Probably texting to tell her how far they'd gone in the last couple of hours. Andi enjoyed that part of Brooke's adjustment to these longer trips, like she had to pull away a little at a time, just like Andi. But that wouldn't last many more years, Andi mused.

The text wasn't from Brooke, though. It was from Zeke: Yacht club is having music tonight. Want to walk over, maybe around 8?

Hmm...did she ever. She texted back:

Would like that. See you at the store a little b4 8?

Taking the phone with her, she went back to the bow. She was ready to call this a date. Just like the trip to Elmwood Pond was a date. Like every time they were together, whether it was sitting together on the deck talking, or when she helped out in the store, felt like a special time. A date.

Later that afternoon, before she fixed herself a quick dinner and took a shower, Andi sat at the table with a glass of iced tea and searched job listings. She had to face facts. The bulk of the boat work was nearly over, from the galley to every corner of the staterooms.

Even as she looked around, though, she envisioned a bride, only a few years younger than Andi herself, sitting at this very table, maybe writing a letter to her friend describing her storybook honeymoon on the boat.

Andi laughed out loud. What a romantic she could be.

Forcing herself to focus, Andi scrolled through job listings, and responded to a corporate recruiter's inquiry. It wouldn't hurt to forward her résumé to this firm. Her search area wasn't as big as it had been in Green Bay. If she wanted a commute of thirty minutes or less, one of her original requirements, her choices were limited. So far, nothing much had turned up in Two Moon Bay, but she still hoped she could work right here in town. In the meantime, she dutifully responded to anything that held the slightest possibility.

Tired of even thinking about her job search, let alone doing anything more proactive than sending out résumés, Andi checked her email. One from her mother brought a smile to her face.

Andi—Brooke and her new family arrived. She'll stay with us tonight and we'll all be together tomorrow. She's grown so much. I guess you were right about her camp. Riding lessons up here wouldn't have been the same. Your dad and I can't believe she actually likes living on what she calls "the dreamer." You know how I hate being wrong, but I admit you didn't need rescuing. Brooke says she made a new friend, and now can't wait to see Perrie Lynn.

What about you? Is a job in the works?

Brooke says you like that boat work, but summer will be over soon. Miles looks wonderful. He seems happy. Hope you are, too.
Love you,
Mom

At the moment, Mom, yes I am happy.

She wrote her mother a quick reply, apologizing for being brief. She had plans, and didn't want to run late. Andi had no inclination to say what her plans were.

She sent the email and then read the incoming texts, one from Brooke announcing her arrival at her grandparents' house, and one from Zeke: Instead of meeting, I'll pick u up.

Well, well, a man coming to her door… more or less. It had been a long time since that happened.

ZEKE CAME THROUGH the back door of his home holding a handful of zinnias.

"Thanks, Zeke, but you didn't need to bring me flowers," his dad said, from his chair near the fireplace. He peered at Zeke over his reading glasses and newspaper.

"Very funny, Dad." He was too old to feel

this much like a teenager. Was this what love felt like when you were staring at a fortieth birthday? The same as it did when he was twenty?

"Are you bringing those flowers to a woman? Maybe a woman named Andi?"

"That's the plan."

"Then put them in a vase. We must have one around. All she'd have on that boat are empty varnish cans."

"I was planning to scare up a vase. I think I know where we put them." Zeke opened a cabinet where they stored things they almost never used and spotted a couple of vases on the top shelf. He pulled one down and arranged the flowers inside it before adding water.

Art let out a low whistle. "I haven't seen you bring flowers to a woman in a long time."

"It's been a long time. That's a fact," Zeke said.

"Look, Zeke, you can tell me if you're interested in Andi."

"I know, Dad."

He didn't know how to respond. He was getting serious, but he didn't know about

Andi. With his back to his dad, he said, "I like her for lots of reasons, Dad. I think she likes me, too. That's all I can say right now."

Art let out a soft grunt. "So, I suppose you're going to want me to move out, huh?"

"Move out? Why would you even say such a thing?" For a few seconds, Zeke assumed his dad was joking.

"I'm not going to hang around and get in the way." Art turned the page and slapped the middle to straighten the fold. "If you and Andi get serious, you won't want to be bothered with me."

Zeke pushed the flowers away and planted his palms on the table, determined to stay calm and not overreact to this nonsense. "Is that really what you think, Dad?"

Art flapped his hand toward the door. "You go on and get outta here."

"Not just yet," Zeke said, moving closer to him. "You do know I'm always here for you, right?"

"Until now. I see the way you look at Andi. You two always have your heads together chewing over something. It's all about that boat. Now you're going out." He let the newspaper drop to his lap. "How do I know you won't just take off?"

Zeke's body was buzzed. Disbelief, anger, confusion. Resentment, usually mild and easy to handle, didn't feel so benign. *"Because I never have."*

His words reverberated through the room. He stayed by the table, but looked squarely at his dad, whose features softened.

"You better go right now. Don't want to be late." Art picked up the newspaper again.

"You sure you'll be okay here for a couple of hours?" Zeke asked, just like he always did. He went on to repeat his usual words, behaving for the moment as if nothing had changed, even though they'd shifted into new territory. "You have the phone. I can be here in minutes. But call 911 first if something happens or you don't feel well."

"Am I going to have to kick you out? Go on, go."

There went that flapping hand again, Zeke thought. Same old Dad.

Zeke was halfway out the door, when he heard his dad call his name. "I'm still here, Dad. What is it?"

"Can you come back in for a minute?" He

matched the words with a big gesture, beckoning Zeke closer.

"I don't want you worrying about me, Zeke. I'm not going to be some old man getting underfoot."

"Dad, please." Zeke sighed. "You're not—"

"Let me finish," his dad said, jabbing his finger in the air at him for emphasis. "You heard the doctor. I might not get worse, but these blips in my brain aren't going to get better. No, sir."

Zeke might have argued, but he had to let his dad get this off his chest.

"I'm ready to go to one of those places. You know, where they help you if you need it, but leave you alone if you don't."

He couldn't help but smile. "Assisted living, Dad, that's what they call it. But it's not on the table for you. Not now." He took a couple of steps closer. "I heard the doctor, but I also heard you point out you have a business to run. And yes, you do worrisome things now and then. I won't deny it. But we work around your problem. Most of the time we're fine—*you're* fine."

Art took off his glasses and pointed them up at Zeke. "You already check the work I do. So now, I'm thinking I'll let you handle most of our paperwork and ordering stock from now on. I'm still good with the customers. They know me. But I get more tired than I used to."

A big concession, Zeke thought. Huge. He crouched down in front of the chair. "Then you'll rest more. We can make that happen. Together, like we always do."

Art responded with a quick shrug. "Okay."

"But, Dad, I'm not saying that things won't change. I don't know what's going to happen, but I really like Andi." He didn't wait for a response, but left out the back door, trying to sort out his mixed feelings. He and Dad were both right. He wasn't ready for assisted living, but he wouldn't get better, either. But Zeke would not stand by and watch his dad feel like he was in the way. Never.

He walked down the street carrying the vase of flowers, still a little torn between what always felt like a risk leaving his dad home alone and his eagerness to see Andi. There was some comfort in knowing Andi would get it. That was the thing about her. She understood things. Or, at least she seemed to understand him.

A PLEASANT LITTLE zing traveled through Andi's body when she and Zeke walked into the dim light of the yacht club. The music hadn't started yet, but almost all tables on the wide verandah outside and the main room inside were filled with couples or groups of four or six. Most of the light came from the candles on each table.

"I see a table outside not far from where the band is setting up," Zeke said. "Is that okay?"

A table for two, Andi thought. "Sure, looks good." She'd brought a long scarf to wrap around her bare shoulders if the night turned cool, so sitting outside was fine with her.

Zeke the led the way through a maze of tables. Andi waved at a couple of women she recognized as instructors from Grassy Shore, and another woman at the same table had an herb booth at the weekly farmer's market downtown.

"I know quite a few people here. And I've only been in town a couple of months."

"Doesn't surprise me," Zeke said. "Not a bit. You're not exactly shy."

"No, not shy, but I've been an introvert for

years. The office and Brooke." She glanced at the lake, calm under the moonlit night sky. "I won't let that happen again."

"Are you job hunting now?"

"A little, but I'll really get down to it after Labor Day." She gave his hand a light pat. "My work with you will be done soon. Then I'll get serious." She could have mentioned the corporate recruiter, but held that back, mostly because she didn't care to dwell on it.

"I'm sure you'll find something that's right for you."

"Thanks for the vote of confidence."

"I only speak—"

"Hey, you two," Melody said cheerily, approaching the table with an order pad in hand.

"Melody? I didn't expect to see you here," Zeke said, looking surprised.

"This is only my second night," Melody said. "They need to hire waitstaff on music nights. So, here I am. What can I get you?"

Andi ordered a glass of the Silver Moon merlot, but Zeke stuck with ale from a local microbrewery.

"Be right back," Melody said.

"Melody is like me," Andi said. "Two

Moon Bay has worked its magic on her and she'll find ways to stay here and make it her home. She loves it as much as I do."

Andi occasionally played with the fantasy of putting together a living by contracting out her skills. "You were a contractor with your restoration work, weren't you? Architects hired you a project at a time. Right?"

Zeke nodded. "And private individuals, too."

Andi's mind lit up with more questions, but Melody came back with their drinks and then the musicians came out and got ready to start. Andi picked up the blurb about the trio. "Can you believe their name? Three Student Loaners."

"I saw that in the paper the other day. It's one of the reasons I thought it might be fun to come over for it. Clever name for a young group."

"And probably picked out of frustration with piles of student loans."

"They must be doing something right," he said drily. "From I what I hear, the yacht club members are very picky about their music. Not just anybody gets one of the prized weekend gigs."

"And now you're the owner of the most elegant yacht in town. You could join the yacht club yourself."

Andi expected him to groan and brush off that idea as not his thing, but he nodded and seemed to give it some thought.

The trio had a woman on piano, a man on drums and the other guy on sax. Zeke moved his chair to face the musicians and edged closer to her. They sat shoulder to shoulder while the trio started their set, starting with jazz so mellow Andi quickly became aware of only the music and Zeke next to her. Already in a dreamy mood when Zeke took hold of her hand, they swayed in sync to the rhythm. But the trio didn't stay mellow for long—they began intense solos that brought everyone in the packed room to their feet and applauding loudly. Then they slowed it all down again and ended with a romantic rendition of "Come Away with Me."

Once the long standing ovation was over, the room began to empty, but Andi and Zeke stayed behind until the crowd thinned. "If they keep playing like that, they won't have to worry about their student loans for long," Zeke said as they rose to move toward the door.

"Are you okay walking in those shoes?" Zeke asked once they were outside.

Andi stuck out one foot, comfy in the wedge sandals. It was the only time she'd gotten to wear them recently. "See? My life isn't all sanders and varnish. But I can walk fine in these. Where do you want to go?"

"A little detour downtown," he said. "You know about me and the Bean Grinder, but I'd like to show you something else right here in town."

"Lead the way." She was curious, but even better, their date would last a little longer.

"It's just a couple of blocks." He took her hand as they followed the path.

"I like walking around downtown," Andi said. "One reason I like living on the boat is that it's so close. I hope I can find an apartment that's within walking distance to everything."

Zeke pointed ahead. "Do you recognize it? It's the town's World War I memorial."

"Sure, I've seen it before. I specifically noticed the wood pedestal. Your work?"

Zeke nodded. "Like Settlers Hall, I managed the project. Got other people involved."

As they approached the front of the stone

pillar, Zeke talked about the architect who asked him to help preserve it and keep it in the downtown park. He pointed to the top of the monument. "Some on the town council wanted to dismantle it and move that metal piece listing the names to the lawn of city hall, and just get rid of the pedestal and base."

Andi stared at the names of dead and wounded from Two Moon Bay etched in the metal ring atop the pillar. "Was it a big fight to keep it in the park?"

"It was, and it went on for a year," Zeke said. "But the architect managed to find people to fund the work and keep it in place. I got involved, because I think this memorial belongs in the park, where people walk every day."

Zeke's soft but determined voice got to Andi deep in her heart.

Taking her hand again, Zeke sighed. "I should get back. I don't usually leave my dad this long."

"I know. I've had a really great time tonight, too, but to be honest, Art crossed my mind when we left the yacht club."

It only took a few minutes to get back to

the boat. When they passed the leg of the path that led to the Bean Grinder, Andi asked Zeke what it was like to see these town landmarks almost every day and know what he'd done to preserve them for the town.

"That's giving me too much credit," he said with a laugh.

"No, it isn't," she insisted. "You did the work."

"Truthfully, what I *do* think about is how much I miss the work itself."

She'd had a feeling that was true. "I got so busy that for years I forgot how much I enjoyed restoring our house. It took seeing *Drifting Dreamer* to remind me. And when it's done, and I've gone back to regular office work, I'll miss it terribly."

"I bet you will." He led the way across the stretch of grass at the marina.

When they reached the dock Andi felt a little shaky inside, a nervous kind of reaction to Zeke standing so close in near darkness, with only the moon providing some light. She tried to keep her voice breezy when she said, "Thanks so much, I had such a good time tonight."

Silently, he looked past her to the still lake

for a couple of seconds. “I need to ask you something.”

Maybe it was his soft tone, but her heart beat a little faster. “Sure. Go ahead.”

“Do you think what we did tonight, you know, music at the yacht club, was a date?”

Andi laughed, maybe from relief. “I’m laughing because it’s such an easy question, Zeke. When a man shows up at a woman’s door with flowers that’s a pretty good clue.”

Zeke threw back his head and laughed. “If my dad was listening to me now, he’d say, ‘real smooth, son, real smooth.’”

Andi pointed to her ear. “I can hear him saying that. But while we’re on the topic, our trip to Settlers Hall was a date, too, at least to me.”

“Really? Good to know.”

Did or didn’t he think they were dates? Andi wondered. “Maybe it goes back to high school and college, but I don’t think about dates the way my parents seemed to. I like hanging out together here on the boat, working on it together and figuring out its past.” She considered her next words, and went ahead and spoke them out loud. “All those times have been like dates.”

Even in the darkness, Andi saw Zeke's expression soften in pleasant surprise. "Well, okay, I get that. So, let's go out again. I'll call it a date and you can call it hanging out."

Laughing, Andi cocked her head. "Oh, really. Where are we going next time?"

"Since yesterday, I've been sitting on some information. Sort of a surprise. It's another clue in discovering the boat's history. It could fill in all the missing pieces."

She groaned. "You're killing me. What is it?"

"I located Quinn Peterson. Up in Ashland." He leaned forward and whispered, "Want to go see him."

She threw her arms open in excitement. "Do I want to see him?" Then she put her finger over her lips. "Oh, wait, let me think about this." She gave his upper arm a playful whack. "Of course I want to go. When?"

"One day this coming week. I've talked to him, and now he's curious about what we know about the boat, and about his family, too."

"The sooner, the better. Just keep me posted."

"I will." His expression suddenly changed, as if something distracted him. "I better go."

She touched his arm. "Go, go. I know you're concerned about Art."

He nodded, and then drew her to him. His arms tightened around her and with his mouth close to her ear, he murmured, "I had such a good time tonight." He kissed her cheek and slowly brushed his lips lightly across her skin to reach her mouth. She kissed him back, not settling for one kiss, but needing more of his warm lips and his fingers in her hair as he pulled her closer. Her eyes closed, she inhaled his scent, spicy like ginger.

Breathless, she finally stepped back. He slid his hands down her arms. He held her hand to his cheek for a few seconds. He kissed her palm before he lowered her hand and whispered, "Good night, Andi."

He broke into a light jog across the grass.

She couldn't see his face when he turned to wave, but she was sure he was smiling. Like her.

CHAPTER FIFTEEN

ZEKE GENTLY PULLED on Teddy's leash to get him to come up the stairs and into the apartment. "We can solve Andi's problem, Teddy." Why had it taken him so long to think of this obvious idea?

Zeke started by pulling the old sheets off the living room furniture, remembering the day his dad had chosen the deep gray couch and the dark red chairs. The hardwood floors were dusty, but in good shape overall. Zeke had refinished them himself during one of his college breaks.

He went into his dad's old bedroom, empty now, since his dad's bed had been moved to Zeke's house. The apartment was junked up, but supplies, old stock, empty boxes and a couple of broken appliances could be tossed out. His eye caught an old chest of drawers and a sturdy oak rocking chair. They showed up one day after his dad went to an auction with Nelson. He bid on them just because he thought Zeke would like them. Bringing furniture back from the dead didn't especially appeal to him, but maybe Andi would like a crack at them.

Wandering through the apartment and seeing that making it livable was about hauling stuff out more than bringing things in, he couldn't think of a reason not to offer it to Andi.

Most of all, he wanted to offer her everything he had in his heart. It's as if he'd known from the day he'd walked down to the boat to see her, that she'd become the one, the only woman he'd ever met who felt like the missing piece he'd hoped for. Standing in the empty apartment, he closed his eyes to savor the memory of her kisses and breathing in the sweet aroma of her hair when he held her in his arms.

Maybe his dad had sensed the shift in—in everything, and that's what prompted his fear. Fear of being abandoned. It wasn't as if Zeke himself didn't understand that feeling in pit of his stomach. Those childhood fears of being left behind had been calmed only by the steady presence of his dad. Now it was Zeke's turn to provide the security.

More was going on within him, especially his thoughts about the future. Maybe he could make it happen, maybe not, but he so easily envisioned a sign on a door—Donovan & Sterling Restoration. Andi had the skills, she shared the passion. Hadn't she said as much? The other day, she'd said this was the best summer of her life. Same for him.

He'd gone over and over the idea in his mind. Since the other night at the war memorial downtown he couldn't squash the pesky inner voices nagging him to find a way to put his skills to work again. For years, he'd made those voices go away, but no more.

The other night he'd acted like a teenager, talking about dating and making a big deal about going up to Ashland. But he wanted more than dates on weekend nights. Work was one thing, but he hoped Andi was in his life to stay.

Zeke accepted the choices he'd made. No one had forced him to keep Donovan Marine going for however long his dad chose to run it. It wasn't only about what he owed his dad. It was about loving the guy.

And now he loved Andi, too.

Zeke pulled out a chair and dropped the small spiral notebook he kept in his back pocket on the table. First things first. Andi—and Brooke—needed a place to live. He had that covered.

Instead of texting Andi, he called her cell. Frustrated to get her voice mail, he had no choice but to leave a message asking her to come to the store when she was free.

Where was she? Her schedule was usually predictable. But then, she didn't have Brooke with her now. He was impatient to tell her everything. He hadn't felt this kind of fire inside in a long time. Over these last years, the embers had all but burned out. But now he'd figured out what he wanted, and even better, he could have it.

So much of what he yearned for was pretty ordinary. Like walking over to the yacht club on a weekend night and having a beer or a glass of wine and listening to music. *Together.* He wanted to make what even his dad called first-rate lasagna for Andi, Brooke and his father. Brooke was a great kid. She had Miles, but Zeke would still like to watch her grow up. As for his dad, well, he'd said himself, not long ago, that things change.

Too restless to sit still, Zeke looked at this phone. Where was she?

ANDI STOOD AND reached across the desk to shake Brianna's hand. "Thanks so much. I appreciate the opportunity to talk with you."

"You'll be hearing from me," Brianna said, taking Andi's hand. "Soon. Most likely by the end of the week."

"I'll look forward to your call whenever you can get back to me." She worked hard to inject a little enthusiasm in her voice.

"And you said you're available to start after Labor Day. Is that right?"

"Yes, that's correct."

Brianna walked her as far as the corner of the reception desk, and then Andi left through the front door. Escaped was more like it. Andi steered her car out of the parking space, and, as if guided by an invisible hand, she headed to the Bean Grinder. Minutes later, she went out to the patio with a large coffee and a bag of super chocolate supreme cookies to bring back to the boat. She was jumpy, though, from nervous energy.

Various emotions—relief, optimism—were engaged in a fierce battle with resignation.

She went to the far end of the patio to claim the only empty table. She'd scheduled two meetings that day so she'd traded her cutoffs and T-shirt for her red suit and beige heels. The first interview had been almost two hours long. Three people asked the questions, and two of them were rude, leading her to conclude that dental practice was a bad fit all around.

Andi inhaled the aroma of the coffee, still too hot to drink. She rested her chin in her palm, thinking of the shorter meeting. Brianna, the administrator of a newish outpatient surgical center, was frank in her need for an office manager *now*.

Andi knew the correct answers to every question, not because she had special knowledge, but because the problems were predictable and she had a grasp of ways to solve them. Not to boast, but she could handle that job in her sleep, she thought. They needed customized patient tracking systems and an old-fashioned flow chart to define roles within the nonclinical team. She could recite the lingo like a pro.

Now, sipping hot coffee at her favorite place in town, if the sudden thud in her gut could speak in words it would have yelled, "blah, blah, blah." Who cares about their charts and teams, anyway? Her mind could spit out answers at a good clip, but her heart dragged sluggishly.

Rubbing her temples, she reasoned with herself. Brianna was nothing if not warm and competent. The center was near the hospital, only a mile or so down the road. An apartment complex was a stone's throw away. If she'd read the signals correctly, Andi expected Brianna to make an offer. Soon. The surgical center was in trouble, and they needed someone just like her.

Andi pulled a cookie out of the bag and bit into it. The sweet, chewy texture melted in her mouth, but did little to erase her growing frustration. She took a gulp of coffee and burned her tongue. She winced in pain, but took another bite of the cookie, anyway.

"Are you okay?"

She looked up, into the face of Dawn, who stood several feet away.

Embarrassed to be caught out of sorts and doing something as mindless as burning her own tongue, she saw no point in trying to cover it up. “Oh, I’m okay. I let frustration get in the way of my good sense.” She looked past Dawn to see if Jerrod or Lark were with her. “Are you alone?”

“I am. In search of lemonade and something—anything—sweet.”

“Do you have time to join me?” Andi asked, relieved for the distraction.

“Give me one minute,” Dawn said, heading for the café’s front door.

While Dawn was gone, Andi debated confiding in her about her job dilemma. Probably not a good idea. She should tweak her mood and be *grateful* she’d landed a couple of interviews.

Dawn came back with her drink and a brownie and sat across from Andi.

“Where are your cute kids?”

“Gordon’s off on his bike with his dad and Carrie’s running errands with Melody. Probably getting ice cream, too.” She cocked her head. “So what’s up with you? You were looking a little…what’s the word? Forlorn.”

Andi scoffed. “You saw right through me. I have a bad case of end-of-summer blues. No more aching back and sore muscles and squeezing into lockers and reaching around corners. In other words, I'm sad to see the work I love so much come to an end."

"You like all that sanding and scraping *that* much?"

Andi lowered her head in a definitive nod. "I had a couple of interviews today for jobs in the so-called regular world. I was sitting here trying to muster up a little gratitude rather than feeling sorry for myself about the prospect of being in an office again."

"I see," Dawn responded. "That's how I felt years ago when Gordon was young and I needed to work part-time but got a sick feeling in my stomach when I started making the rounds."

"I couldn't have said it better myself." She looked down at herself and plucked at the lapel of her suit jacket. "That's exactly how I felt when I got dressed this morning."

"Speaking for myself, that dread gave me the nudge I needed to start my business." She nodded to Andi. "Is there a business in your future? Consulting? Training?"

"Something to think about." Then she groaned. "Who am I kidding? If I'm going to go back to management, even doing it on my own wouldn't make a difference. After the real joy I found bringing that old yacht back to life, the management work holds no interest at all. That's what sent my mood south."

"Ah, a career change is in order."

"Maybe so." Andi closed her eyes. It hit hard knowing that she might have to accept the job at least for now. On the other hand, maybe it would be only a first step. She couldn't—*wouldn't*—spend the rest of her life behind a desk. "Wait a minute. What am I saying? No maybe about it. I *do* need to change direction."

"You sure look determined," Dawn observed.

"I have to figure this out. It's likely I'll get a job offer by the end of the week."

"Really? How do you know?"

"I got that feeling from the interviewer. Besides, I saw for myself they need help." She shrugged. "Frankly, I have the skills they need." Andi took another big bite of her cookie.

"Then offer to be a consultant," Dawn said offhandedly.

The tightened fist in her gut opened a little

and eased the tension in her body as ideas started spinning.

"You could work up a contract," Dawn said. "Tell them you'll train their staff and define the position they want you to fill. But then you could help find the right someone to fill the position permanently."

Andi laughed out loud at the bubbling excitement filling every cell in her body. It wasn't the first time she'd mulled over the idea. Even Miles had mentioned it years ago. But it was different this time.

Like a sponge, Andi soaked up Dawn's ideas about selling her services to Brianna. By the time Andi and Dawn walked back to the parking lot she was filled with hope. The resignation weighing her down had vanished.

"You've helped me so much, Dawn. I don't feel so stuck anymore, as if I have only one path forward," Andi said. "I never saw it coming, but one summer on *Drifting Dreamer* changed everything." The memory of Zeke's kisses floated into her mind like an image from a lovely dream.

Dawn grinned and glanced down at her round belly. "I've cut back my schedule this summer. I just wanted to enjoy this pregnancy, and spend time with Carrie. But I sometimes forget I have a mind for business." She tapped her temple. "It's served me well. I should be thanking you for the chance to brainstorm."

"I'll let you know how it turns out," Andi said.

"You be sure to do that." Dawn waved as she walked away.

Andi got into her car and pulled out her phone to check for messages. Zeke called? Odd, he usually texted. She'd turned off her phone for her interview and missed his call. Listening to his message, he didn't give a reason he wanted her to stop by. Maybe he needed help. She smiled to herself. Maybe he didn't need a reason. Filled with the rush that came from her eagerness to see Zeke, she drove straight to the store.

When she walked through the front door, Art was behind the counter. "Look at you, all gussied up."

Andi let out a hoot. "Oh, Art. Gussied up? I haven't heard that old expression in years!"

"I know, it's older than me, I think." Grinning, he said, "Anyway, you look real nice. And even taller, too, in those shoes."

"Only a few inches taller, Art," she teased, but offered no explanation why she was in a suit and heels. "Uh, Zeke called earlier, and I missed it. Is he around?"

"I'm here," Zeke called from the back. "I was upstairs. There's something there I'd like to show you. Do you have time to come up?"

She followed Zeke to the apartment, familiar from her trips to soak in the tub and get the kinks out of her back after a long day of boat work.

"Were you on a job interview?" Zeke asked.

"Two, actually. One is a no-go for sure." She was about to say the other interview could lead to a job offer, but she changed her mind. After talking to Dawn, she would no longer consider a regular job her only option. "The other, I said I wasn't available until after Labor Day. I refuse to leave *Drifting Dreamer* with too many loose ends. Well, more to the point, I don't want to."

Stepping deeper inside the apartment, she noticed something had changed. "Looks like you cleaned up in here." The living room furniture was uncovered, for one thing, and boxes were stacked in neat piles near the door ready to be hauled away.

"I'll get right to the point," Zeke said, sweeping his arm to encompass the large open space. "This is a two-bedroom apartment, mostly furnished. I think it would work for you and Brooke."

Andi cupped her cheeks in happy surprise. Relief rippled through her. A problem solved. And she'd never thought of this place as a possibility. "Are you sure? I mean, I'd love it. But you use it, don't you?"

Zeke waved her off with a quick swat of the air. "Oh, sort of. But mostly just to stash things we should throw out or give away down the road, but those roads never appeared. I can move stuff out of here fast, so you can move in when we haul *Drifting Dreamer* out of the water for the winter."

Andi hurried to peek into the room Zeke said was his old bedroom. "Perfect for Brooke," she said. "I'll add a few of her things. She'll love it, Zeke."

The room where Zeke had been a little boy, the small kitchen table where he and Art had eaten their meals. Her heart ached knowing Zeke invited her into this slice of his past. She also liked the idea of still living so close to him. She'd been sad about the summer winding down, but her life had changed and now the fall stretched out just as sweet as the summer a couple of months ago.

She looked out of the big windows in the living room and flopped down into a comfy red chair. She kicked off her heels and put her feet up on the footstool. Leaning back, she sighed, "Ah, nice."

"Have at it," Zeke said. "Make yourself at home."

"I will. I accept your offer. But since there's no restoration or remodeling or even redecorating involved here, what's the rent?" She stood and thrust her feet back into her shoes.

"We can talk about that later. On our trip to Ashland."

"Day after tomorrow," Andi said, about to make a joke about their date, their third. She closed the space between them and wrapped her arms around him in a big hug. "Thanks for this. For me, but for Brooke, too."

Zeke stepped closer. "When I tell my dad, he'll think it's an okay idea. But he doesn't even realize himself that it's been good for him to have you two around."

That was a little too vague for Andi. "So, he might balk? That's what you're really saying, isn't it?"

Zeke stepped back and held both of Andi's hands in his. "It could trigger…something. He might suddenly think he should move back here."

Andi studied Zeke's face, nearly able to see him struggle with his thoughts. "In other words, if he's not doing well that day you think he might feel displaced."

Zeke nodded and glanced around the room. "He'll never live here again. But he forgets that sometimes."

They stood in silence a few seconds, but then Andi squeezed his hands before telling him she'd see him later. She was heading to the boat to change out of her unusually dressy clothes. Thinking about the furniture she'd need to take out of storage, Andi waved to Art on her way out. Once she was out the door and on the grass, she took off her shoes again to feel the cool grass under her feet on the way to *Drifting Dreamer*. She turned around and looked at the Donovan Marine

Supply sign on the water side of the building. Big and bold. And a home for Brooke, at least, for a while.

She chuckled to herself. Her day was improving. She had a new home, a business idea incubating in her brain and she was dating a really great guy.

Dating. She was beginning to like the sound of that. Maybe it was the safety of it. Dating a man didn't mean opening the door to making another marriage mistake.

CHAPTER SIXTEEN

"I WISH MY father was here to answer some of your questions," Quinn Peterson said as he opened a battered leather photo album. "I keep saying I'm going to make a digital file of these old pictures, but I never get around to it."

Zeke glanced at Andi, who was eyeing the album. She'd brought a flash drive of photos taken over these last weeks of the boat renovation: before, during, after. But Quinn hadn't shown any particular interest in them. Surprising. But this visit was odd in ways they hadn't anticipated.

Quinn, a lumbering guy in his midforties, with scraggly gray hair, appeared to live alone in a rambling beach house with a wraparound porch and huge windows. Zeke could see it in a movie set—the lived-in beach house, full of shabby chic and just plain shabby furnishings. Outside, the shingles had been weathered—battered—by ice and snow and winds blowing in hard off Lake Superior. Zeke would have liked to see more of it, but Quinn didn't offer to show them around.

The location on the shore alone would command an eye-popping price tag, but it needed sprucing up or would soon go the way of *Drifting Dreamer.* They'd been invited for lunch, and Quinn ordered pizza a few minutes after they'd arrived. Zeke offered to pay for it, and Quinn didn't protest. And he'd made it clear he wasn't interested in talking about the yacht until after they'd had their fill of sausage-and-pepperoni pizza at a table on the porch.

"You know, you might have the only surviving early photos of *Drifting Dreamer,*" Andi said as they helped Quinn deal with the empty pizza boxes and used paper plates. "Your grandfather might have owned her for longer than anyone else, as far as we could tell."

Quinn stared out to the lake, a quizzical expression once again taking over his face. From the moment they arrived, Quinn had admitted being puzzled by his grandfather's history with the yacht. "No one in the family could figure out why he didn't sell the boat after Charles and Mary died."

"We understood Mary served as a nurse in the war and died on a troop ship in the Pacific. But it wasn't clear how Charles died," Zeke said.

"Everyone used words like 'he died from the war,' or 'or he wasn't ever right after the war.' All I know is what my dad told me," Quinn said. "Charles was badly burned in France and was supposedly recuperating at home with his parents, but then he died suddenly not long after the war ended. Complications from his injuries, I guess."

"Did your dad talk about *Drifting Dreamer*?" Andi asked. "I mean, his dad inherited it from Charles, and from what we can tell he likely spent part of a summer on it with Charles and Mary. The summer of '41. From what you've said, your grandfather Quinn hung on to it for a long time."

"I guess, but he didn't mention much about the boat, or about Charles." Quinn shrugged, his expression indifferent. "Sure, at one time, the family had a lot of money. Back then, my grandfather could afford to put her in the water every spring and keep her at the dock in a boatyard in Duluth. He paid other people to keep her up. He *hired* the crew to take the family out, too. And then, when he was pretty old he lost a ton in the stock market, and he had to sell the boat, along with his home. My dad found a buyer—they let that boat go for cheap, too, just to make a few dollars. But we knew the family who bought her. They didn't get much use out of her, either."

Quinn contacted the old family friends in Duluth who'd purchased the yacht and they filled in the rest of its history, right up until the sale to the man who brought *Drifting Dreamer* to Wisconsin.

"Odd how little the boat has been used," Andi said sadly. "Your family, the next owners and the couple in Wisconsin all had dreams, but they were never realized. And the man, Smyth, who left it to Zeke's dad never put the boat in the water."

Quinn was clearly puzzled again. But he shrugged and said, "I guess. I never really gave it much thought. All I know is that my grandfather was no fan of his brother,

Charles. Bad blood of some kind. Maybe over money. I wouldn't be surprised."

Quinn patted the manila folder. "I can't say these are all the missing pages of the log you were curious about. But it's all that's left. My dad kept these, but some are still missing. He found the pages of the log in one of the staterooms, when he was going through the boat before he sold it."

"Are you saying they were deliberately hidden?" Zeke asked.

"Yep. We're thinking Granddad might have torn apart the logs." Quinn nodded. "Once he lost his money, he was kind of erratic. My dad said he was always kind of troublesome. I couldn't make out too much of it. Water splotches wiped out big sections." He laughed. "Maybe they wiped out a few secrets. I always wondered what was up with Quinn and Charles."

"Those are the originals?" Andi asked, pointing to the file.

"Sure. You've got the boat. You might as well have the rest of it. No one in my family wants these pages." He scoffed. "We don't have much family, anyway. Me, my older sister in Florida and a cousin on my mom's side. I don't have kids."

"The copies of what we have are on the flash drive with the pictures."

Zeke gave Andi a pointed look. They'd brought the log pages and the list of possible names for the boat. He'd been prepared to hand them over, thinking he was obliged to give the documents to the family and only make copies for himself. But he'd changed his mind now. He and Andi would take the originals and preserve them.

Quinn handed the file to Zeke. Andi took the flash drive from her tote and put it on the table.

"What did your grandfather do?" Andi asked. "We saw that Charles was with the family law firm."

"Investments," Quinn said with a snicker. "He invested money—money he inherited from Charles—in all sorts of stuff. Kind of like a venture capitalist. Lived pretty well, too. Until he didn't."

Andi smiled. "I see. I was just curious."

"My dad went to law school and worked at the firm. They dissolved it and Dad got a job over here in Ashland. Then he and my mom bought this house." Quinn pushed his chair back and said, "Well, thanks for supplying our lunch. I'm glad I could help you fill in a little background about the boat."

That was it? The visit was over? Zeke got to his feet, and so did Andi.

"Do you mind if I take a few pictures before we leave?" Andi asked, tentatively, gesturing at the curving sand beach.

"Sure, go ahead."

Andi pulled out her phone and went down the porch stairs to the wide stretch of sandy beach between two rocky points. She turned one way and then the other, getting shots from every angle.

"She's a really good photographer," Zeke said, making conversation. "Maybe someone will want those photos she took of the restoration work."

"I have a niece in Florida. I'll send them to her. Let her decide."

"Uh, do you live here full-time?" Zeke asked.

"Uh-huh. My dad left the place to me. I tend bar in town. Helps me pay the taxes."

"I see. Well, it's an amazing house."

Watching Andi take her pictures, he thought

of *Drifting Dreamer*, ready now for its first trip on the water. Hearing the sketchy stories, seeing Quinn's indifference, that old yacht had never felt more like his—and Andi's.

THEY WERE SILENT in the car as Zeke drove the quarter mile or so down the road back to the highway. Then Andi snickered. "That wasn't exactly the visit I expected."

"No? Can't imagine why." Zeke sputtered a laugh, again trying to understand why Quinn bothered to invite them in the first place.

"If that guy, Terrance Smyth, was alive today, I'd give him a big hug," Andi said. "Aren't you glad he decided to settle that debt with your dad?"

"You bet I am. It was the lack of Quinn's interest that floored me." He gestured to the folder. "Go ahead and open it up. Maybe we'll discover a family secret."

Andi wanted to wait until they could look at the papers together, and as they drove out of town, she spotted a park and public launch. A low fishing pier extended out into the water. She pointed to it, suggesting they pull in and sit at the end of the dock. "Looks fairly empty and quiet."

After Zeke parked, they walked the length of the wooden pier and took off their shoes so they could sit with their feet dangling in the water.

"By the way, I caught that look you gave me when I was just about ready to hand over the originals like we planned."

"I got kind of stubborn. Quinn couldn't care less about them, so why should we let them go? Art Donovan is the official owner of the boat now. Far as we know, no one cares about *Drifting Dreamer* the way we do."

Andi opened the envelope and pulled out a handful of loose pages. She scanned them quickly. "These look like the log, all right. Most are in what we think is Mary's handwriting." She handed Zeke a couple of sheets from the top.

"Not much is legible, but Quinn's name appears." He pointed to a line. "Here. Part of the name is smeared, but this looks like it says, 'Quinn on board for two days so far.' Then it's blurry, but it picks up here—'Charles unhappy with…' I can't make that out."

"I can see the *ing* there." Andi's index finger landed on the small spot where the letters weren't washed out. "I'll bet you anything that says something about Charles being unhappy with Quinn's complaining." She ran her finger down what were probably three or four lines of writing. "Here she says, 'Q doesn't like stew or fish.'" It was one line, but it was clear.

For the next few minutes, they looked at the dates and put the pages in order. The entries covered six days in August, and Q, or Quinn, was mentioned in every one of them. Andi waved one of the pages in frustration. "This is so annoying. Here on this page, Mary says something about leaving the boat for the afternoon, and then the ink ran and the next line I can read says, 'Q and C fighting over a loan.' I think that word is *loan*."

"Quinn was probably right," Zeke said. "The bad blood he mentioned was probably about money."

"Maybe the loan started it all," Andi said, sifting through the papers. "There's a piece of old-fashioned stationary in here. It's got a floral border on it." She pulled the page and although the writing was faint, she recognized it. "Oh, Zeke, this is Mary's writing. It's a letter to her mother." She scanned down the page. "Wow, listen to this.

"October 9, 1941
Dear Mama,
I hope this letter reaches you before the first snow! We will be moving off *Drifting Dreamer* and heading home in about two weeks. I do have mixed feelings. I miss all of you at home, but it was a wondrous summer. I've finally mastered our little kerosene stove, so now I cook up our bacon and eggs without burning everything to a crisp.

My only regret is that we had Quinn aboard for ten days. But I can't say you didn't warn me about marrying a family, not just a man. I know it's selfish of me, but his visit was the only cloud over our trip—well, we had plenty of real clouds, but that was okay. We were always dry inside. Thelma hoped Quinn's time with Charles on the boat would force the brothers to settle their quarrels, but that didn't happen. Quinn even ended up borrowing more money for a business scheme. I took your advice and stayed out of it. And breathed easier when Charles put Quinn on the bus headed for home.

I wrote back to accept the job offer I mentioned in an earlier letter, so when we return I'll be a daytime private nurse for an older woman who needs full-time care. My first job as a real nurse. I'm very excited, and Charles is happy for me. I can't say if Charles really wants to return to his father's firm, but he doesn't complain, so I leave it at that.

No matter what happens in the future, I want to come back to the lake every summer and bring along our children, when we have them. I want our children to know the beauty of hidden coves and morning fog over the lake, and the clear water washing over the stony beaches. It's as much their heritage as the farms and the peaceful Ash River at home.

As for Charles, I can only hope we can make our honeymoon last and last, even when we're home and we're busy with all the things that make day-to-day

life work. I love him more and more each day. I'll never forget this summer. See you soon, and lots of love to Dad,
Mary"

He didn't speak, and neither did Andi. Like him, she stared at the letter she held in her hand. Finally, she looked at him with tears in her eyes and pressed the letter to her chest. He put his arm around her and cradled her head against his shoulder. "So now we know for sure they had that one special summer," he whispered.

"It just touches me so, Zeke. I wonder how many more letters Mary wrote in the next year," Andi said. "I'll always wonder."

"I'm glad we have these papers, the two letters. We care about the boat and about Charles and Mary. From what I can see, no one else does. But we've solved the mystery, or so I've been calling it."

Andi lifted her head and nodded. "Somehow, I get the feeling Quinn number three is a lot like the Quinn written about in the pages."

"I bet he's hiding something. There has to be some reason he's holed up there in that big house all by himself. Who knows what secrets he's keeping?"

Hiding? Secrets? What was she thinking? Andi had been telling herself she'd confide in Zeke and come clean about Roger when the time was right. As if a right time would appear by magic. Besides, she'd been way too preoccupied with falling in love. Roger never crossed her mind. Feeling queasy, she sighed and said, "Oh, Zeke."

"What? Are you okay, Andi, you look pale."

She pressed her fingers against her temples, as if warding off a headache. "I've wanted to tell you something. But I've been afraid."

"Afraid? Of me?"

"No, no. It's just… I need to tell you about Roger." Lifting her feet out of the water, she tucked her legs under her. Then with her arms crossed over her chest and her shoulders drooping forward, she told him the truth about what she considered the darkest time of her life, start to finish. The worst mistake, the worst consequence. Namely, the shame she'd never put all the way in the past. She kept glancing at it through the rearview mirror and there it was, following her. It gained on her, but could never outpace her.

"So, the truth is, even before my thirtieth birthday, I signed my second set of divorce papers. Roger was the closest thing to a con man I'd ever met," Andi said, feeling hot tears pool in her eyes. "So different from you. And from Miles, for that matter."

When Zeke put his arm around her, she let her head drop to his shoulder. "I should have told you this a while ago."

"I'm glad you finally told me."

"So what now, Zeke?" Andi asked.

Zeke checked his watch. "We should probably get on the road. We've got a good five-hour drive ahead."

Huh? What was he talking about? How did he feel? "No, Zeke. I'm serious. You wondered what Quinn was hiding. But what about me? And what about us? We've been dancing around each other all summer. And now we're finally using the D word—*dating*."

Zeke took his arm from her shoulder and picked up her hand and kissed it. "Us? Like Roger has anything to do with us?"

"Well, doesn't it?"

"I can't believe you were afraid I'd hold

some mistake you made years ago against you," Zeke said, reproach in his voice. "Like we have a scorecard."

"But *I* hold it against me. It's the one thing I've done that resists healing, like a stubborn infection."

"Slow poison is more like it." Zeke shook his head, sadly. "Oh, Andi. I have a past. My mother ran off with another man. I was *nine*. From that first day on our own, Dad poured everything he had into me to try to give me a normal life. He must have been heartbroken. But he did the best he could for me all the same."

"And you do your best for him, Zeke."

"I promised myself that. But he's getting old before he should and these lapses..." He abruptly stopped talking. "Why am I going on about me? Or my dad. This is about *you*."

"No, not really," she said wistfully. "It's about me learning more about you. Your words about your dad really are like notes of music."

He kissed her hand again, and then took her in his arms and kissed her, a long, sweet kiss filled with promise. He tightened his arms around her and when he eased back he brushed loose strands of her hair off her face. "I don't care about Roger, and I don't want you to care about him, either."

She closed her eyes, relaxing against him, aware only of the sound of his breathing, the feel of his warm arm around her.

"Know what?" he said, lifting his head.

"What?"

"My feet are getting numb in this cold Lake Superior water."

After planting a kiss on his cheek, she broke their embrace and stood. "And like you said, we have a drive ahead."

"We have lots of things ahead."

Holding hands, they walked to the car. Suddenly, it struck Andi that Roger had been like the all-powerful man behind the curtain. She'd given him all the power when he was nothing more than a sham.

CHAPTER SEVENTEEN

"I NEVER THOUGHT I'd be put-putting around the lake on a fifty-foot motor yacht," Zeke said, turning the wheel to change course. They'd left the dock around ten o'clock after making sure they'd secured every loose tool and bolt on the boat.

"No? You saw yourself as more of a sailboat type of guy?"

"Absolutely." He lifted his chin and squared his shoulders in a show of mock captain behavior. "But now that I'm steering this ship, I've changed my mind. Motoring demands a lot more attention."

"I never imagined myself out here on a boat of any kind other than a ferry to go to Washington Island, or maybe out for a day on *Lucy Bee*."

With so much hope and so many ideas turning over in his mind, Zeke had slept very little. But when the morning came, he wasn't tired and left as soon as Melody arrived to spend the day at the store helping his dad.

Zeke pointed to a cluster of sailboats far off their port side. “In a few days it will be Labor Day weekend, and that means those boats will soon line up to be pulled out of the water and stored for the winter.”

“And our time is just starting, such as it is. At least we saw a red sky last night,” Andi said, a dreamy look passing over her face. “And we got the ‘sailor’s delight’ weather that old saying promises.”

“Fair skies, a light breeze, sun sparkling on the water.” Zeke glanced at Andi. She looked as if she didn’t have a worry in the world. He was a content guy himself and sighed to prove it. Louder than intended.

“You’re a happy man, huh?” she teased. “And why not? You’ve got the best-looking boat on the water today.”

“It led to much more than I’d ever imagined.” Zeke cast an intimate smile Andi’s way. Earlier, Zeke noted even Nelson sensed something special about this first cruise. Telling Zeke he didn’t want to miss seeing *Drifting Dreamer* pull away from the dock in such pristine condition, he’d come by and taken photos and shot video. Not at all camera-shy, Andi smiled and waved at Nelson as he recorded her energetically flinging the lines to the dock as they motored away.

Zeke steered clear of the rocky shoals to their starboard side and soon picked up speed heading to the open waters. Now they were several miles offshore and Two Moon Bay looked like clumps of green broken up with horizontal white lines, the beaches, and dots, the cottages and other buildings ashore.

Zeke watched Andi, who stared at the shore behind them. “My town now,” she said. “I like seeing it from this distance and yet know Brooke and I are a part of Two Moon Bay.”

“Me, too.” Zeke’s his heart raced just from the pleasure surging through him when he looked into her face. She’d been radiant when he’d arrived that morning and was still beaming.

They covered a few more miles before Andi broke the silence. “I don’t want to bring down the mood, but I can’t help but think about Charles and Mary. At least they had that one summer cruise to hang on to when the war separated them.”

Zeke reached out and cupped Andi's cheek. "That's always going to stick with us. We don't have much detail to fill in, but I'm going to think of it as their summer of drifting and dreaming."

"Okay, let's think of them fulfilling a shared dream, like the letter implied."

"That crossed my mind last night." And so did the image of the two of them having a summer like that. One day. He knew it was way too soon to even mull over a dream like that, let alone make concrete plans for it. But his imagination didn't play out on a small screen, like next year or the year after. His feelings for Andi propelled the two of them decades into the future.

She held up her hands and wiggled her fingers. "Having had my hands on the boat all summer, it brings it all home to me about Mary. Sometimes musing about worrisome clouds, sometimes noting that her brother-in-law doesn't like stew. Those pages make her seem like she's an old friend telling me her news."

Her wistful tone made his heart ache with love. She put into words how he'd been feeling about Charles and Mary, and now the two of them. And the boat herself. "The magic of boats. Especially wooden ones." He patted the mahogany console. "*Drifting Dreamer* is alive and ready for new adventures."

Zeke guided the boat on a course to the north and closer to a protected cove. "Maybe we'll see some eagles while we're having lunch."

"Just the change of scene will be fun." She pointed to cottages hidden behind dense woods bordering on a county park. "They're like secret retreats back there."

"Well-kept secrets, too, with mostly winding dirt roads leading to them."

They soon passed the Cana Island lighthouse, majestically surrounded by trees on its own small island. People were walking around the grounds and stood on the lookout balcony near the top.

They didn't speak until they rounded a wooded point, where small pines seemed to grow right out of the rocks. Zeke checked the chart on-screen against the depth sounder. "The data matches. How about that? We're anchoring in fourteen feet." Using the engine, Zeke turned the bow into the light breeze and let the lighter of the two anchors drop, feeding out six feet of chain followed by line. "We're secure long enough for lunch on this nearly windless day."

Side by side, they brought out the containers of local cheese and roast beef from the deli. Zeke cut thick slices of rye from the bakery and piled tomatoes and greens on top of slices of cheese and meat. Andi spooned out potato salad and they sat on the deck and washed down the food with sparkling water and ice.

"Talk about the good life," Andi said. But suddenly, her pleasant expression changed and her eyes were troubled.

"What's wrong?" he asked.

She surprised him with a cynical smirk. He didn't know what to say to that.

"You'll think I'm ungrateful for my reaction to what should be good news…*is* good news. I tried to forget about it just for today. But being out here with you, away from everything else made it hit home."

Resting her elbows on the table, she steepled her fingers and rested her hands under her chin. "I got a job offer yesterday. Last night, I should say. It was from the surgical center near the hospital."

"That was fast. You just interviewed the other day." Frustration burned in the center of his chest. He was furious. With himself. He'd waited too long to bring up his idea.

"Uh-huh."

He spoke slowly. "And from the look on your face, you're not happy about the offer?"

"Pretty confusing, isn't it?"

Curious, he responded, "Yeah, I admit it is."

She explained how she was certain she had exactly the skills they needed. "I expected the offer, and the salary was in the ballpark I'd assumed."

"That's good, isn't it?"

"Oh, sure. I'll probably take the job," she said, drawing out the words and pretending to yawn.

"What if you were offered a better option?" Zeke blurted.

She leaned toward him, at least appearing receptive. But then she told him about running into Dawn at the Bean Grinder right after the interview. "She suggested offering to be a consultant to rework their systems and train staff."

Shaking his head, Zeke laughed. "That's Dawn for you. But it's actually a great idea."

"I'm mulling it over. I'd not thought of it before, but I could work up a proposal."

"What did you tell the administrator?"

"I was professional about the offer. I thanked her, but told her I needed to think about it over the weekend."

"So you're considering Dawn's suggestion?"

She bobbed her head from side to side. "It's intriguing. I didn't realize how much I want a change until the interview went so well. I was actually dreading the offer more than I admitted, even to myself."

She'd handed him his chance. He folded his arms across his chest in a show of determination. "Well, I think that's great. Because I've been thinking about something, too. And it could be part of your solution."

Opening her eyes wide, she leaned in. "I'm listening."

"It all started here." He patted the table. "With *Drifting Dreamer* herself."

She sat up a little straighter.

"Every day I've seen how you feel about this work." He played back what he'd just said. Way too weak. "What I mean is we share a real passion for restoration. Bringing back the beauty of something. Buildings like your house, and Settlers Hall. And now a classic boat from a long-gone era."

He also leaned forward and took Andi's hand. "Here's my idea. I'd intended to keep my restoration business going while I helped my dad in the store, too. But gradually, I cut back during the summer because we got so busy. I tried to keep it going in the winter, but it didn't happen. The store had grown so much Dad needed me more. I accepted fewer and fewer jobs." Zeke tried not to hang on to regrets over those past decisions. "I couldn't do both, though."

Zeke lifted Andi's hand, gave it a quick kiss and watched her smile. "But, it's time to revive it, and with you working with me, I think *we* can make it happen."

"Restoration." Andi said the word slowly. "Really? Fill in the details. And why now?"

"The easy answer is that people keep calling. Architects and contractors. Even the owner of a gone-to-seed Victorian mansion in Green Bay. In the past few years I've turned down projects that would be perfect for you. I've said no to other jobs we could work on together."

"What about the store?"

"I've thought about that. We can figure it out, get people in to help. I'm not worried about it. And you could even do the consulting work if you wanted to."

Andi put her hand over her chest. "Wow, Zeke, this is so exciting, I can barely breathe."

"It's a huge change—for both of us. But, Andi, it's about us. What's happening between us. Growing closer every day."

She cupped her hands over her mouth as if surprised. "This could work. All of it. What an adventure!"

He leaned across the table, took her face in his hands, kissed her softly and said, "Falling in love with you has been the best adventure of my life."

She kissed him back, then whispered, "And completely unexpected, at least for me. I never imagined anything like this would happen. But then I met you."

He kissed her again, murmuring, "It's new to me, too. And I like it."

"But what about Art?" Andi asked. "How is he going to react to what will seem like such a sudden change? What will he think of me sharing your life now?"

*Andi sharing in his life...*he said the words to himself, feeling the electric charge in the air. And only a couple of months ago he wasn't sure he believed in such a thing.

Love in the air or not, Andi's questions deserved answers. Zeke lowered his hands and folded his arms again. "Honestly, I'm not sure. Some of the signals he's sent aren't so good." Zeke thought back to his dad's talk about moving to a retirement center, but that wasn't going to happen. "He's slowing down, not always putting in a full day."

"But you can't leave him all alone in—"

"Of course I wouldn't do that," he interrupted.

He saw the force behind his words when Andi jerked her head back.

Lowering his voice, he said, "I'll need help. But nothing has to be handled or decided today. My dad may get a little testy now and then about my being away more, but he'll get over it." Zeke glanced down at his plate. "We've barely touched lunch."

"And I'm really hungry." She picked up the sandwich and bit into it, her face thoughtful as she chewed. "I've already made one decision. I'm going to talk to Brianna about consulting, but no matter what she says, I'm *not* accepting the job."

A warm wave of satisfaction spread through him. "So, we're in this together."

She looked into his eyes and grinned. "You bet I am. I'm all in, Zeke."

He reached across the table and gently put his hand on the back of her head and brought his lips to hers. She returned the kiss and touched his face with soft fingertips.

"Nice way to seal a deal," she said, lowering her eyes flirtatiously.

"I thought so," Zeke said, lifting his glass of sparkling water. "Let's have a toast. We just changed our lives."

And it was only a start.

ANDI HAD BEEN too caught up in the emotion of the magnitude of what she'd just done to get practical. Even while they finished lunch and got under way again, they were both in a dizzying place.

"I'm feeling kind of mellow," Zeke said, "like the mood of the slow jazz that night at the yacht club."

"Right. We have a lot of plates spinning, but they're good plates." She giggled. "I wonder what Brianna will think of my response to her job offer."

He reached out and squeezed her hand. "Even if she doesn't go for it, it's a good idea. And now you have lots of irons in the fire. Once we firm up some plans, I'll fire up my old network and spread the word. I'm back in business." He grinned. "With a bonus. You."

They covered the miles back to Two Moon Bay as if there was no need to rush. Just like their plans.

His hands still holding the wheel, Zeke got out of the chair and stepped aside. "Here, you take over."

"But I've never driven a boat," she protested.

"It's okay. I'll show you how."

She moved into the captain's chair and Zeke stood behind her, his hands over hers to help her get a feel for the wheel. The closeness of him left her energized, every nerve ending on alert. No words were needed as the minutes ticked by. Only the low hum of the engine broke the silence as *Drifting Dreamer* moved through the water.

She'd let down the barriers, she mused, and let in the heady, nearly overwhelming feeling of falling in love. Fear tried to creep in, but she wouldn't let it ruin her joy. A new feeling, she thought. She liked it. So this was what falling in love, grown-up style, was all about.

They stayed quiet all the way back until they turned into the bay and Zeke motored past the park and the marina and stopped at his dock. Together, they secured the lines.

She went below to pour them each a glass of wine. "Everything okay?" she said, coming back to the deck and seeing his phone out on the table when she sat next to him.

"Looks like it." He gave her a rundown on the day in the store. "Dad texted about walking the dog. Fascinating."

"Exactly what you wanted to hear, I imagine. I did a quick check of my phone. All's fine with Brooke up in Minnesota, too."

Zeke took hold of one of her hands. "Look, Andi, I've got so much to say to you. It's so simple to me now. I love you, you love me. I could go on and on about how I've come to feel about you over the summer."

"Oh, Zeke, I can say 'I love you' with a sure heart now, no doubts," Andi whispered.

"Well, then, what are we waiting for?" he asked.

"What do you mean?" Andi asked, puzzled. "Won't we start working together once we have a plan?"

He waved her off with his free hand. "That's just details. We can handle that. No, I'm talking about us. Why don't we really seal the deal? Marry me, Andi. Will you?"

She yanked her hand out of his and stood. She took a few steps back and stared into his expectant face. *"No!"*

CHAPTER EIGHTEEN

To avoid *Drifting Dreamer*, Zeke took Teddy inside the store. It was almost closing time and he hadn't seen Andi all day.

"Why did you take the dog out now?" Art asked from the office, where he was sitting at the desk. "I was going to take him for his usual walk around the building before we lock up."

"No reason, Dad, just felt like stretching my legs."

The chair squeaked as Art rocked back and forth. "I was just thinking that I haven't seen Andi. Is she off somewhere?"

Of course, Dad would notice Andi hadn't stopped by. And since her car was in their lot, he wouldn't likely think she was off somewhere.

"She's probably working inside today, that's all." He unleashed Teddy, who immediately padded across the floor to join Art.

"By the way, Zeke, you never told me

what happened with Andi and the apartment. What did she think of it?"

No sense letting this go on. "I'm not sure that's going to work out. Could be their plans have changed."

"You and your girl had a little spat, huh?"

That was it. He couldn't let him act like they were a couple of schoolkids. "Dad. Andi's a grown woman, a mom. She's not my girl. I'm not her guy. We're having some… disagreements, differences."

Right.

Zeke shuffled papers on the counter, and straightened out a stack of catalogs. He glanced at the clock. Fifteen minutes to go 'til closing.

"You don't really know her that well, Zeke. So, it's no surprise you wouldn't always agree on—" Art shrugged "—on whatever."

That was unbearably annoying. "What do you mean I don't know her?"

"She only showed up here couple of months ago. You haven't had time to argue before now. Seems a shame she and Brooke won't be upstairs."

Zeke got a sinking sensation in his gut. *A couple of months*. "You're right, Dad. But that doesn't change my feelings for her."

"When?"

Zeke sighed. "What do you mean?"

"When are you going to patch it up with Andi?"

"I don't know." Zeke walked to the office and leaned against the doorjamb. "Somehow, I blew it, Dad, I might as well tell you. I asked Andi to marry me."

"*Marry* you."

It was a statement, not a question, Zeke noted, as if his dad had to repeat it to believe it. "She didn't just say no, she *shouted* it."

"And you're just telling me this now?"

Zeke shrugged and stared at the floor. "I didn't want to bother you with my troubles."

Art scoffed dismissively. "Don't know why not. I bother you with mine all the time."

Since the door was open, Zeke decided to take a chance and walk through it. "I didn't know if you'd be okay with Andi being so important to me. And Brooke, too. You tried to hide it, but I saw you get irritated when I left to spend time with Andi. You knew it wasn't all about the boat."

"Change, Zeke. It's scary, especially when you're old like me." Art swiveled in the chair to face Zeke. "I want you to be happy. And

I don't want to get in the way…you know, cramp your style."

"You're not in the way," Zeke said with a groan. "You'll never be in the way. Like I said before, I'm not leaving you. But I want to marry Andi, too, and have a life with her."

"Well, you're getting in *my* way today. You're hanging around here when you should be over at Andi's to tell her that you didn't mean to scare her half to death." Art reached down and scratched Teddy's neck behind his ears. "If it's any help, son, I think she likes you. I don't know much about women, but anyone with eyes in his head can see how she looks at you. The gal likes being around you—got a good sense of humor, that one."

"She says she loves me, like I love her. So what's the problem?" He'd reached out. He sent two messages last night, two more today. All he got was silence.

"She's already been married once and it didn't work out," Art said, "so maybe she just needs a little more time to be sure."

"Twice. She had a second marriage—it was bad and she ended it really fast."

"Good one, Zeke," Art said, his voice rising on each word. "Andi's had more than her share of troubles and you ask her to marry you a few months after she showed up at our dock. Don't forget, she's new to you—no matter how much you love her." Art paused and sighed.

Zeke shook his head and tried to find the words to explain himself. That job was becoming more challenging by the minute. His dad didn't have to say any more.

Zeke had thought his spur-of-the-moment proposal was romantic and fun. A major miscalculation. "Can you close up here and take Teddy home, Dad? I have to see if I can fix this."

Art shooed him away. "Get outta here, Zeke. Teddy and I will get along just fine."

As Zeke headed across the grass to the boat, his phone signaled a text. He took in a breath and glanced at the screen. *Andi.* He stopped to scan it. Let me know if u need help in the store... I made that commitment to u and Art. Finishing cabin details.

What was all that supposed to mean? That she wouldn't leave the job unfinished before packing up and going on her way? No, he wouldn't let that happen.

It had taken her all day to send the message, but once she did, she couldn't stop watching her phone. She'd sent the text for a couple of reasons. For one thing, she owed it to Zeke to assure him she wasn't running out on her end of the bargain they'd made many weeks ago. As long as she was living on *Drifting Dreamer* she'd keep her promises. Big deal. This wasn't about doing the honorable thing.

The text was meant to create a crack in the door. He could fling it open all the way. She wanted to tell him why his misunderstanding of her and what *she* needed had hurt so.

"Andi, Andi!"

She opened the cabin door. "Zeke. Come aboard, please."

"I don't want to start this conversation where we left off, Andi. I want to start it all over again."

He wasn't beating around the bush, and neither would she. "I want that, too…do you want to come down here?"

Zeke shook his head. "Come up and join me on the deck. I want to see your beautiful face full-on, in the light."

Jittery and aware of her shallow breathing,

Andi went up to the deck, where the breeze blew her hair forward.

Zeke reached out to gently brush the strands off her face. "Your silky hair, Andi, dark like midnight."

"Oh, Zeke." She started to laugh and gestured to the chair.

Ignoring the invitation to sit, he opened his arms. She had only to walk into them. So, would she? The shock and confusion over Zeke's proposal had dissipated over the last twenty-four hours, but the conviction behind her response to his proposal hadn't. But who was she kidding? She wanted him.

She took two steps forward and Zeke's arms closed around her, pulling her close.

"This is where I want to be," he murmured.

She lifted her face to welcome his urgent kisses. She could have stayed in his arms enjoying his lips, hungry for hers. His fingertips caressed her face, the feel of his strong back under her hands. But it wasn't that simple. She broke their embrace and stepped away.

"Let me explain."

He shook his head. "Even my dad was

quick to point out my mistake. But I love you, and I want us to be together."

"I want that, too. But..."

"But it's too soon to start setting a wedding date."

Andi took Zeke's hand and led him to the table. For a moment Andi stared out at the marina and then looked back toward the Donovan sign on the building. "I love it here in Two Moon Bay, Zeke. Making friends with Dawn and Joy, knowing Brooke is happy here with her riding friends and the horses. It's home. But I found my real *home* with you, Zeke..." She had more to say, but stopped to form her thoughts.

"I hear another *but* on the way," Zeke quipped.

Andi pointed to herself. "It's me, Zeke. I never anticipated this. Never. I'd cut myself off from the possibility of loving anyone ever again."

"Well, you saw for yourself I've been a hermit for a while now. When you more or less tossed me out of here last night," Zeke said, "I walked away thinking I'd lost you."

"Believe me, I didn't mean for that to happen." Andi shrugged. "But I felt so misunderstood. I told you I married two men I'd known for only a little longer than I've known you. In that moment it was like you didn't know me at all."

Zeke groaned. "And I took what we said about falling in love and ran with it."

"And it's true. I'm in love you. *For real.* I have the racing heart and crave the delicious kisses, but it's the deep kind of love, too. The kind I want to keep, Zeke. I want to cherish it, like I haven't done before."

"I have a new idea," Zeke whispered.

"I'm listening."

"So, marriage is off the table—for now. But if you promise not to run away, I want to ask you another question."

She rolled her eyes at his teasing. "I promise not to go any farther than the cabin."

"To say we're dating, well, that seems a little weak for what's going on here." His brown eyes were full of fun, and a smile tugged at the corners of his mouth. "I think we need something in-between. I mean, I'm not planning to ask anyone else out on dates."

Andi laughed. "Me, neither." She wasn't sure what was coming, but she had a feeling she'd like it.

Zeke picked up her hand and held it in both of his. “So, Andi Sterling, will you go steady with me?”

She titled her head, deliberately being flirtatious. “Go steady?”

“That’s what I said.”

“Now you’re talking, Zeke Donovan,” Andi said, laughing.

Zeke made a show of looking shocked. “You’re laughing at me?”

“Oh, sort of. It’s funny.”

“Maybe so, but I’m waiting for my answer.”

“Well, then, my answer is yes. I’ll go steady with you.” She lifted her head and initiated a kiss.

“I see us having a lot of fun, Andi,” Zeke murmured, his voice hoarse with emotion. “And not just us. But fun with Brooke, too.”

“And your dad.” Andi clasped her hands in front of her chest. “Whatever happens with Art, I’ll be here with you. I know it won’t be easy. That’s what I meant by loving deeper than I ever have before. I see the four of us as a family, Zeke, and all that comes with it. That’s why I need to let our feelings grow and discover more about you along the way.”

"Odd to think I met you because of my dad's old written-off debt."

"I'm not forgetting *Drifting Dreamer*. And Charles and Mary, who had only that one summer," Andi said. "But even after that one day on our mini-cruise, I started to imagine new dreams for us and for *Drifting Dreamer*."

"That's what I want, too."

Andi leaned into Zeke's chest and rested her chin on his shoulder.

"We don't need glasses of wine for this toast." He pressed his lips against hers, and then, breaking the kiss, he said, "To the future, Andi. Our future."

"Yes, Zeke, to our future."

* * * * *

Don't miss more Two Moon Bay romances from talented author Virginia McCullough:

GIRL IN THE SPOTLIGHT
SOMETHING TO TREASURE

Available now from www.Harlequin.com!

Get 4 FREE REWARDS!

We'll send you 2 FREE Books
<u>plus</u> 2 FREE Mystery Gifts.

Love Inspired® books feature contemporary inspirational romances with Christian characters facing the challenges of life and love.

YES! Please send me 2 FREE Love Inspired® Romance novels and my 2 FREE mystery gifts (gifts are worth about $10 retail). After receiving them, if I don't wish to receive any more books, I can return the shipping statement marked "cancel." If I don't cancel, I will receive 6 brand-new novels every month and be billed just $5.24 for the regular-print edition or $5.74 each for the larger-print edition in the U.S., or $5.74 each for the regular-print edition or $6.24 each for the larger-print edition in Canada. That's a savings of at least 13% off the cover price. It's quite a bargain! Shipping and handling is just 50¢ per book in the U.S. and 75¢ per book in Canada*. I understand that accepting the 2 free books and gifts places me under no obligation to buy anything. I can always return a shipment and cancel at any time. The free books and gifts are mine to keep no matter what I decide.

Choose one: ☐ **Love Inspired® Romance Regular-Print** (105/305 IDN GMY4) ☐ **Love Inspired® Romance Larger-Print** (122/322 IDN GMY4)

Name (please print)

Address Apt. #

City State/Province Zip/Postal Code

Mail to the **Reader Service:**
IN U.S.A.: P.O. Box 1341, Buffalo, NY 14240-8531
IN CANADA: P.O. Box 603, Fort Erie, Ontario L2A 5X3

Want to try two free books from another series? Call 1-800-873-8635 or visit www.ReaderService.com.

*Terms and prices subject to change without notice. Prices do not include applicable taxes. Sales tax applicable in N.Y. Canadian residents will be charged applicable taxes. Offer not valid in Quebec. This offer is limited to one order per household. Books received may not be as shown. Not valid for current subscribers to Love Inspired Romance books. All orders subject to approval. Credit or debit balances in a customer's account(s) may be offset by any other outstanding balance owed by or to the customer. Please allow 4 to 6 weeks for delivery. Offer available while quantities last.

Your Privacy—The Reader Service is committed to protecting your privacy. Our Privacy Policy is available online at www.ReaderService.com or upon request from the Reader Service. We make a portion of our mailing list available to reputable third parties that offer products we believe may interest you. If you prefer that we not exchange your name with third parties, or if you wish to clarify or modify your communication preferences, please visit us at www.ReaderService.com/consumerschoice or write to us at Reader Service Preference Service, P.O. Box 9062, Buffalo, NY 14240-9062. Include your complete name and address.

LI18

Get 4 FREE REWARDS!

We'll send you 2 FREE Books
plus 2 FREE Mystery Gifts.

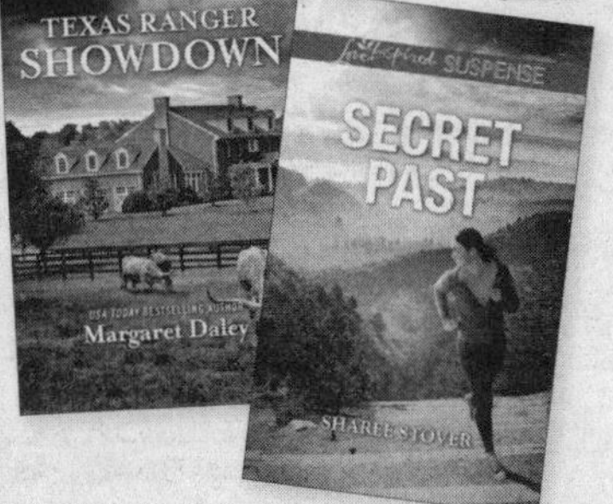

Love Inspired® Suspense books feature Christian characters facing challenges to their faith... and lives.

YES! Please send me 2 FREE Love Inspired® Suspense novels and my 2 FREE mystery gifts (gifts are worth about $10 retail). After receiving them, if I don't wish to receive any more books, I can return the shipping statement marked "cancel." If I don't cancel, I will receive 4 brand-new novels every month and be billed just $5.24 each for the regular-print edition or $5.74 each for the larger-print edition in the U.S., or $5.74 each for the regular-print edition or $6.24 each for the larger-print edition in Canada. That's a savings of at least 13% off the cover price. It's quite a bargain! Shipping and handling is just 50¢ per book in the U.S. and 75¢ per book in Canada*. I understand that accepting the 2 free books and gifts places me under no obligation to buy anything. I can always return a shipment and cancel at any time. The free books and gifts are mine to keep no matter what I decide.

Choose one: ☐ **Love Inspired® Suspense Regular-Print** (153/353 IDN GMY5) ☐ **Love Inspired® Suspense Larger-Print** (107/307 IDN GMY5)

Name (please print)

Address Apt. #

City State/Province Zip/Postal Code

Mail to the **Reader Service:**
IN U.S.A.: P.O. Box 1341, Buffalo, NY 14240-8531
IN CANADA: P.O. Box 603, Fort Erie, Ontario L2A 5X3

Want to try two free books from another series? Call 1-800-873-8635 or visit www.ReaderService.com.

*Terms and prices subject to change without notice. Prices do not include applicable taxes. Sales tax applicable in N.Y. Canadian residents will be charged applicable taxes. Offer not valid in Quebec. This offer is limited to one order per household. Books received may not be as shown. Not valid for current subscribers to Love Inspired Suspense books. All orders subject to approval. Credit or debit balances in a customer's account(s) may be offset by any other outstanding balance owed by or to the customer. Please allow 4 to 6 weeks for delivery. Offer available while quantities last.

Your Privacy—The Reader Service is committed to protecting your privacy. Our Privacy Policy is available online at www.ReaderService.com or upon request from the Reader Service. We make a portion of our mailing list available to reputable third parties that offer products we believe may interest you. If you prefer that we not exchange your name with third parties, or if you wish to clarify or modify your communication preferences, please visit us at www.ReaderService.com/consumerschoice or write to us at Reader Service Preference Service, P.O. Box 9062, Buffalo, NY 14240-9062. Include your complete name and address.

LIS18

HOME on the RANCH

YES! Please send me the **Home on the Ranch Collection** in Larger Print. This collection begins with 3 FREE books and 2 FREE gifts in the first shipment. Along with my 3 free books, I'll also get the next 4 books from the Home on the Ranch Collection, in LARGER PRINT, which I may either return and owe nothing, or keep for the low price of $5.24 U.S./ $5.89 CDN each plus $2.99 for shipping and handling per shipment*. If I decide to continue, about once a month for 8 months I will get 6 or 7 more books, but will only need to pay for 4. That means 2 or 3 books in every shipment will be FREE! If I decide to keep the entire collection, I'll have paid for only 32 books because 19 books are FREE! I understand that accepting the 3 free books and gifts places me under no obligation to buy anything. I can always return a shipment and cancel at any time. My free books and gifts are mine to keep no matter what I decide.

268 HCN 3760 468 HCN 3760

Name (PLEASE PRINT)

Address Apt. #

City State/Prov. Zip/Postal Code

Signature (if under 18, a parent or guardian must sign)

Mail to the **Reader Service:**

IN U.S.A.: P.O. Box 1867, Buffalo, NY. 14240-1867

IN CANADA: P.O. Box 609, Fort Erie, Ontario L2A 5X3

* Terms and prices subject to change without notice. Prices do not include applicable taxes. Sales tax applicable in NY. Canadian residents will be charged applicable taxes. This offer is limited to one order per household. All orders subject to approval. Credit or debit balances in a customer's account(s) may be offset by any other outstanding balance owed by or to the customer. Please allow 3 to 4 weeks for delivery. Offer available while quantities last. Offer not available to Quebec residents.

Your Privacy—The Reader Service is committed to protecting your privacy. Our Privacy Policy is available online at www.ReaderService.com or upon request from the Reader Service.

We make a portion of our mailing list available to reputable third parties that offer products we believe may interest you. If you prefer that we not exchange your name with third parties, or if you wish to clarify or modify your communication preferences, please visit us at www.ReaderService.com/consumerschoice or write to us at Reader Service Preference Service, P.O. Box 9062, Buffalo, NY. 14240-9062. Include your complete name and address.

HRCBPA18

Get 4 FREE REWARDS!

We'll send you 2 FREE Books plus 2 FREE Mystery Gifts.

ROBYN CARR Any Day Now

CARLA NEGGERS the RIVER HOUSE

FREE Value Over $20

B.J. DANIELS HERO'S RETURN

KAREN HARPER SHALLOW GRAVE

Both the **Romance** and **Suspense** collections feature compelling novels written by many of today's best-selling authors.

YES! Please send me 2 FREE novels from the Essential Romance or Essential Suspense Collection and my 2 FREE gifts (gifts are worth about $10 retail). After receiving them, if I don't wish to receive any more books, I can return the shipping statement marked "cancel." If I don't cancel, I will receive 4 brand-new novels every month and be billed just $6.74 each in the U.S. or $7.24 each in Canada. That's a savings of at least 16% off the cover price. It's quite a bargain! Shipping and handling is just 50¢ per book in the U.S. and 75¢ per book in Canada*. I understand that accepting the 2 free books and gifts places me under no obligation to buy anything. I can always return a shipment and cancel at any time. The free books and gifts are mine to keep no matter what I decide.

Choose one: ☐ **Essential Romance** (194/394 MDN GMY7) ☐ **Essential Suspense** (191/391 MDN GMY7)

Name (please print)

Address Apt. #

City State/Province Zip/Postal Code

Mail to the **Reader Service:**
IN U.S.A.: P.O. Box 1341, Buffalo, NY 14240-8531
IN CANADA: P.O. Box 603, Fort Erie, Ontario L2A 5X3

Want to try two free books from another series? Call 1-800-873-8635 or visit www.ReaderService.com.

*Terms and prices subject to change without notice. Prices do not include applicable taxes. Sales tax applicable in NY. Canadian residents will be charged applicable taxes. Offer not valid in Quebec. This offer is limited to one order per household. Books received may not be as shown. Not valid for current subscribers to the Essential Romance or Essential Suspense Collection. All orders subject to approval. Credit or debit balances in a customer's account(s) may be offset by any other outstanding balance owed by or to the customer. Please allow 4 to 6 weeks for delivery. Offer available while quantities last.

Your Privacy—The Reader Service is committed to protecting your privacy. Our Privacy Policy is available online at www.ReaderService.com or upon request from the Reader Service. We make a portion of our mailing list available to reputable third parties that offer products we believe may interest you. If you prefer that we not exchange your name with third parties, or if you wish to clarify or modify your communication preferences, please visit us at www.ReaderService.com/consumerschoice or write to us at Reader Service Preference Service, P.O. Box 9062, Buffalo, NY 14240-9062. Include your complete name and address.

STRS18

Get 4 FREE REWARDS!

We'll send you 2 FREE Books
plus 2 FREE Mystery Gifts.

Harlequin® Special Edition books feature heroines finding the balance between their work life and personal life on the way to finding true love.

YES! Please send me 2 FREE Harlequin® Special Edition novels and my 2 FREE gifts (gifts are worth about $10 retail). After receiving them, if I don't wish to receive any more books, I can return the shipping statement marked "cancel." If I don't cancel, I will receive 6 brand-new novels every month and be billed just $4.99 per book in the U.S. or $5.74 per book in Canada. That's a savings of at least 12% off the cover price! It's quite a bargain! Shipping and handling is just 50¢ per book in the U.S. and 75¢ per book in Canada*. I understand that accepting the 2 free books and gifts places me under no obligation to buy anything. I can always return a shipment and cancel at any time. The free books and gifts are mine to keep no matter what I decide.

235/335 HDN GMY2

Name (please print)

Address　　　　Apt. #

City　　　　State/Province　　　　Zip/Postal Code

Mail to the **Reader Service:**
IN U.S.A.: P.O. Box 1341, Buffalo, NY 14240-8531
IN CANADA: P.O. Box 603, Fort Erie, Ontario L2A 5X3

Want to try two free books from another series? Call 1-800-873-8635 or visit www.ReaderService.com.

*Terms and prices subject to change without notice. Prices do not include applicable taxes. Sales tax applicable in N.Y. Canadian residents will be charged applicable taxes. Offer not valid in Quebec. This offer is limited to one order per household. Books received may not be as shown. Not valid for current subscribers to Harlequin® Special Edition books. All orders subject to approval. Credit or debit balances in a customer's account(s) may be offset by any other outstanding balance owed by or to the customer. Please allow 4 to 6 weeks for delivery. Offer available while quantities last.

Your Privacy—The Reader Service is committed to protecting your privacy. Our Privacy Policy is available online at www.ReaderService.com or upon request from the Reader Service. We make a portion of our mailing list available to reputable third parties that offer products we believe may interest you. If you prefer that we not exchange your name with third parties, or if you wish to clarify or modify your communication preferences, please visit us at www.ReaderService.com/consumerschoice or write to us at Reader Service Preference Service, P.O. Box 9062, Buffalo, NY 14240-9062. Include your complete name and address.

HSE18